THE LOST ONE

L.G.PACE III

Copyright © 2014 by L.G. Pace III
Cover design by Michelle Preast of Indie Book Covers
Formatting and interior design by JT Formatting

Printed in the United States of America
First Edition: March 2013
Second Edition: October 2014
Library of Congress Cataloging-in-Publication Data
  Pace III, L.G.
   The Lost One – 2nd ed
    ISBN - 13: 978-0-9889418-0-9

https://www.facebook.com/LGPaceIII

To my parents who taught me to have a love of books that has become a lifelong pursuit.

To my children who inspire me every day.

To my wife who taught me to love life.

PROLOGUE

THE CHASE

OVER A CENTURY of wear had left its mark upon the concrete outside of 1421 Mason Ave. Its surface was a mottled tapestry made up of chips, discolorations and cracks. These cracks ranged from hairline fractures to those deep enough to support grass and, in one case, a sickly looking daisy. The building it stood in front of, while newer, was not in much better shape. The crumbling facade had pitted bricks hanging precariously over gaps where the mortar had fallen away.

Through the years, the area surrounding it had undergone a period of gentrification. Retrofitted townhouses offered old world charm with all the modern conveniences to those that could afford it. It was a place caught in the midst of a metamorphosis from the old to the new. Signs of the improvements were all about all down the street. Construction material lay beneath tarps and huge metal dumpsters were nearly overflowing with debris. Bright orange fencing encircled holes with new wires, cables and pipes jutting out. Along the street shiny new luxury cars sat parked next to old jalopies further reflecting the ongoing changes to the neighborhood.

Far down the block from the old building sat a quaint little park and it was here that the night was disturbed. In the heavy shadow of the largest tree, a stately oak, a pale blue mist flowed from near the roots. It expanded with unnatural speed to encompass the confines of the tree's shadow. Roiling and twisting it thickened until no part of the ground could be seen.

Within the mist, a figure slowly resolved itself. Stooped and bleeding it carried a small burden clutched to its chest. Stepping into the light, the diminutive figure, barely three feet tall, glanced around. The harsh streetlights showed fresh cuts bleeding sluggishly.

Deep blue skin held yellow patches where the pigment was discolored from bruises. Luminous blue eyes scanned the area looking for signs of danger. Seeing nothing, the figure relaxed a bit and stepped away from the tree. With a sigh he set his bundle down on the ground for a moment and stretched, working his shoulder to relieve a knot forming there.

Adjusting a black felt bowler hat on his head, he looked down blankly at his formerly fine suit of clothes. Scuffed wing tipped shoes, one with a loose and flapping leather sole, held one tattered spat, the other having been lost somewhere in his flight.

His fine coat and splendid waistcoat were torn and covered in blood and gore. Tailored pants were little more than rags held up by his suspenders. Although this once would have caused him great stress; the clothes now seemed meaningless compared to the task at hand.

Moving further from the tree he glanced behind at the ground. With relief he saw that he was not leaving a bloody trail as he went. Cradling the bundle in his arms, he started down the street towards the old building at the far end. He caught sight of a bedraggled daisy pushing its way valiantly up through a crack in the concrete. *Ah, see my little friend. Even when everything seems lost hope, and daisy's spring eternal.* Grinning like an idiot he started forward then winced as the dangers in his way made themselves apparent.

With exaggerated care, the small man swung wide to avoid a parked car, then a metal lamp post, and then an iron manhole cover. An exclamation of pain escaped when he was forced to press between a parked car and a metal fence. Smoke rose off his hand as it brushed the wrought iron fence. Grimacing, he stumbled forward, holding his cargo in one hand. Once he was free of the fence he scowled at his appendage and examined the burn the metal had given him. Luckily the damage was not severe; still it stung as he flexed it. A moment later he was relieved to be at his destination. Squinting, he read the words on the sign near the door.

St. Michael's Orphan and Foundling Home. Established 1895. Pausing at the base of the stairs, he opened the bundle and peered inside. From within came a soft coo and a small hand came up and grasped one of his blue fingers.

"Ach, lad. I hope you will be safe. Know that your Uncle Martin loves you. I will lead these beasts away and come back for you once it is safe."

Wrapping the baby in a soft hug, he wiped a tear from his face. He glanced around and quickly made his way up the stairs to the door. Gently, he laid the mismatched collection of blankets holding the child on the doorstep. Carefully pulling the top layer aside he saw that the baby inside had fallen asleep. He took a moment to look at the boy. A beautiful child, he had his father's eyes and his mother's gentle face.

Get a hold of yourself, Martin. It is time that you are off, before they catch up to both of you. Leaning down, he whispered again to the sleeping baby, "Goodbye, boy. I love you." Closing the blankets around the child, he knocked on the door and slid back into the shadows to watch.

The lights came on inside the building almost immediately and he saw someone walking to the front door, turning lights on as they went. Finally, the exterior light came on and the door cracked open. The face that peered out into the night was that of an older woman with streaks of gray in her hair. Her garment was an old-style sleeping gown, buttoned up to the neck with the figure of the cross stitched on the front of it.

At first, she glanced around in irritation until her eyes fell upon the small bundle near the front door. Cautiously, she reached out, moved the blankets aside and peered in. With a small smile, she picked up the bundle and began scanning the surrounding area. Cradling the baby to her chest, she stepped out on to the porch.

"I don't know if you are still out there," she said. "You did a brave thing here tonight giving the child over into our care. I don't know your circumstances or what led you to us tonight. You should know that you have made the right decision. We'll take good care of the baby. If you change your mind and decide to return and reclaim the baby, you are most welcome. Should circumstances make this impossible, then we'll find a place for it in the world to be loved. May the Lord bless and keep you."

With that, she stepped inside and closed the door. He stood across the street and wept silently as he watched the lights go out in reverse order until the building stood dark again. Turning, he retraced his path quickly, giving the fence a wider berth this time. Having seen the child to safety, he had to get far enough away that no one would find him.

Heading up the block, he cringed back from an old clunker that looked like it was made of tons of iron. *Damn technology. Between iron all over the place and all the new technology being created this world is becoming more toxic by the minute.* Returning to the small park, he headed for the large oak to reenter his portal. As he neared the tree, he had the feeling that he was being watched. From behind the oak, a familiar figure stepped out to greet him. His heart sank as he recognized his brother, Felinor.

"Well, well, well . . . if it is not my dear little brother, Martin. What brings you to the glare of the city on such a busy night?"

Martin could see from the look in his sibling's eyes that he knew exactly why he was here. He slid his hand behind him, placing it on the hilt of the sword secured at the small of his back. "Felinor! What are you doing here?"

A look of disgust crossed Felinor's face as he stepped forward, drawing his own blade. "What do you think I am doing here, you twit? I have no idea what madness has possessed you, to shame our family like this. It cannot and will not stand!"

Pausing, Felinor looked his brother over carefully. "Where is the child, Martin? I know you took him from the crash site. Give him to me now and there may still be a chance I can smooth this over. Perhaps they can be convinced that you were ensorcelled by your friend. Turning over the child may be enough to get the Sahae to forget your past transgressions."

Moving slowly, Martin put one of the larger trees to his back and drew his sword. Looking around, he saw no movement. "Where are the rest of them, Fel? Hmm? Will you sit and watch while your brother is tied to a tree and tortured for information? Have we really grown that far apart?"

Felinor sighed and balanced his sword blade lightly on his shoulder.

"You really are an idiot, are you not? I cannot believe how long I have allowed an embarrassment like you to muck things up for me. Do you really think I would humiliate myself by bringing others to witness your revolting behavior? No. I saw you leaving the area and I followed after you. As if I would need assistance to deal with the likes of you."

He came alone. Martin felt a burst of hope. If no one else knew where he was, then perhaps all was not lost. As if reading his mind, his brother gave a derisive snort.

"You truly are a fool, Brother. What shame I feel even calling you that; it truly sticks in my throat. I have a better label for the short remainder of your life: Betrayer. Betrayer of family, of race, of sanity. The time has come for this little drama to play itself out. There is no way you can escape. I am more than your match in wits and you have little skill with a blade. In short, Betrayer, you are finished. The best you can hope for is to turn the child over. If not, I shall torture it out of you or simply kill you and set trackers to find it. I am sure the child cannot be far. It should be a very short search."

Martin felt the strength leaving his legs. He had known he was in trouble as soon as he saw Felinor. It had never occurred to him, thought it should have, that it would be this bad. Because looking at his brother's face he had no doubt that he was going to die. His brother, who had once been so loving and carefree, seemed like a twisted monster now. To hear Felinor speak so casually of torturing or killing him chilled Martin to the bone. His mind raced as he tried to think of any way to escape, any plan that might spare him from this fate. It must have shown on his face as he realized the futility of his situation. Felinor misinterpreted his expression as surrender and relaxed a bit.

"Do not worry, little brother," Felinor said. "Once he has the child he will be more than willing to overlook what you have done. We may even be able to work this to our advantage. After all, he has been turning over the countryside trying to verify if this child was dead or not. Now you and I will give him the pleasure of seeing to its fate himself."

As he moved closer, Felinor's weapon slid just out of position and it was then that Martin struck. The thought of anyone hurting the boy was more than he could bear. He leapt forward and with all his strength drove his blade deep into his brother's chest.

Twisting the sword, he felt bone break and flesh tear. He yanked the blade back and forth in a frenzy, trying to pull it back out to stab again, yet it was stuck fast. Felinor roared in pain and brought his sword down on his brother, opening a grievous wound on Martin's torso. Both brothers collapsed in the dirt near the large oak.

Felinor stared at his brother in shocked fury. "Why, you imbecile? You've killed me, you ass, and for what? A stupid half-breed bastard?!" Blood flew from Felinor's mouth as froth began to build at the edges.

Martin forced himself to speak through the pain of breathing. "Left . . . me . . . no . . . choice . . . Everyone deserves . . . only a baby."

Felinor glared at him, trying to stand. After a moment, he gave up, lying heavily on the ground. "Who would have thought my useless little brother would be the one to finally kill me? I hate you, Martin. I hope I have killed you. I hope . . ."

With a crackling gurgle, the last puffs of air left Felinor's lungs and the light faded from his eyes. With a sob, Martin used a fallen branch as an improvised crutch and levered himself up off the ground. Tearing up what was left of his pants and shirt he bound his wound with tears streaming down his face. When he was finished he stood for a moment, looking down at his fallen brother.

I cannot leave him here. It could lead them to the boy. Better to leave him somewhere else, to lay a false trail. Leaning down, he grabbed his brother's arms and dragged him to the portal. Pulling the body through Martin used the Way to close the gateway behind him.

The portal disappeared with a popping sound sending a blast of wind out in all directions. By the time it reached the orphanage it barely ruffled the petals of the stalwart daisy.

1

TILLY CRAYES

THE STEAM CLOUDS filling the roadway cleared, showing the flash of passing traffic as she stepped from the sidewalk into the alley. With a quick glance behind her, the odd-looking woman strode away from the light.

Tilly Crayes had never been accused of being a pretty girl. At five foot four, she had straight dirty blond hair, parted in the middle, with very little body. Brown eyes glared beneath eyebrows in desperate need of a good tweezing; a wide, pig-like nose led down to thin lips and a less than defined chin. And if nature had not been cruel enough, her cheeks were slightly puffy and resembled the outer curve of a croissant that had been taken out of the oven just a few minutes too soon. An especially virulent strain of childhood measles had left her skin mottled and she self-consciously tried to cover the pockmarks with too much makeup.

Physically, she would be best described in modern terms as "having a few extra pounds." She tried to disguise this flaw by wearing outlandish outfits. The normal response she got from her wardrobe choices ranged from shock, laughter and, on one unfortunate occasion during a visit to Chicago, a stern dressing-down from a fashionably dressed older woman. The matron had seemed mortally offended by her clothing choices and spent almost ten minutes loudly taking her to task. This unpleasant incident made her avoid traveling and she now spent her time almost exclusively in a thirty mile radius of her apartment.

Currently, as she stomped down a grease-splattered alley between businesses, her ensemble was striking. It consisted of bib overalls, a lime green sweater, yellow cowboy boots and a bright orange head scarf tied in a tight knot behind her left ear. Although Tilly maintained a harsh front, she was well aware of her physical appearance and how the world saw her. She had decided a long time ago that the world would not accept her no matter what she did. So she did what she wanted and the world be damned.

Sadly, instead of this giving her a devil may care attitude, it caused her to approach life with vindictiveness soaked in rage. While it was not entirely her fault, years of abuse and ridicule had twisted her inner self to mirror her outer appearance, it was her choice to behave the way she did. The hatred she felt for the beautiful people of the world, those that "had it easy," festered inside of her until it left pockmarks on her soul to match those on her skin. She reveled in tormenting the world that tormented her.

As luck would have it she had discovered the perfect platform long ago to enact her revenge. After trying a few different jobs in her youth, she had found that working at the County Clerk's office was the perfect place for her. Not only was it a cushy government job with great pay, excellent benefits and lots of paid holidays off, it was also a gateway to power. Her initial discovery of the possibilities of her new position started with a simple mistake. The error on her part caused havoc for some poor, innocent citizen. When the bungle came to light, she panicked, afraid she would be fired. Instead, a tenured employee, who had absolutely nothing to do with the problem, inexplicably took the fall and was summarily dismissed. The next time she screwed up, it happened again—someone else took the blame. When it happened a third time, she realized that it was not luck, she was inexplicably blessed.

Over the next few years, she built an empire. Through guile and brazen action she eliminated tenured employees in the office, making sure every decision had to go through her. This left her free to torment the local residents with all manner of bureaucratic hell. The county started to get complaints from consumers that never checked out. From overdue taxes sent to collections to impounded cars, all had a paper trail that validated them.

For the poor citizens, it was as if the worst urban legends of red tape had come to life. Cars were towed, impounded, and destroyed, always with the proper documentation. Checks sent with traffic tickets were lost en-route, leaving residents with suspended licenses. There were even cases where she managed to have people declared dead and their possessions auctioned off while they were at work.

Her ability to conceal these actions and scapegoat others bordered on the mystical. Even when she expected to be caught, circumstances would play out so that some poor schmuck in her office took the fall.

Tempting fate, she came out again and again smelling like a rose. Having lost all fear of retribution, she set herself as the final power in the government for millions of citizens. In short, Tilly Crayes became something of an administrative goddess.

Tonight, she was aglow with a new personal triumph. There was a man in her building, an incredibly gorgeous man, who had been studiously ignoring her. It had been child's play to arrange for him to be ticketed and then delay the ticket for a considerable amount of time. She magnified the charges for towing and storage after having his car impounded. This had the desired effect of driving the man to distraction. When she casually let him overhear that she worked in the clerk's office, she could tell she had gotten his undivided attention.

She had no doubt, especially with the amount of money he owed, that he would waste no time trying to sweet talk her into taking care of his bill. He had tried to get away cheap—like she was that easy. Thinking back to her evening, she grinned evilly. In the end, she managed to get dinner, dancing and a quick roll in the back of his rental car. Having drained the man of his self-respect and virtue, she told him she would see what she could do and left him with a parting smile. Sneaking a peek back around the corner, she watched the transition from his false smile to a worried look of self-loathing. Somehow that was almost more satisfying than the rest of the evening.

The walk home had been a calculated move on her part. A cab would have been alright, but she had not spotted any yet in this low traffic area. Walking home let her avoid any pressure from him on how she would take care of his issue. Before the evening had even begun she had decided there would be no mercy for this pretty boy. As a matter of fact, the best he could hope for was the damage she had already done. If he crossed her or disappointed her this evening, she had planned a few things that she would have been able to add to his long list of woes.

Performance review: adequate. Cackling wickedly, she stepped around a pile of refuse and found herself suddenly surrounded by dark, shadowy figures. The lights from the street disappeared and the noise of the city was abruptly silenced. Tilly's first thought was to flee, but she saw that was impossible. While she had been busy gloating over her evening she had walked right into their midst. Now she was at the center of an unbroken circle of gray forms. Looking around wildly, she only found one discernible visage staring back at her.

The man . . . no, the creature looking back at her was breathtaking. Too slim to be real, his body was like a stick figure with supple muscles lining the thin frame. His face was as pale as a plate of snow; two burning black eyes glared at her from above a sharp nose and almost sneering lips. The effect he had on her was immediate and disturbing; she found herself both terrified and excited by his presence. The man's nostrils flared as he inhaled deeply. Staring at her for a moment he nodded as if confirming something for himself. With no apparent command given the rest of the figures suddenly withdrew to a wider circle, leaving him alone in the center with her.

For many moments he stood there simply staring at her. As she was beginning to wonder whether she should try to break through the circle and make it to the street, he spoke.

"Hello, child," he said with a soft, melodious voice. The sound sent shivers down her spine and she was again awash in confusing emotions. It was a heady mix of longing and fear. She had jumped as he spoke and only then realized how much tension she was holding in her frame. Her hand crept inside her jacket pocket and the handle of a razor sharp switchblade pressed into her palm, giving her some small comfort.

"Who are you?" she asked in a voice that quavered far more than she liked. Granted, this was freaking her out, but she would be damned before some pretty boy and his band of geeky, costumed freaks were going to get the best of her. She assumed that the entire company surrounding her must be wearing some sort of mask that kept her from seeing their faces.

But I've seen you, pretty boy, haven't I? I bet I could pick you out of a line up push come to shove. Feeling a bit more confident, she took a step forward, took a deep breath, and stared him in the eye.

"And what the hell do you want?"

The man stood stock still for so long she wondered if he was even going to respond. Maybe she had taken it too far and pissed him off. She could be in real trouble here with so many of them surrounding her. Finally, he smiled at her. His smile took her breath away. It was a thing of beauty which at the same time terrified her to the core of her being. Something told her this was not a creature she wanted smiling at her. No, this was not a creature she wanted noticing her at all.

"What interesting things to start a conversation with. To the former, let me say I am many things; you may call me Elder. As for the latter . . . I would say a great many things would not even begin to cover it."

Without seeming to move, he was suddenly there, in her face, inhaling as if smelling a pie just out of the oven. Now she could hear the rush of air as it entered him and he stood silently, eyes closed for many moments again before speaking. The fear was now overcoming the attraction and she looked around franticly but could see no avenue of escape.

"You, my poor unfortunate child, are one of the lost ones. Normally we would not even have noticed you. However, you were projecting malevolence all over this area. It overcame our normal aversion to traveling amidst all this putrid technology. So we slipped into the city to come and seek you out." He again did not seem to move but was on the far side of the circle. "Your hatred is what drew me. It is like a sweet vintage; a fragrant flower that pulled me from my path. Once I had your scent, I just had to find you."

Tilly felt quickening beads of sweat begin to wash down her back like the tickling fingers of the dead teasing her. Again, she looked toward the street and was dismayed by what she saw. Where the entry to the alley had once been was a gray wall of mist. She noticed that the circle around her was a bit more distinct.

She could make out portions of faces, although none of them were more than a blur. As she turned her attention back to the creature that called itself Elder she tried to find her voice.

"What exactly is a Lost One?" she asked, giving the name more emphasis, as one would a title. "And where exactly am I supposed to be lost from?"

Elder turned and looked at her with what might have been pity, or it might have been malice. She had never had this much trouble reading someone's face. Then again, this creature did not seem to be normal in any way.

"Well, let me answer the last part first and the first part last." He said this with some small amusement tipping up the corners of his eyes and mouth, as if he had just told some sort of private joke. "Before you were born, one of your parents came from another place. A magical place filled with beautiful layers of inky night."

He watched Tilly for her reaction and, seeing no discernible change, continued. "It is hard to say which one it was or even if it was intentional. After all, the best of us have slipped during a visit and taken our amusement where we saw fit."

At this there was a smattering of muted laughter from the surrounding ring. With growing dread, she realized it was much easier to make out faces and she was able to almost hear the words they were saying, thought she still could not understand what language they were speaking in. With a deep feeling of foreboding, she realized that these were not people in costumes. The sweat dripping down her back became a torrent. She tried to speak, tried to make some witty comment, but her mouth was dry and tight.

The distinct concrete and refuse of the alley were gone, and she realized she was now standing on an old dirt path with giant trees on either side. The sudden change reminded her of her one visit to an amusement park; she had walked through a gateway and found herself in another land. Her stomach started to churn and her pulse began to race.

No way! No way is this happening! That pretty boy bastard must have slipped something in my drink. Yeah! That must be it. This is all some sort of hallucination. Looking around she realized that as much as she would like that to be true, it did not seem to be the case.

Elder watched as her eyes scanned the area and smiled nastily. "Yes, you are far from where you were. I would not expect your simple mind to grasp the particulars of the Way. It is more pleasant to speak here rather than having to endure the putrid cesspool you call a city." He began walking around the inner perimeter of the circle of beings. "As I was saying, when one from our beautiful world dallies with one of your world, a half-breed is created. In your case, like so many others, the creature is out of place. They can find peace neither in your world nor in ours."

He increased the speed of his pacing now, getting into his explanation like a practiced teacher delivering a lecture to a class. "They are dangerous, disruptive and are an Abomination to all we know and love. This is why, long ago, we forbade the making of your kind. If there were ever any such creatures made, it was the responsibility of the parent to see to the child or others would come to solve the issue themselves."

Tilly tried to wrap her brain around what he was saying. "What do you mean, I can't find peace? I'm doing just fine, thank you very much. And F.Y.I.? I am a little old to have my parents see to me."

Elder turned to her with a look of mild exasperation. She noticed that the beings behind him in the circle were extremely clear and defined. All of them seemed to be smiling at her in the same horrible, beautiful way.

She could hear the wind whispering through the branches of the trees, although, save the wind, there were no sounds of nature that she would expect to hear in the woods. No birds, no insects, nothing. It was as if Mother Nature herself was holding her breath.

"I phrased that poorly, my dear. You have not been able to fit in here. The world rejects you and you, in turn, reject the world. It has turned you ugly and mean. The only pleasure you take is in the torture of others. Their pain is like a sumptuous meal to you. The lack of connection you feel for those that surround you keeps you for forming a lasting bond to anything."

Tilly glowered at him. "Shows what you know! I have five cats!"

Elder ignored and continued her as if she had not even spoken. "In short, you are a misfit . . . a freak. With each passing day, you become more and more determined to destroy the world around you. Ultimately, you lack the drive to follow through on your ambitions. In the end, you will simply make those that dwell in the light a bit more aware of the dangers that surround them and put them on their guard. This cannot be allowed."

"So what?" Tilly sneered with all the bravado she could muster. "You're here to tell me to stop being such a bitch? Good luck with that." The air around her went very still as Elder slowly turned and fixed her with an incredulous stare.

"Well now. You do have spirit, I will give you that. And, despite your rudeness, I feel obligated to share a bit of wisdom with you. I have been alive longer than your pathetic species has been out of the trees. My eyes have beheld such beauty and horror as to crack that little mind of yours into jagged fragments. If you had even a small inkling of the intrinsic glory of the Sahae, you would have ended your life years ago. If you became so enlightened now the reality of being born half human would drive you mad. Although it is not your fault, you must know that in our eyes you are an Abomination, a corruption of beauty with ugliness. You are unclean and cannot be tolerated."

As he finished, Tilly felt iron-hard hands grip her arms, legs and torso. Elder leaned in and she nearly fainted from the sheer terror she felt with him this close. "You see, my dear child, I do not mean to say you could not survive. Rather that you would not be allowed to survive. Although I have to say, for sheer vile temerity, you definitely place high among the bastards that have come before you."

Tilly saw him raise his hand and he seemed to gently touch her chest. There was a sharp flare of searing agony and she saw him holding a bloody, twitching lump in his hand. As the light faded from her eyes, she had time to realize that lump was her heart that he had plucked from her chest like a fruit from a basket.

2

NIGHTMARES

ERIC WOKE FROM the dream drenched in sweat and scrambled for the notebook on his bedside table. Scribbling furiously, he tried to record as many details from his dream as he could. For an instant, the face of the woman blazed in his mind along with the face of something else glaring down at her. He wrote as quickly as he could but the last wisps of the nightmare slipped out of his mind. Frustrated, he looked down at the gibberish on the page.

Garbage piles, an alley, a circle, trees . . . none of it made any sense and nothing jogged any memory of the dream back into his mind. Dropping the notebook back on the table, he ignored the pen as it bounced off the wood and ricocheted across the bedroom floor. Flopping back onto his sweat-soaked sheets, he glanced over at the clock. The little metal hands read three o'clock exactly. "Great," he said aloud, "another early morning."

Lying back, he tried closing his eyes and laying still, hoping that he would be able to fall back to sleep. When he glanced at the clock a short time later, he saw that only ten minutes had passed. Now wide away he realized that there was no chance of falling asleep again. With a resigned sigh, he levered himself up and sat on the edge of the bed. He caught sight of his reflection in the mirror on the wall and smiled wryly at the image. His thick, dark brown hair was sticking out in every conceivable direction. It actually looked like he had stuck his finger in a light socket. His dark green eyes were a bit bloodshot today and he rubbed some grit out of the corner of one of them.

Standing up, he stretched up to his full six foot height and glanced around the room. The room was barely furnished, a reflection of his long standing spartan lifestyle. There had never been a lot of possessions cluttering up his room back at the orphanage, either. Here, other than the bed and the mirror, he had a beautiful, old oak dresser and a brilliant green oval area rug.

An old, carved mahogany trunk he had gotten from his foster parents for his 15th birthday sat on the far side of the room. That had been two days ago, a few months after he had come to stay with the Greens. The chest was an impressive relic from another age, when travelers had seen the world out of their steamer trunks. Inside there were all manner of compartments and racks to keep even the messiest world traveler organized. They had bought it for him after he had been fascinated by seeing one in a movie. It was currently his favorite, if somewhat eclectic, world possession.

In his best Jimmie Stewart voice he said, "One day, old chest, old pal, we're going to travel the globe. I'll be a man of means and you'll be my faithful sidekick. Together we'll blaze a path across all the continents." Grinning, he patted the top of the chest and sat down on it to gaze out the window.

Outside a heavy mist coated the ground. It gave the trees across the road the look of an ancient forest rather than the suburban green space he walked through on the way to school every day. Leaning back on the chest, he rubbed his eyes and thought about how much things had changed in such a short time.

He had been the oldest kid living at the orphanage when Mrs. Clark, his social worker, had come and told him that she had a new family to place him with. It had come as kind of a shock, since he had left his last foster family five years ago after it had most definitely NOT worked out.

They had been a nice family with two teenage kids of their own. The dad was a doctor and the mother was a stay at home mom. They had been given all of his background information and medical files and apparently thought that his malady was overstated. His "condition," as everyone liked to call it, was paroxysmal parasomnias, or night terrors. It meant that he had nightmares and would wake up screaming and yelling. As traumatic as they apparently were, he very rarely remembered his dreams.

Because of this most of the specialists were unable to help him. One of the doctors he had seen had suggested that he keep a dream journal. It seemed like a good idea but now years later he had little to show for it other than some random notes.

It was frustrating, but he hoped that one day something would click and he would make his own breakthrough. The doctors had been so ineffective he figured he might do better on his own.

According to a book he had read, keeping a dream journal was supposed to help work out his subconscious issues, but so far it helped him work out jack squat. Still, he figured it did not hurt to keep the journal so it still sat next to his bed. It sure worked better than the medication his last foster parent, Dr. Young had given him. At least the journal had no side effects.

Eric had felt like a lab rat not like a member of the family. The drug regimen had been sadly ineffective. The side effects of rash and nose bleeds just made him even more irritable than he normally was.

After a month of his screaming and general freaking out, they had called it quits and sent him packing. They had been so very apologetic, telling him how if it were just the three of them, the parents would stick it out. They were just watching out for their other kids. He could understand that, but it still pissed him off. They had been so arrogant, thinking they could fix him and then they just sent him back like all the rest.

After this final, crushing disappointment, he had gone into a funk that lasted nearly a month. In the end, he had achieved a Zen sort of peace by deciding to take charge of his own destiny. He gave up on the idea of getting adopted. It was obvious that he was fundamentally broken in a way that made him undesirable. By admitting this truth he found a new well of strength. Rather than wasting his energy pointlessly, wondering if he would ever find a family, he decided to focus on his goals. Figuring that he would be staying at the home until his 18th birthday, he started making his plans for the future.

While others were dressing up and meeting with prospective families, he spent time researching funding opportunities for orphans to go to college. Though there were plenty of options, he decided not to make scholarship handouts his primary plan. At first, he focused on working odd jobs to start earning money for his college fund. After he had earned some money he invested it by buying broken electronics.

He would repair them and then sell them through the local consignment shop. The more complex the device was, the more he enjoyed it. And the more it paid.

When word got out where the consignment shop owner was getting his used electronics Eric started getting called by people with broken things they wanted him to fix. Once word got around he was barely able to keep up with the demand for his services. Even stuff that people had given up hope of fixing he found a way to repair. He loved to go to the repair places to dig through their trash. Most of what was there was deemed hopeless, yet he still found a way to fix it.

One of the local repair shop owners got angry, thinking his employees were slacking off and turning away customers with easily repairable stuff. After all, if a kid could fix it then his staff should have been able to as well. Eric heard about this from an angry clerk who lost his job after a customer told his boss about Eric fixing something the clerk turned away. Feeling bad about it Eric went to the shop with the clerk. After talking to the owner he asked him for something that was beyond repair, just as the computer was that the clerk had turned away. The owner and the clerk both inspected an old clock radio and both agreed it should be junked. Using their tools and equipment Eric fixed it with ease. Both men stood their slack jawed as he plugged it in and turned it on. After having him do this a few times most of the owner got his number. And the clerk got his job back.

They worked out an agreement. Eric would stop fixing things on his own, which was cutting into the repair shops bottom line. In return they called him if they ever had some repair that stumped them. He earned a hefty commission, far more than a normal employee.

This paid a lot better than doing it himself and it kept him from having to take care of all the administrative parts of the business. It made the work a lot more fun when he did not have to keep track of all the customer information.

Before long, he had a pretty decent start to a college fund. So when he got pulled out of the reading room to go meet with Mrs. Clark, he thought she was there to reprimand him for begging for work or maybe even to talk to him about college. The last thing he expected was what she said after he sat down.

"We have a new family for you."

"I'm sorry, what?" Eric asked.

With a beaming smile, Mrs. Clark nodded vigorously and handed him a folder full of papers. She was pushing her late forties, with red hair that could only come from a bottle. Her pantsuit was only a few years out of date and she still made a valiant attempt to keep her makeup done. The laugh lines around her twinkling green eyes dug into her face as she looked at him with glee. He could tell by her level of excitement that not only was she serious, she thought this was the real deal.

"I know, Eric, I know! After so many years and your . . . well . . . your special circumstances, it was a real surprise. Apparently the Greens, there's more on them in that folder you're holding . . . go ahead and flip through it. As I was saying, the Greens have been part of the foster system for the last forty or so years. They've hosted three different children and their last child left them for college a year ago. When they were asked about another placement they said they were getting too old to be able to raise another child with the attention and energy needed. But then, last month they came in and started asking about any older children that needed a home. When they found out about you they jumped at the chance to have you placed with them."

Eric looked at the folder in front of him with shock and a bit of apprehension. He sighed and plastered a halfhearted grin on his face.

Seriously? Another family? Do I really have to go through this again? Like it will turn out any different this time? I have moved beyond this. So I haul all my crap, not that there is much of it, to some new house for a month or so. Then they figure out when the file says, "wakes up screaming" it actually means "wakes up screaming." Then I have to go through the rejection all over again? No way. He looked at Mrs. Clark and felt the stab of irritation melt away. She looked so hopeful it made his heart ache. *It isn't her fault. She's really nice to keep trying like this, even on a lost cause like me.*

Opening the folder, he saw a color photo of a nice-looking older couple paper clipped to the front page. They looked to be in their sixties. Both of them had gray hair and lots of character in their faces. Which is to say that they had wrinkle lines on their wrinkle lines. But even in the picture, their eyes seemed to emit a kind light and gentleness that had Eric suddenly wondering if this would be different. Maybe he could find a place to belong . . . He clamped down on that train of thought. Tenth time will be the charm? Yeah right, he thought mockingly.

Flipping through the pages, he saw that the Greens lived on the other side of the state. *At least I can try out what it will be like when I move away to college. If I want to reinvent myself then I might as well get some practice in now I suppose.*

Looking up at Mrs. Clark, he knew from her expression how he looked. She was trying for a poker face, but he could see the exasperation hiding there. *She thinks I should be happier. After all the trouble she apparently went through to orchestrate this she deserves that, even if this turns into another fiasco.* Turning his smile up to a tentative happy, he looked back down at the file and then back at her. "They . . . they know about the past placements?"

Sudden understanding dawned in her eyes and she nodded, placing her hand on his. "Eric, they know everything about the past. As a matter of fact, they have asked more questions and read more of your file than any other couple ever has. They even spoke to a few of your past doctors, from both sides of the fence."

Eric knew she meant those that thought he was suppressing a childhood trauma and those that thought he could just be an attention-seeking nut job.

"They're both well-educated people with experience with several foster children over the years. Nothing they read about you deterred them one bit from having you as part of their family. Now, I do want to apologize for just springing this on you. You've been through this enough to know that we ordinarily proceed slowly and introduce you all and then begin the process." Eric nodded at this. Mrs. Clark flushed in embarrassment.

"Well, in your case, with all the disappointments you've faced with past foster homes and failed adoptions, I wanted to make sure that everything looked promising before I mentioned it. I had to call in more than a few favors but in the end I was able to make everyone see that my way was the best way. Once everything else checked out, I told the Greens that I'd tell you about them. Truth be told, I have bent quite a few of the rules and regulations. Let me be clear though, I wouldn't even be here if I didn't think that this would work out. I know how hard it has been on you in the past."

He could see the tears starting to build in her eyes and he just could not take that, not from her and not now. Since he was barely old enough to remember, Mrs. Clark had been there. She was not a mother, more like a crazy aunt, but she had been there for him through everything and he could not stand to see her cry.

Standing up, he nodded. "So, when do I meet them?" The sudden change in him had the desired impact, and he saw the sheen disappear from her eyes as she took the folder back from him and turned toward the door on the far side of the room.

"How about right now? They drove up with me, and if you've no objections, I thought you could leave with them today."

He experienced a mild panic attack, things were moving too fast for his liking, but he was now committed and had no choice but to see this through. "Sure." He pasted a more believable smile on his face as the two people from the picture walked into the room.

They smiled as they strode over and the man reached out and shook Eric's outstretched hand. "Hello there, Eric. I've heard a lot about you. My name is Edward Green and it's wonderful to meet you. This is my wife, Claire."

Mrs. Green stepped up as her husband released Eric's hand and folded him into a hug. "It's a pleasure to meet you, Eric."

"So, Eric," said Mr. Green. "Have you decided if you'd like to come and live with us?"

Eric was overwhelmed by the intensely warm welcome they had given him and stumbled a bit before replying. "Yes. Yes, I think that would be great." The rest of it was a mad rush in Eric's memory. He was soon leaving the orphanage and heading across the state to his new home with the Greens. True, it wasn't all a done deal. There were still papers that needed to be filled out and a few meetings before they left. There were follow ups that would be done later on, to check on him and his placement. Still, it seemed like almost no time had passed before he was in the car with his latest set of foster parents.

During the drive, they three of them talked more than Eric had ever talked with another pair of adults. As they neared the outskirts of the town, Mr. Green began telling him more about his new home.

"Seaverville, Iowa. Population, give or take, about twenty thousand. Not a giant metropolis, but a pretty good-sized town. It used to be a lot bigger, but over the years the industry tapered off. Recently, we have experienced a mini boom with a few new companies moving into town. Seaverville is one of the original riverboat towns. At one time this town was a hub for overland travel on the rail line and river traffic up and down the Mississippi. It was an important artery for the survival of the nation. Of course, that was back before modern railroads and interstates. Ah, now there is something I wanted to point out to you. Look up there; you see that tower up on the bluff?"

Eric gazed up and saw a rather impressive square rock tower shaped like an old fort. Something about it seemed familiar, though he could not quite figure out why.

"That's Ft. Silverstrike. Matthew Silverstrike was one of the first to settle the area. He didn't have any children from what I know of local history, but his legacy lives on in the form of that fort and this town. When the settlers first arrived there was nothing here but trees and rocks."

Eric smiled as he looked out at the tower in the distance. "Is it open to the public?"

Mr. Green paused for a moment in thought. "I believe that they're closed right now. They close from about this time until late spring. They want to make sure no one takes a tumble off the bluff; something about having difficulty getting snow removal equipment up there and liability insurance. We can head up there come the end of the school term and take a look around if you like."

Eric nodded and pointed over towards the town. "Are those mansions up on the bluff?"

Mrs. Green smiled. "Yes, the mansions from the three biggest river barons who lived in Seaverville. Jonathan Seaver, Francois Seville and Matthew Silverstrike. The first two are bed and breakfasts the last one is privately held by a foundation of some kind." She looked askance at Mr. Green, who shrugged.

"Something like that I think." Pointing down towards the water, he directed Eric's eyes to a few large docks. "Down near the river we have a few steamboats like back in the day. One is a museum and the other is a functioning paddle wheel that takes passengers out during the warmer months. They're probably getting her dry docked about now. That's the problem with the weather in Iowa; you could have a hard freeze in September or be mellow all the way into January."

Cresting a high hill, the town spread out below them and Eric got a good look at his new home. The older section of town was near the river and appeared to be full of shops and tourist spots. Farther out he saw a few restaurants, some fast food joints and a movie theater. *Nice to see there are actually some modern amenities here.* Near the northern part of town on a bluff overlooking the river he saw a large grouping of buildings.

"What's that over there," he asked.

Mr. Green looked where he was pointing. "Ah, that's one of the most important parts of town. Seaverville College is one of the finest technology colleges in the country. Just this year it was ranked within the top twenty technology schools to attend, boasting some of the best and brightest working on the next big thing."

Eric gave him a confused look. "Here? I mean no offense, but when I think technology I think Berkeley or MIT, not Iowa."

The Greens both laughed and nodded. "I know," said Mrs. Green. "Most of the time when we travel and people find out we're from Iowa they start treating us like Ma and Pa Kettle." She laughed and patted Mr. Green's shoulder.

"Well," he said, "I think you'll be surprised at the things you find around here. After all, this entire town was built by a few sharp men who chose to strike out in an area that others had dismissed. Never judge a book by its cover and all that."

Eric nodded and stared down at the distant campus. "Do you think we could go check out the campus sometime?"

Mr. Green smiled at Eric in the rear view mirror and nodded. "Matter of fact, if you're interested, I think they have a mentoring program that helps high school students figure out a career path with job shadowing, that sort of thing. Remind me and we will make an appointment to go and meet with some people."

The road turned and the view ahead changed to show the high school and football field. Eric was unable to suppress an involuntary shudder. His old school had been a football school in a football town. You were either on the team or you were a pariah. He hated being on the team, but it had beat being tormented like he had been before he joined.

Mrs. Green seemed to notice his change in demeanor and followed his gaze, "Worried about the new school, dear?"

Looking up to meet her gaze, he nodded and found himself telling the Greens about his past experiences with football. He hadn't meant to include all the details, but once he started, they just came spilling out. Mrs. Green's expression grew distraught and Mr. Green looked angry.

Realizing he had probably said too much, he clamped his jaw shut and sat back in the seat. Way to overshare Eric. *Well, that was quick. The way they look right now, they may just decide to turn around and drive me back to the home.*

The car pulled up in front of an old Victorian style house and Mr. Green cleared his throat. Putting the car in park, he turned in his seat and fixed Eric a piercing gaze. "That's a terrible thing you've been through, Eric. Sounds like that old school was full of bullies and cowards. Here, if you don't want to be in football, then you feel free to stay clear of it. If anyone gives you a problem with that, you just let me know. You're a part of this family and we take care of our own. It's amazing how fast a bully will retreat when faced with a united front."

Eric looked on in astonishment as Mrs. Green nodded and put her hand on his shoulder. "That's right, Eric. You're a Green now. If anyone messes with you, they mess with us. And we may be getting on in years but that doesn't mean we still can't raise a little Cain!" Smiling, she opened the car door and together they ushered him into his new home.

They had both been as good as their word. From the beginning, they had done everything they could to ease his way into his new life. Mrs. Green took him to social events and introduced him to his new classmates. Once the celebrity of being new wore off, Mr.

Green took him to a lot of "townie" things and made sure everyone there knew that Eric was not just a new kid in the school.

He was Eric Green and he was as much a member of town as anyone who had been born there. He was not completely free of problems, though. There were still a few football jocks that gave him grief for not being in sports.

It did not help that for some unknown reason one of the cutest girls in town, Emily Randall, seemed to have decided that he was interesting and wanted to hang out with him. Since her ex-boyfriend, Dave Mackenzie was captain of the football team and two years older, it had made his life a bit complicated. He smiled as he thought of it.

It would be great if the only complication in my life was some iron-pumping rich boy wanting to take my head off. Rising up off the trunk, he padded silently across the room and grabbed some clothes from his dresser. Heading downstairs, he took a shower and then grabbed a book and settled into the easy chair near the fireplace.

The book was one of the new purchases that Mrs. Green had gotten at the secondhand bookstore downtown. Even with the resources of the local and school library, it was necessary to supplement his growing need for reading material. Even so, it was not unusual for him to reread books several times, so he relished each unread book he received.

Being up half the night has its advantages and its disadvantages, I guess. Cracking open the book, he saw that it was an old technical manual for an electric range. Far different from the current owner's manuals, this one included a detailed wiring schematic as well as a section on repair and replacement of parts. It was so engrossing that he failed to notice the lightening of the sky until he was startled out of his book by Mrs. Green calling from the doorway.

"Had trouble sleeping again?" Eric closed the book, set it on the table and grinned up at her.

"Sleeping is never the trouble. Staying asleep, now that's a bit more problematic." He saw the tightening around her eyes and knew what she was going to say before she said it.

"I still think it'd be a good idea for you to go see Doc Mason to talk to him again about getting on a sleep aid. I know you don't like taking them, but I worry about you not getting enough sleep. It isn't healthy. Most boys your age have to be pulled out of bed by a tow truck."

Eric smiled at the mental picture. "I know you worry. The thing is, the sleep aids don't work on me. I've tried all of them. Instead of making me sleepy, they make me hyper. And no one needs that. From what I've read about the new medications, they're just remixes of the same old thing."

Mrs. Green gave him an amused smile at that. "I should've known if it was written somewhere, you would have read about it."

Eric nodded seriously. "I'm always willing to try something new. I just don't see the point in repetition. But you don't need to worry about me. I know it seems unnatural, but this is normal for me. Even though I don't sleep a lot, I'm not tired. Do I look tired?"

Searching his face, she tried to find some sign of his shorter sleeping hours and saw no ill effects. "Well, it wouldn't hurt to go see him."

He crossed the room and gave her a hug. "How about I let you know if I start to feel tired and then you can make an appointment, okay?"

Looking at him for a moment, she finally nodded. "Alright, but remember that I trust you to tell me the minute you start having problems. And trust is a gift . . ."

Eric smiled at what he had learned was a common phrase from the Greens. "That should always be honored. I know. Now," he said with a grin. "What's for breakfast?"

3

SCHOOL

MR. GREEN WAS IN the kitchen making coffee when they strode in. "And the early riser appears!" He smiled, picked up the newspaper, and settled into his chair. Glancing up, he nodded towards the volume in Eric's hands. "So, what great escape are you reading this morning?" Eric laughed and showed him the spine of the technical manual and saw a twinkle appear in his foster father's eyes. "A little light reading, eh?"

The two discussed the finer points of electric ranges as Mrs. Green made breakfast. The smell of frying bacon and eggs soon filled the room and by the time his plate was placed before him, Eric was positive he was completely hollow. Three helpings later, he pushed himself back from the table and stretched his legs out.

"That was an amazing breakfast," he said. His foster parents looked at each other in amusement.

"All three of them?" asked Mr. Green. Eric grinned unabashedly.

"Well, I'm told that I'm a growing boy and growing boys need food." To emphasize this point, he grabbed a large sweet roll from the plate in the center of the table and his jacket off the hook nearby. With a quick bit of juggling he had the coat on, backpack over his arm, and still managed to take a big bite out of the roll as he headed towards the door. "Have a good day!" he said around the mouthful and before Mrs. Green could bring up the subject of the doctor again, he slipped out the back door.

Taking a shortcut through the side yard, he walked across the road and headed through the trees. There was a well-worn footpath through the grass and in a minute he wound his way out of the trees and onto the sidewalk on Elm Street. Eric exited the path and saw a dark-haired figure crouched behind a large blue mailbox. He appeared to be desperately trying to hide from a large group of high school boys on the far side of the road. Eric grinned evilly to himself then slipped up behind the boy and tapped him on the shoulder.

"Gotcha," he exclaimed in a low menacing tone.

With a yelp, the boy spun around and dropped into a clumsy fighting stance, wide-eyed and pale. Seeing Eric behind him, he relaxed and stood up. "Good God, Eric! Don't do that to me! I thought you were Mackenzie! That black-hearted fiend swore that he was going to pound me down for that crack I made in English yesterday."

Eric smiled at his friend's, as usual, overly dramatic speech and glanced at the group down the street. He spotted the aforementioned Dave Mackenzie, senior and captain of the football team, walking with his normal posse. At just over six feet two inches with thick blond hair that he kept about a gallon of product in, Dave was the poster child for the stereotypical jock. While not the strongest, best looking or smartest boy in school he was most definitely the richest. Coming from money he had no qualms about splashing it around, something that made him immensely popular with his classmates. He was always dressed in the latest, most expensive fashions and seeing him surrounded by his adoring public gave Eric a small stab of envy. Sighing, he clapped Matt on the back.

"I think we're safe. They're pretty far down the road there." His friend looked both up and down the street before he relaxed and leaned back on the mailbox.

Matt Claughin stood to his full five foot six height and glared at Eric. Straightening his Doctor Who t-shirt, he brushed some grass off his black cargo pants before leaning down to grab his backpack. Smacking Eric playfully in the arm, he mock-glowered at him. "Thanks man, I was just thinking what do I need today? A heart attack! Yes, that would be perfect."

Eric grinned and the two started walking towards school. Matt was the very first boy that Eric had met after moving to Seaverville. Their meeting was a setup, as Eric's foster parents wanted him to make friends and Matt's mother was desperate for him to have a friend at all.

Matt had lost his father when he was very young, something that he did not like to talk about. From what little Eric had been able to learn, his dad had died in an accident at the plant he worked in. His mom had raised him alone since then.

Growing up without a father would have been hard enough on any boy, but with Matt there were a few other complications. First, he had suffered from pneumonia as a baby and lung damage had made him a chronic asthma sufferer. Second, and only slightly less crippling, his mother was an overprotective nut. After coming so close to losing him, Matt's mother was obsessed with preventing her son from doing anything that might spark an asthma attack. Because of this, Matt was not even allowed to participate in the normal gym classes. So as a pale, dark haired asthmatic with a borderline crazy mom he had two strikes against him already.

Then there was the coup de gras of uncoolness, a rabidly deep love of science fiction. It went far beyond collecting action figures and boxed sets of his favorite shows. Matt actually had memorized almost every science fiction movie and show ever made. Whether appropriate or not, he was known to spout phrases and quotes that fit into any given situation. In a larger city, he might have been the head of his own avant-garde clique, who would have appreciated his off-color humor and numerous science fiction references. In a town like Seaverville, his uniqueness made him an easy target for ridicule and abuse from his much stronger, if not smarter, classmates.

Due to his odd behavior, at least in comparison to most of the rest of the town, he had become used to being considered a "freak." Instead of being ashamed of his "geekdom," as he called it, he had embraced it and flew his freak flag high and proud. And while he was not swimming in social invitations from his peers, he did get along with a lot of them. The adults in town, as they actually got a lot of his references, found him more entertaining.

With his endless supply of one-liners from the science fiction universe, coupled with his quick wit, Matt was able to verbally destroy an opponent in seconds.

He had taken to calling his mouth 'The Great Equalizer,' a term he ripped off from an old gun advertisement. When it came to being fast on his feet, Matt might be last in line, but he was at the head of the class when it came to smartass comments and quick comebacks.

Despite Matt being a certified oddball, he and Eric had hit it off immediately. When the guys at school had teased Eric about being friends with the 'Court Jester,' as they wittily called Matt, they had been surprised when he had not only stood up for Matt, but told them to "back off or else." They, of course, wanted to know what "or else" meant. Eric had been forced to provide some helpful demonstrations after school. The results had not been pretty for the challengers. Apparently they were used to easier prey. Once word got out, the constant abuse that was normally heaped on Matt stopped.

The downside of this was that Matt, who had once had to watch his mouth or get pounded into jelly, had started being a bit more vocal in his interactions with his detractors. It was nothing short of setting a verbally abusive dork monster on the school, and Eric had finally been forced to tell Matt to scale it back, not that his input had really helped. Eric could not always be around and more than once he had found Matt stuffed upside down in his locked locker. As the two of them had very few classes together, Eric could only imagine how Matt skirted the line between humor and death on a regular basis.

As they walked towards the school, Matt regaled Eric with his latest verbal exploits against, as he dubbed them, 'The ogrish louts that proliferate our school.' Eric was only half-listening as his mind went over the schematic that he had been studying that morning. He pictured the diagram in his head and began modifying it, trying to improve its performance. The design was more than twenty years out of date, but he figured he could look up a more recent version to see if he was on the right track. It had him so engrossed that he did not notice someone standing in his path until it was too late.

A rather large hand reached out and grabbed him by the shirt-front and pulled him up into the air. Eric found himself staring into the rage-filled dark blue eyes of Donny 'Moose' Calig, the current state champion heavyweight wrestler.

At six feet six inches, he weighed in at a solid two hundred and twenty pounds and towered over Eric. Eric looked to his left and he saw that one of the senior boys, Darrin Viceroy, had come up behind

Matt and Dave Mackenzie was standing in front of him, smiling a very unpleasant smile.

"I've got you this time, Jester. I even have your boy out of the picture, so it's just you and me. Not so smart now, are you?"

Eric saw the look on Matt's face and suppressed a groan. He had seen that look plenty of times. It was Matt's brain engaging the smartass engine before the logical side could stop him.

"Yep, it's just you and me...and your buddy behind me. Damn Dave, I didn't think I was that tough." Dave's face flushed red in anger and he grabbed for Matt with one hand and pulled his other fist back. Whatever he said was lost to Eric because, at precisely that moment, Moose's fist slammed into the side of his face. Things went fuzzy for a second and then the world seemed to move. One moment, Moose was holding his shirt and the next Eric was standing over the prone forms of Moose, Dave, and Darrin, with Matt looking at him in outright terror.

"Eric! Eric, man! Chill out, man! Chill out! What the heck? Calm down, just calm down! Jesus man, what did you do to them? Are they dead?" Eric shook his head and it was like a red fog cleared from his mind. Looking down, he saw a bit of blood smeared on the back of his hand. A groan came from Moose, who turned over. Eric saw that Moose's nose was bleeding but it did not look broken.

His eyelids fluttered open and he stared up at Eric in puzzlement for a few seconds before his eyes went wide and he actually scrambled backwards away from Eric on all fours, like a crab. Once out of arm's reach, he took off at a dead run down the street. As Moose fled, the other two jumped up and headed after him, not even stopping to throw threats back over their shoulder, leaving Eric staring at Matt in confusion.

"Matt, what just happened? One minute Moose is bashing me in the skull and the next . . ."

Matt stared at him for a minute in suspicion before his mouth dropped in disbelief. "Seriously, dude? You don't remember going all Bruce Lee on those guys? It was intense! I only saw part of it because Dave had a hold of me, but you basically dropped Moose and then pushed me out of the way and wailed on the other two. It was unbelievable, man!" Matt was still staring at him and the way he was looking at Eric was making him really uncomfortable.

"What are you talking about? There's no way I could drop Moose like that, he's huge." Matt looked at him suspiciously.

"You're telling me you don't remember anything that just happened? Nothing?" Seeing Eric look at him in honest confusion Matt started nodding rapidly and shaking his finger at Eric in excitement. "I know what this is, man! You must've had one of those hysterical strength things like we're learning about in Science! Your endorphins must have kicked in and bam, you cleaned house! Wow, that was unreal! Did you see the looks on their faces when they took off? Classic!"

Eric brushed off his pants and wiped the blood from his hands onto the grass. His stomach was churning and he felt like he was going to be sick. "Matt," he began and then he felt breakfast come up fast. Grabbing a nearby signpost, he emptied the contents of his stomach into the grass.

"Eww!" cried Matt, scrambling back out of the way. "Hey, man, are you okay?" Eric waved him off as he wiped his mouth and leaned heavily on the post. His stomach slowly quieted and he straightened up.

"Come on," he said thickly to Matt. "We better hurry up or we're going to be late for class." Without waiting to see if Matt was following, he grabbed his backpack and hurried down the path.

He set a fast pace, so fast, in fact, that by the time they neared the steps poor Matt was wheezing and pulling out his inhaler. As luck would have it, Mr. Callin the industrial arts teacher, was on door duty and, seeing Matt, mistakenly thought they were late because of his asthma.

Giving them each a pass, he told them to stop by the nurse's office if necessary and let them continue inside. Matt tried to talk to Eric again at the lockers, but his lungs just were not up to the task yet.

Eric looked pointedly at him.

"Hey, Matt...Let's not talk about what happened this morning, okay? I don't want to get in trouble for fighting again." Matt looked at him for a moment and then nodded finally catching his wind.

"S...Sure, man," he gasped out. Eric watched him take a long hit off his inhaler and waited for Matt's breathing to steady before heading down the hallway to History. His mind was still reeling over what had happened. As hard as he tried to remember, all he could see was Moose lying on the ground. Maybe it had been the blow to the head. Or maybe Matt had a point with his hysterical strength theory. After all, the people who did that stuff normally did not remember it. He entered the classroom, gave Mrs. Arnold his late slip, and took a seat near the back of class. Between the bile in the back of his throat and a splitting headache, he had trouble concentrating on the lesson.

He almost ran headfirst into Emily Randall leaving class. As always, she looked amazing, blonde, perky and perfect. She grabbed onto his shoulder to stop her momentum and her blue green eyes lit up as she saw it was him. Normally, just being in her presence made his heart skip a beat and tied his tongue in knots. She smiled at him and then her expression changed to one of horror as she saw the side of his head.

"Eric! Oh, my god! What happened to your face?" Before she could say anything more, he slipped around her and entered the boy's bathroom. Under the harsh light, he saw a large purple bruise, unsurprisingly about as ham-sized as Moose's fist, covering most of the side of his face. Gingerly, he touched it and found the area extremely tender. Groaning, he leaned back against the wall.

There's no way I can hide this. Great. I promised Mr. Green that I would try to stay out of trouble after the last fight and here I've gone and broken my promise already.

He barely made it to second period on time. Mrs. Perkins, a mid-forties career teacher with graying hair and an eclectic style, gave him a disapproving look as he slid into his seat. Luckily, she was on the wrong side to see the bruise. The rest of the day went by in a blur. During lunch, a lot of conversations stopped when he walked by and he could feel his ears burning. He could only imagine what wild stories were going around.

Matt was nowhere to be found until the last bell rang and then he showed up just as Eric was walking out the front door. They silently moved away from the school as quickly as possible. Eric tried and failed to ignore the looks and whispers as they passed. It was obvious that word had spread like wildfire and he could only imagine having to explain himself tonight to the Greens.

One of the problems with living in a small town is five seconds after anything happens, everyone knows about it. He was angry, and felt his heart growing heavier the closer he got to home.

Matt switched sides to avoid a hole in the sidewalk and caught sight of Eric's head. "Holy bashed cranium, Batman! Man, have you seen yourself? That bruise is almost as big as your skull."

"Yeah, Matt, thanks," he said sarcastically. "Emily pointed it out to me after first period."

"Emily Randall? Wow. So did she go all Florence Nightingale

on you? She want to patch you up with a—"

Eric was not in the mood for this line of conversation and interrupted him. "Look man, I need to get home and face the music. I'll call you later tonight . . . if I'm not grounded until the next ice age."

Matt's face took on a look of remorse. "Frak. Dude, I never thought about that. Hey! Tell them it was all me. Well, it was all me anyway, running my mouth, never knowing when to shut up . . ."

Eric shook his head and crossed his hand between them in a hard slash. "No dice, Matt. It doesn't matter how it happened, you know how the Greens are about this kind of thing. It's my responsibility to control my temper. And they're right."

Matt looked a little uncomfortable but doggedly tried to argue his point. "But they know I've got a mouth on me," he began. "They know that if anyone started anything it was because of something I said."

Eric grinned at him in genuine amusement, for a moment at least forgetting how much trouble he was in. "Well, we all know what a pain in the butt you can be." The smile fell off his face as he thought of the Greens faces. "But it's like I said, they hold me responsible for my actions. And they should. I don't remember a lot of what happened, but what if I'd really hurt them, Matt? Did you see what I did to them? I didn't. One minute I'm getting hit and the next I'm standing over the guy that hit me. How can I be in control if I don't even remember what happened? Yeah, I took a pop to the head, but does that excuse me losing it? If I don't even remember what happened, how do I know I was in control?" Eric shuddered as the full impact of what he could have done shot through him and he felt his stomach begin to twist.

Matt put up his hands in a calming pose and slowly patted the air with them. "Okay, okay, you feel remorse. You lost it. But you need to think about this. You could've hurt them, but even when you were out of it you only did what you had to so they'd stop. I saw the whole thing, Eric, you probably could have killed them with those moves but all you ended up doing was bloodying Moose's nose."

Eric looked back at him and for an instant he let himself believe what Matt was saying; then it all came crashing down around him. "That could just as easily been blind luck. I don't even remember doing it! One misplaced blow and someone could have died. Maybe even you! The Greens and the doctors are right, if I don't find a way to control my temper…"

Matt tried to argue, but Eric turned away and almost ran across the street to the path through the trees. No matter what Matt said about how okay it was, Eric had seen the fear in his friend's eyes. Not fear of the bullies, fear of him. And that more than anything made him feel sick.

4

S.P.A.R.K.

THOMAS CRAWFORD WIPED his brow with a red checkered handkerchief. He had just finished stocking the nail aisle and still needed to shelve the new shipment of paint that came in yesterday afternoon. At twenty-seven, he was a bit old to be the stock clerk in a hardware store, even in a small town like Seaverville. He had been promised a new position as store manager later in the year, if Mr. Crandall retired as planned. In the meantime, Thomas enjoyed a good salary and benefits to do work that he loved. And it kept him free to work at his true full-time job.

It was this job that jumped to the forefront of his attention when his phone began issuing an obnoxious alarm. Dropping the paint can he was holding, he ripped the phone out of his pocket and stared at the message on the screen in disbelief.

CODE 1. IMMEDIATE RESPONSE.

Tearing off his apron, he ran to the front of the store and flipped the sign to "Closed," slipped outside and locked the door behind him. As casually as possible he walked over to the alley. Once out of sight of the street, he ran as fast as he could to the back of the building. There, between two overfull metal dumpsters, was a heavy metal door. He heaved it open and rushed down the stairs leading to the basement of the store.

Once he was in the basement, with the outer and inner door secured behind him, he stopped to verify that he was alone. Satisfied that no one was secreted behind any of the odds and ends around him, he moved to the far wall and began a complex series of adjustments to two wall brackets. It took him two tries to get it right but then a panel slid open in the wall.

"IDENTIFICATION, PLEASE," a cold metallic voice grated.

"Thomas Crawford. Gold Division."

"PLEASE ENTER AUTHORIZATION CODE INTO KEY-PAD."

Taking care, he managed to get the code entered correctly on the first try. The panel slid closed and a section of the floor parted, revealing a set of spiral stairs heading down. He cautiously walked down the staircase, making sure to keep contact with the handrail at all times. The stairs were so steep that one slip could send him rolling down, an extremely painful if not fatal prospect. After two hundred and forty-two steps, he came out into a small four by six room. He stood directly in the center of the room and waited.

"BIO SCAN COMPLETED. HOMO SAPIEN MALE. ELEVATED READINGS INDICATE HIGH STRESS LEVELS. ALL PARAMETERS WITHIN NORM. PLEASE STAND BY FOR ENTRY."

The metallic voice seemed to come from all around him. After a moment, the floor began to sink, slowly at first and then with increasingly alarming speed. A few moments later he came to a stop in a room almost identical to the one above, save for a large steel door. He placed both palms on the door and pushed. It swung open quietly on well-oiled hinges, revealing a large control room filled with monitors and workstations. Multiple steel doors stood spaced around the perimeter, entry points from different locations in town. On the far side of the room, a yellow light was flashing over a central workstation. Hurrying to the terminal, he sat down and logged in. What he saw on the screen sent his pulse further into the red.

With a trembling hand, he reached over, picked up the phone and hit the emergency button that took up most of the top of the dialing pad.

"Sir? It's Crawford, sir. We have a confirmed Code 1 hit. I repeat, we have a confirmed Code 1 hit. We have a Level A contact. Verified, Level A contact. There has not been a repeat reading and the system is in active scan. Timestamp shows that it occurred a little before eight this morning. The system was in diagnostic mode and it delayed the report until it was done scanning the entire town."

"Well, that's a nice software feature," the voice of the man on the other end of the phone dripped sarcasm.

"Holy Mary, Mother of God! With equipment like this we could all be dead before we even know anything is going on. Alright, Crawford, it's time to remember your training. Protocol demands that we call everyone in. Get as many as we can without causing a panic. I want another full scan done and diagnostics run. Soup to nuts, Agent. I want to make sure this is not another one of those damn bugs causing an error. Clear?"

"Yes, sir."

"Do we have a location?"

"Yes, sir. Based on the sensor data, we show the reading near Elm and Grace Streets, not far from the school."

"Oh, wonderful. That close to the school we could have an absolute nightmare on our hands if the thing decides to get aggressive."

"What if it hits again? We don't have a standing protocol for dealing with a Level 1 threat, sir."

"There is a reason for that, son. The only thing we can do if we have a Level 1 threat is to try and mitigate the damage."

"What do you mean, sir? There is no way to stop a Level 1?"

"Oh, there's a way; just not one that leaves anything alive in the area for the next few thousand years. Get that place staffed and get me that info A.S.A.F.P., clear?"

"Yes, sir."

Hanging up the phone, Thomas spun his chair and wheeled over to a panel on the wall. Opening the glass cover, he hit the center button. All over Seaverville cell phones began to ring.

5

MATT

MATT WAS MISERABLE as he made his way home. Yet again, he had let his mouth run away with a situation. It was not like he did not try to control it, he just had a knack for seeing an opening. Once you saw the target, it was hard not to try and hit the bull's-eye. As he drew near his house, he saw a familiar figure standing on the front porch. *Oh for crying out loud Mom, every friggin' day? Get a hobby.* Looking around, he could not see anyone, but knew other kids must have seen her lurking on the porch as they passed by.

As she caught sight of him, her eyes lit up in a mixture of joy and relief. Mary Claughin was a woman who still got admiring looks from men half her age. Her brown hair was neat and fashionably styled and her makeup was subtle, done to accentuate the natural beauty underneath. Over the years, she had managed to stay trim and fit, keeping herself healthy enough to do double duty as both parents for Matt. The only thing that took away from her appearance was her eyes. Her brown eyes had once been described as deep and soulful, eyes a man could get lost in. Now, they held a haunted look that left you feeling like she was not quite all there.

It was a well-known fact that his mother had never gotten over his father's death. From what his grandparents had told him, she had faded to a shadow of what she had been before. They had been afraid she might have slipped away completely if it had not been for Matt. Shortly after his father died, Matt was sick with pneumonia and ended up in the hospital.

When he got sick, his grandfather told him it was like she flipped a switch and shut her own pain away to focus on getting him well. Since he recovered, she had hovered over him, waiting for any reason to swoop in and help him. No matter how much he protested that she was infantilizing him, the attention had not abated over the years. Knowing that she did it out of love, he still found himself resenting the fact that she would not let him do anything. Steeling himself against the coming argument, he climbed onto the porch.

"Matt! Where have you been? I expected you home five minutes ago." She looked pissed, which was stupid because he usually got home about this time.

"Why? You got a timer on me now? Geez, Mom! Why not just install a GPS tracker in my rear?" He regretted saying it the second that the words left his mouth. Pain flared in his mother's eyes and she gasped.

"What did you just say to me? How dare you!" Her voice rose high enough for the neighbors to hear and Matt winced. Dropping her voice to a deadly low tone, she glared at him. "I don't know who you think you are, young man, but I'm your mother and it is my job to keep track of where you are."

Matt raised his hands in surrender. "Okay, Mom. Okay. I'm sorry. Open mouth, insert foot. Really, I'm sorry. I just had kind of a rough day." His mom looked like she was about to tell him what kind of night he would have, and in a panic he played the sympathy card. "Eric and I got jumped on the way to school today and..." He realized that he had made another mistake immediately; she started visually assessing him for damage.

"What do you mean 'got jumped?' Did someone hit you? Are you hurt? Why didn't you call me? That incompetent school! I told them if this happened one more time I was going to get a lawyer and sue them! It's their responsibility to make sure you have a safe environment to learn in."

"Whoa! Slow down, Mom! It wasn't at school. We had a run in with Dave and a few of his boys on the way to school. And they didn't lay a glove on me, but Eric took a pop. Then he cleaned house. It was beautiful. He took them all down so quick if I'd blinked I would've missed it."

"Matthew Claughin, you know I don't approve of fighting! If that Eric boy is so violent perhaps it's best you don't hang out with him anymore."

She was spinning up for a real tirade and Matt realized he needed to do some damage control fast.

"Hey, Mom, chill. Seriously, you need to think about drinking some decaf, okay? My boy Eric is totally not about violence. Yeah, he took the three guys down who were about to beat us up. But after they lit out, you know what he did? He worried that he might have hurt them and it made him so sick he ended up blowing chunks. It was gross."

His mother looked at him suspiciously. "You sure you're not just humoring your idiot mother so she'll let you hang out with your friend?"

Matt looked at her in outrage. "Mom! That totally offends me. First off, I don't lie to you. Second, if I was going to lie to you, I would come up with something way less complicated than this." His mother grinned at that and then sighed.

"Alright, Matt. Why don't you just tell me what happened?" Matt gave her the highlights, downplaying most of the story, making it sound much more minor that it had been. By the time he was done, he had a feeling she was not buying it entirely. Still, she had calmed down enough that he did not have to worry about being under house arrest. He led her inside as he was finishing and sat down at the table, waiting for her to bring dinner.

She was quiet while they ate, which was not necessarily good or bad. Once he cleared the plates from the table, she called him into the living room. "Matt, sit down." She waited for him to take his seat and stared at him a moment before she spoke. "Look, I know that things have not been easy for you. I make allowances for that. But you have to know that I'm not going to put up with you being a smart aleck to me. Your medical condition is a fact of life. I know you want to be able to do the things that your healthy friends do. The reality is that you could die if you overexert yourself." Matt rolled his eyes and his mother's face flushed. "Yes, I am quite aware that you think I'm an overprotective nut case."

"But—" He tried to interrupt her to argue, but she plowed right over him.

"Facts are facts, young man. I will not let you endanger yourself by taking risks, nor will I let others threaten your health with their bad behavior. I like Eric. I'm glad he was there to help and I'm going to take your word for it that things happened fairly close to what you said. So I'm going to drop it for now. If you have any more trouble with this boy, Dave, let me know. I'm the parent and it's my job to take care of problems like that. Understand?"

Matt managed to limit himself to a rather neutral, "Absolutamente."

She sighed, "Do you have homework?"

"Of course I do, Mom. What education would be complete without infringing on my free time with pointless, repetitive exercises?"

She pointed to the den with a smirk. "Get to it, young man. And I had better not hear any TV, radio or computer until you are done. Clear?" Matt groaned and nodded, grabbing his bag and heading into the den. Once the door was closed, he plopped down and zipped through his homework.

Not hard if you have half a brain and actually pay attention in class. Stowing his books back in his bag he went out into the hallway. "Hey, Mom, I'm going to hang out in the dungeon for a while, okay?"

His mother was in the bathroom, getting ready for her night class. She poked her head around the door. "Just remember to turn on the air filtration and dehumidifier, alright? I don't want you inhaling any mold spores from hanging out in that dank basement. And I'm going to have Mrs. Taylor check in on you while I'm in class tonight. I don't want you giving her a bunch of crap about it. She's a good neighbor to help out like this. Understood?"

Matt made sure his face was turned away so she would not see him roll his eyes. "Sure thing, Mom." Slipping out into the garage, he pulled on a rope that led to the pulley that helped raise the large sheet of inch thick plywood from the opening to the basement. Tying it off, he dropped a few feet to the top step and pushed open the door to his dungeon. This was his favorite place in the world. It was here that he game-mastered his role playing games, worked on models, and created objects of science fiction lore for conventions. It was also one of the few places in the house that reminded him of his dad.

Granted, the basement itself did not hold a lot of the memories. It was what he had stored there. Far from his mother's prying eyes, he had put together a sort of shrine to his dad. From what little Matt could remember, his dad had been awesome. He had been strong enough to lift Matt and his mother up at the same time. Matt remembered riding his father's back up the stairs to his room while his father carried his mother in his arms. The memory of her laughter was bittersweet. He never heard her laugh anymore.

On the far side of the basement, away from anywhere his mom could see, he had set up an office like his dad once had in the den. Here he kept all of his dad's old things that he had been able to spirit away after his death. At the time, he had no reason for taking his father's stuff. He had done it on impulse. It had taken five hours to carry the boxes of paper, knickknacks, and other tchotchkes down to the basement. He hid them behind a tarp and had just made it back upstairs when the men had arrived.

The first thing he had seen were multiple headlights pulling into the driveway. At first, he had dared to hope that it had all been a mistake and they were coming to tell him his father was alive, that he had not been killed by a falling crane at the factory. Instead, the doorbell rang and his mother answered the door.

"Mary. I'm sorry to bother you in your time of grieving."

"Anthony. You've got a lot of nerve coming here…"

"I know, Mary. You've made your feelings about both me and the organization crystal clear. I'm more than willing to honor your wishes that we leave you alone. We're just here to collect any material that Steve had from the office. I'm sorry, but we can't leave that kind of thing lying around."

"God! Steve's not even cold in the ground, you bastard. I hate all of you! If your group hadn't recruited him, he would still be alive today!"

"Mary! Get hold of yourself. Someone might hear you. The boy might hear you."

Their voices dropped low enough that Matt could not hear and when he moved closer, the floor squeaked and alerted them to his presence. At the front door was an older man wearing a long trench coat and holding a fedora. At the time, Matt had not known who he was, but later he surmised that it was Anthony Harris, the mayor of Seaverville. Taking a knee, the man had placed his hand on Matt's shoulder.

"Matt, I am so sorry for your loss. Your father loved you very much. He talked about you all the time to me."

Matt nodded although he had wondered why his father, a factory worker, would be talking to the mayor all the time. The whole thing made him uncomfortable and he had told his mother that he was hungry. He had not been he had just wanted to get away from the man and all those behind him. They all looked so sad and Matt did not want to have to hear them all tell him how sorry they were that his dad was dead. His mother had directed the mayor to the den and taken Matt to the kitchen for lunch. By the time he was finished eating the mayor and his men had left. When Matt went back into the den, the things he had not taken down to the basement were gone.

Looking back, he realized how lucky he was to have moved those boxes, as it provided him insight he otherwise may not have had. It was years before he looked at any of the stuff again. Even then, most of what was there did not make any sense.

It was much later, after years of science fiction conventions and reading that he had gone back into the material and realized what he had. Case files that would make the worst X-file look like a joke. *Eat your heart out, Agent Mulder*. The files were amazing and painted a much different picture of his father than what he had known.

All his life, he had been told his dad worked on machines and died in an accident involving a falling crane. From what he could tell from reading through the files, his father had not been a simple factory worker. He had been a certified badass, literally. The files included certifications in combat training, military grade tactics and things that Matt did not even begin to understand. Every time he looked at the files, he came away with something new. Lately, it had become one of his favorite things to do when he was feeling down. Looking at the notes written in his father's hand writing made him feel closer to the man he had spent so little time with. He picked up the folder he had been studying last night and flipped to the notes section.

"Creature X is highly adaptive. After repairs were completed to the import valve on the dam, it tried to damage the mechanism again by feeding hardwood into the pipe. New diversion screening deflected material back into waterway. Recommend installation of stainless steel grate to intake pipes to deter further interference. Creature is avoiding all areas of processed steel on the dam structure." Looking at the words, touching them with his own hand, he imagined his father scribbling on the paper.

It had taken some time but he was starting to get the big picture. The world was a hell of a lot scarier than he had ever imagined. As far as he could tell, the Grimm Brothers were writing a survival guide, not a story book. There were files on creatures that resembled vampires, werewolves, monster animals, and all manner of faerie creatures on acid. Things the Science Fiction Channel would kill to get a script about. *Whoa. If Mom knows about all this stuff, it might explain her overdeveloped overprotective side. I suppose I should cut her some slack. This is some heavy stuff to be carrying on your shoulders.*

Carefully, he placed the folder back in the box. He took a black strip of cardboard and set it in the next file to mark his place. *It's hard enough going through these things without losing my place.* With a smile, he turned back and flopped down on his beanbag chair, cracked open a can of soda and drank half of it down.

I should bring Eric down here sometime and show him all of this. Of all the people I know, he is the most likely to understand. He's also one of the few people in town smart enough to get it. Well, that and he reads like a mo'fo'; I bet he would be through these files in a weekend. Then maybe I could get those jerks at the organization to take my calls.

A few months back, Matt had run into the mayor at the river. The mayor was fishing and Matt had taken the long way around to avoid Mackenzie, who was pissed about something he had said. The old guy had waders on that ran up to his nipples and was actually standing in the water fly fishing when Matt happened by.

"Hey, Mr. Mayor. How's the fishing?"

"Oh, hi there, Matt. You startled me. The fishing is pretty good. Got about four on my stringer so far. How're things with you? School going well?"

"About as well as ever. It's funny I ran into you. I was just thinking about you the other day."

"Really? You're not quite old enough to be a voter. Still, I'm always ready to listen to future constituents."

"Heh. Well, I don't need a pothole filled on my street or a new street lamp on my block. No, I was thinking about that day you came out to the house. You know, after my dad died."

"Yes. That was a very sad day. I still miss your father, Matt. He was a great man and I know he loved you very much."

"Yeah. Well, the thing is I remember you saying you needed to get some of his stuff that he had borrowed from the organization. I was wondering what you meant by that. Was dad in some sort of club like the Lions or the Masons?"

"Well, no. You see…the thing is…oops got a fish on the line. Just a second, Matt—Oh, nuts! He got away. Boy, I think that was a big one too!"

"So, was he part of a club?"

"Well…um…let me think, that was a long time ago. What were we there for…Ah! I remember. There were some files your father had from the plant that they needed for the safety follow up, for the crane accident investigation. It was pretty important for us to find out what happened and make sure we did not have it happen again."

"Oh. So it did not have to do with any group he was part of?"

"No." The mayor had given him a long calculating look before continuing. "Why do you ask, Matt?"

"Well…the older I get…the more I wonder about him. I don't like to talk to Mom about it because I don't want to bum her out. I figured if he was part of a club maybe I could join it someday."

"Hmm…well, I think he was part of the Community Theater. Does that help?"

"Yeah, sure. I better get home before my mom comes out looking for me. Have fun fishing."

"Good to see you, Matt. Hurry home. We don't want your mother to worry about you."

At the time, he thought that was a funny thing for the mayor to say. That was until he had mentioned offhand to his mother that he had run into the mayor on his way home. She had grilled him about their conversation until he felt like a captured spy strapped to an interrogation chair. He had limited what he told her of their conversation to him asking about the fishing but she kept pegging away at him until Matt had lost his temper on her and been sent to bed early.

She was paranoid and way more overprotective for the next few days, to the point that he had seriously started considering the possibility that she might have snapped. When nothing happened after a day or so she began to calm down and even tried to play off her odd behavior as hormonal "female issues."

Matt had no doubt that she had issues, but the more he read down here the more he wondered if she did not have more than enough reason to act the way she did. The more he read, the more he wondered if any of them were truly safe. Or if they just thought they were.

6

A VISITOR

THE HOUSE WAS quiet when Eric got home. Mr. Green was still at work and it seemed that Mrs. Green was out running errands. *Or she got called to the school,* Eric thought uneasily. Sitting down at the table, he pulled his books from his backpack. The math problem on the first sheet seemed to swim before his eyes and he struggled to keep his mind on his homework. The image of Moose lying on the ground and the look in his eyes just before he ran away from Eric made in impossible for him to concentrate.

He could not lie to himself. Part of him had liked the feeling of power he had standing over his downed foe. He had felt gratified to see Moose on the ground like that. Try as he might though, he could not remember one scrap of action between being struck and standing over Moose's prone body. The shame and horror he had felt after-wards may have left him puking in the grass, but he could not deny the strange sense of contentment he had felt as well. Though he hated to admit it, part of him loved the feeling of standing victorious over his foes and had even reveled in it.

After a while, as the afternoon shadows lengthened enough that he had to turn on the light, it struck him that he could not recall ever being home alone this long in the evening. Looking outside, he noticed that Mrs. Green's car was in the driveway. *Maybe she left a note.*

Shortly after the Greens had brought him home, they had purchased a small chalkboard that they had hung next to the front door. Mrs. Green had forgotten to buy something Eric needed for school and Mr. Green had been forced to run out after he got home from work. It had surprised Eric, because he figured they would just get it the next day. After all, you do not use all your school supplies the day after you start. But Mr. Green had jumped right in the car and picked up exactly what Eric needed without complaint.

He had returned with an extra bag which he had presented to Mrs. Green like a knight returning from the Crusades. Eric smiled as he walked down the hall, thinking back on that day.

"Dear, I have something here that should help remind us all of anything that otherwise might slip through the cracks," said Mr. Green with a grin.

Mrs. Green opened the bag and pulled out a small chalkboard, framed with dark mahogany. A long piece of chalk hung from a string connected to the board.

"Oh, Edward! It's perfect! Where shall we hang it?"

"How about the hall? That way we can see it every time we are ready to walk out the door. Eric, would you like to help me hang it up? Good. Let me get my tools."

It was the first of many times that Eric had felt completely included in what was going on. He also remembered being touched that they had cared so much about something as mundane as his school supplies. That was the day his defenses had begun to crack. A small ray of hope began to shine through his jaded attitude—maybe this could become his new home.

He got to the end of the hallway and saw the message on the board was and old one, a note reminding Mr. Green to pick up some milk on the way home. Turning to head back into the kitchen, he glanced into the living room and froze in place. What he saw caused every hair on his body to stand on end and his heart to hammer in his chest.

Normally, the fireplace in the living room was left unlit during the day as no one was home to enjoy it. So seeing a roaring fire in the grate would have been enough to warn Eric that something was up. However, the scene before him pushed the fireplace far from his mind and set him on edge. Near the hearth, Mrs. Green sat in the wingback chair where she normally read her evening books.

Her eyes were closed and her hands were folded in her lap over a well-worn cookbook. The cookbook lying in her lap told Eric she had been sitting there since school let out. The few times he had seen her deciding what to make for dinner, on the days he came home from school early, she had been sitting in that chair studying on of her cookbooks.

Sitting across from her, in Mr. Green's chair, was a dark blue-skinned figure with odd blue eyes. At first, he mistook the figure for a child in face paint, until it grinned at him and fixed him with a world-weary stare. Stretching, it dropped down out of the chair and faced him. It was dressed from head to toe in black with white and green striped socks and soft, pointy-toed slippers. On its head was a vaudeville-style hat, made of felt rather than straw. The coat and pants it wore looked old-fashioned as well, with the pants pulled above the belly button and a short-waist coat that barely overlapped. While Eric was examining the figure, he felt himself being scrutinized in return. Eric screwed up his courage and stepped forward.

"Who're you and what've you done to Mrs. Green?" The figure looked at him with almost a hurt expression before putting up a placating hand. When it spoke, it was as if it was unaccustomed to using its voice. It had a thick brogue accent and sounded somewhat like the leprechaun from the horror movie Matt had made him watch.

"The lady be fine. She simply sleeps; the least of what is known to a user of the Way. It would never do for her to see me, never do. Quite a time I had finding you, lad." Moving forward, the fellow dipped into a semblance of a bow. "Introductions, I think be the first way of things. Years it has been, and you just a babe then." The way he talked reminded Eric of an exchange student he had once met. His

English was halting but the longer he spoke, the more confident he seemed to get, as if remembering the language.

"My name, which I be trusting you to share with no one, not the Greens or your dearest mate, is Matelisk. You can call me Uncle."

Eric felt his world tip a bit at these words. Half-recalled dreams came to him, a face . . . a blue face . . . could it be? He stumbled to the couch and sat down heavily, his brain full of confusion. His stomach had begun to twist again and his mouth had gone dry. Somehow, he knew that Matelisk was not lying; this was the face he had seen in his dreams. "Mm . . . Matelisk . . ." he stammered.

Matelisk hushed him with a quick hiss. "Tis safer, lad, for you to call me 'Uncle.' 'Uncle Martin' if you must have a bigger name. Bigger names seem to be the way of things these days. But say not the other one aloud. There is power in names and it is a great trust I put in you to share this."

Eric gaped at him for a moment, nodded, and then started again. "Uncle Martin, why do I know you? Who . . . no, what are you?"

Martin looked at the boy and motioned for him to sit back on the couch before flopping down beside him.

"Tis a longer story, lad, than we have time for at the moment. Needs be said that you have been lost to me for far too long. I took a great hurt and by the time I was recovered, you were gone. I have spent a great deal of time searching for you. And twas lucky I did. Your powers awakening have lit up the area like a beacon for any who use the Way to follow right to you." Martin took a moment, and then, seeming to come to a decision, began again. "I was a friend of your parents. Truth be told, your father and I were bosom companions and later when he took to your mother, she became a grand friend as well. I was there the day you were born and helped see to you while your parents were alive."

Eric sat forward at this and looked at Martin with a hungry look on his face. "You knew my parents?" he exclaimed.

Martin fixed Eric with a sharp look and muttered something. A cold chill swept through Eric and he quieted against his will. "Sorry, lad, but we have no time for old home week. Later perhaps, but not now. I need you to come with me. Right now." Standing, he walked over to the big picture window and glanced back and forth.

Eric sat on the couch, stunned. "Leave? What do you mean leave? I can't leave with you, I barely know you." Eric stood from the couch and walked over towards Martin. He was starting to get angry and Martin jumped as if he had been burned and fixed Eric with a glare, again muttering beneath his breath.

The same heavy chill swept through Eric, only this time it was like an arctic wind blasting through him blowing his anger away. Just like that the anger, the fear, even the joy at seeing his forgotten uncle was gone. It did not slowly go or fade away; instead it all just abruptly disappeared.

"Blast it!" Martin growled. "I had not wanted to do this however we do not have time for this, lad. Let me lay it out simple as I can. There are beings out there that want to kill you. Things that you would call monsters and things that are so horrible they are likely beyond your imagination. It does not matter to them who you are near or what collateral damage takes place. If you stay here, you put yourself, your foster parents and anyone else in the area in mortal danger. And that temper of yours! Every time you lose control, you give off power like a bloody bonfire gives off light. Unless you want the whole lot down on our heads, you have to keep it together."

Moving to the window, Martin muttered in a language that seemed familiar to Eric but was most definitely not English. A small light appeared out in the yard and raced away towards the river and vanished into the darkness. "What was that?" Eric asked.

Turning from the window, Martin grabbed Eric's arm and hustled him over to the fireplace. "A diversion, one that I have used successfully in the past to elude my enemies. It will draw any nearby pursuers away. By the time they realize their mistake, we need to be somewhere else, somewhere far away from here."

Martin began to speak in that odd language again while staring at the fire. The fire burst into a kaleidoscope of colors and turned red, then green before finally settling on blue. Swelling to gargantu-an proportions the fireplace suddenly filled the entire wall.

Eric thought he could make out something in the middle of the opening and leaned forward a bit unconsciously. Without a word Martin grabbed Eric by the shirt front and with surprising strength, threw him into the fire.

A scream of surprise tore from his throat before he could stop it as he flew into the flames. His cry was cut abruptly short as he smashed chest-first into a rough stone floor. Groaning, he turned over just in time to see Martin come through an oval opening in the flames and land on the floor beside him. Turning to the fire, he waved a hand and the flames lost their blue color as the fireplace shrank to normal size.

Their entire interaction had only taken a few minutes and in that short time, this little blue man had turned his world inside out. Eric knew he should be angry, or confused, even terrified. But instead he seemed unable to feel anything. Brushing himself off, he spoke in a strangely disconnected fashion. "What's going on? What just hap-pened? And why am I so calm about everything?"

Martin walked over to a stove and Eric realized that they were standing in a kitchen. It looked like something out of a Thomas Kinkade picture. The floor, as he had already painfully discovered, was made of old, round river stones mortared together. The fireplace was made of the same rocks, fitted together with thick veins of mor-tar and topped by a dark wood mantle. The rest of the room kept up the decor with a rough-hewn table and chair set and an archaic sink with an ornate spigot. The walls were stone and the ceiling was sup-ported by dark, square wooden beams that were only a foot or so above his head.

Then there was the stove, a monstrous six-burner top with a huge wood-grate oven underneath that appeared to be formed out of one solid piece of stone. The handles of the oven and grates over the fires also seemed to be made out of stone. There was an ancient-looking teapot sitting atop one of the burners which Martin filled with water from the spigot in the sink. Setting it on the stove, he opened a door at the bottom and tossed a few logs inside.

After lighting the wood on fire he closed the door. Turning, he motioned for Eric to sit at the table. As Eric pulled out the chair, he again felt like his mind was taking all of this in too readily and he turned his attention back to Martin.

"What's going on?" he asked again. "And where are we?"

Martin leaned back in his chair and produced a pipe from his jacket pocket before seeming to think twice about it and putting it away.

"Well now, lad. First, let me apologize for my rough handling of you. I hope you dunna have any lasting damage from the trip. Things were getting a might hairy and I had to get you out of there before anyone knew what I was about." He gave Eric a quick once over and seemed satisfied that the boy was not physically damaged.

"That town has a lot of technology in it and that was helping to mask you until you started to lose your temper. I have never seen a place so small that had so much technology interwoven into it. Our kind finds many man made items painful. The more advanced the item, the more painful it can be. I am hopeful that between the technology and the decoy I used any searchers will be drawn away from the town. With that kind of aversion, they should need little encouragement to keep away anyway. Any excuse to keep their distance from toxic levels of technology would be wholeheartedly embraced." Eric looked at him in confusion and then calmly sat down in the chair. Martin took a deep breath and continued.

"Secondly, I have to apologize for the geas I set on you. Seeing as I have your true name, I placed a spell on you to keep you calm. Knowing a true name is a potent thing. It gives you the power to overcome a person's resistance to your magic, if not dominate them entirely. With a thing's true name, you can turn it to dust or turn it to your whim. Now as to the spell I have laid on you? I would take it off, but I fear you might get a bit riled up. It is important that I get you to understand your situation before I release you. An untrained user of the Way can be volatile in the best of circumstances. When they have a temper such as I suspect you to have it can be even more dangerous." Eric leaned forward and Martin trailed off.

"Geas?" Eric asked. "What exactly do you mean by a geas?"

With a guilty look, Martin continued.

"A geas is a bit of forceful suggestion. Normally, it has to be put on a willing subject. In your case I forced it upon you using your true name. Between that and the fact that you are completely untrained, it was quite simple for me to overcome your resistance. I admit it is an abuse of power, but it was more important to save your life and I will not apologize for that. Nor will I take it off until I am certain you understand what is going on here."

Eric sighed and leaned back in his chair, motioning for Martin to continue. Martin sat back and seemed to collect his thoughts. "Very well, back to the beginning I suppose. Your name is not Eric. Well, your name you use with your friends is Eric and it can remain whatever you like it to be. What I speak of is your name of power, your true name. It is Leicester, which means fort or something like that in the new tongue and blessing in the old. Granted, most of your peers consider the new language old . . . but I digress."

Martin pulled a handkerchief from his pocket and wiped sweat off his face and neck as he spoke. "I apologize for my words. It has been a long time since I spoke, to anyone, and while I am out of practice, it is beginning to come back to me now." Martin pushed his hair back on his head.

"So here begins your first lesson. For what I hope now are obvious reasons, never tell anyone your true name. It holds power over you, as I have demonstrated here. Depending on the power of the one using it against you, it is still possible to resist, however it greatly weakens you. This means that one much weaker than you might be able to control you if they knew your true name."

Eric looked at him in confusion and Martin sighed. "We will cover that more in the days to come. I know that you must be confused. I cannot keep the geas on you forever so I think it best for me to try and give you as many answers as I can now. Hopefully, this will help to offset your anger once I free you from the spell." Eric shrugged at Martin.

"It's not like I have a lot to say in the matter." Martin grimaced. "Yes, well, let me try to answer the questions you have already asked before we go too much further. This place that we are in is called a safehold. Most safeholds are magical constructions set up in a pocket removed from either the Sahae or the human world. This one is also a bit removed from time as well. I will tell you more about that later. For simplicity's sake I will say that this is one of the safest places you have ever been. You are here to learn about who you are and how to protect yourself." Eric looked confused.

"Yes, I am not making a lot of sense yet, am I? Very well, let me share a bit of history with you to give you some point of reference. You were born to one of the greatest of Sahae, a scion of an ancient powerful line. The Sahae is what our race calls itself. It is also the name of our world. It is easier to understand when you understand the nuance and inflection of how to speak about it. English is extremely crude when it comes to nuance. People get tired of talking one way and they just make up a new word to describe something. It is bloody irritating." Martin glanced over at the kettle on the stove before continuing.

"As I was saying, our race comes from another place, the world of shadow. It is a place that has been forgotten by your kind or thought of as fantasy or make-believe. For some time the two worlds were separated by a cataclysm. Before that, one could move freely between them. When the worlds were severed many Sahae were trapped here. Much of what your kind thinks of as folklore is actually the story of the Sahae that remained behind. Humans wrote of them and called them myths and legends.

"The great ones and evil ones of the past are relegated in the human world to children's stories and farce. To put it in terms you can understand more easily, think of the old stories and tales told of Rumpelstiltskin, Snow White, Baba Yaga,

"The Elves and the Shoemaker . . . almost any fairy tale you were told as a child most likely. Even a lot of the superstitions and rituals that have survived to this day in your world come from when the worlds were connected. Or stem from the Sahae that remained when the passages were closed."

Martin rose from the table and rummaged through a cupboard near the sink. Returning to the table, he laid out plates and an odd-looking stone knife.

Reaching into a sack at his waist, he pulled out crackers, sausage and a hard orange wheel of cheese and thumped them down next to the plates. "Help yourself, lad."

Cutting a large wedge of cheese, Eric set about eating with gusto and for a few minutes the kitchen was quiet. He found that other than being made of stone the knife worked as expected. In fact, it was dangerously sharp, cutting through the cheese far easier than he thought it would.

The sausage was familiar tasting, but he could not quite place where or when he had tasted it before. As the food disappeared, Eric realized how ravenous he was. It was only when he took the first bite that he had discovered how empty his stomach had become. Martin got up, poured water from the kettle, and dropped what looked like grass into both mugs. As it settled down into the water, he sat down and gave a long, contented sigh before he began speaking again.

"The way things were, back before the worlds separated, was very different from the world you know today. Humans were not free like they are today. The human population was stringently controlled for all of recorded Sahae history. Depending on who sat at the head of the High Court, well, let us just say that human fortunes rose and fell quite a bit over the centuries. What matters is that there was eventually a disagreement on how the Sahae would deal with humans. The thing blew up and there was a war such as the worlds had never seen before or since. Entire continents were shifted, beings of immense power that had existed since time began fell and the connection between the Sahae and this world was severed. The unspeakable power unleashed in this battle is what caused the worlds to tear apart."

Martin took a sip of his tea. Eric took a sip as well finding it to be somewhat sweet and altogether pleasant. "Those that were on this side of the divide found the way home inaccessible. They were forced to live their lives here and this is where a great many of the human cultures' myths and legends spring from. Some decided to set themselves up as gods, others wanted simply to be left in peace and sought out the most secluded places in the world. "

"Others, driven mad or simply enraged by being cut off from their home turned their vengeance on mankind. Here are some of the monsters that your kind fears in the dark. So much pain was given out in such a short period of time. Eventually, humans would rise up to destroy a Sahae that had terrorized them for too long. In the end, most of the Sahae trapped here either perished or entered the long sleep. The long sleep is as close to our kind comes to death without dying. You drift in the comfort of darkness forever until you finally become one with it, or until you are awoken by another." Martin quieted for a moment and drank the rest of his tea before continuing.

"In any event, humanity was unfettered for the first time in their existence and ran amok. The civilizations that rose and fell in such a short time seemed to forget about the Sahae and we became false tales told for entertainment." Martin looked amused at this. Pouring them some more tea he dripped a few generous dollops of honey into each mug and stirred them with a stone spoon.

Wagging the spoon at Eric, he continued. "Now, mind you, humanity has done some great things. There are things that are wondrous, and the technology they have created is reaching the level of magic. Yet the monstrous things humans have done to each other are as bad as or even worse than anything the Sahae ever visited upon them. The difference is that some of the things humans do with technology crosses the bridge between realms and affects the Sahae. The first real notice of this was when humans tested something called a bomb. Areas on the other world were obliterated with no apparent cause."

Even through the enforced calm of the geas, Eric felt a shiver of horror at the thought of bombs being tested or even used in the human world obliterating unsuspecting Sahae in their world.

It was like hearing about a terrorist attack in a faraway land then discovering your country might be involved. Only here it was not a country, it was the entire human race.

"From what I have learned of your kind's history you first invented bombs all the way back in fourteen hundred in the Orient. It caused quite a bit of a stir on the other side let me tell you. Small sections of damage would be found with no apparent cause.

"Then Sahae began to be killed. First it was a lone Sahae here or there at random. Then it happened to a few at a time and finally large groups were being killed. The areas of damage became larger as well. There was no apparent pattern, no root cause that anyone could discover. It was perplexing to the most learned minds of Sahae. One theory that gained credence for a while was that magic was becoming unstable and, for a time, the use of the Way was forbidden. The next bit of mayhem put an end to this theory, and from that point on we began to search for a cause to our plight." Taking a sip from his cup Martin looked at Eric sadly.

"You must understand, Sahae society was still recovering from the Great War. Old grudges were still being nursed and so suspicions ran high among the great houses. Most of them suspected their rivals had discovered some new form of magic that was untraceable. Tensions were as high as they had been before the war and many feared that a second war was going to erupt. Before anything irreversible had happened one of our scholars discovered that the connection between our realms had been regenerating. The scholar had entered the world of man and discovered that humanity had grown to epic proportions. Returning to Sahae he had announced this and it had caused everyone to become distracted. A great many Sahae came through the gate too see what was happening." Martin stared down into his cup.

"They were horrified with what they found. Humans in numbers that were unheard of in Sahae history. Technology, once unheard of among most humans had grown out of control. Then, there came a startling realization. A giant blight had appeared in Sahae and killed members of one of the ruling houses. It was a few days later that one of the researchers returned home and realized that the area of the blight in Sahae corresponded with damage from the humans battling in the other world. One group of humans had used weapons on the other humans, what they called a grenade.

"The explosion and loss of life to the human's reflected a far greater bit of damage than what had occurred in Sahae. The greatest minds in Sahae began looking into this and realized that the connection between worlds was strong enough for waves of technology to pass over and impact our world." Eric felt mild shock even against the power of the geas.

"How could that happen? I mean an explosion should limit the damage to where it occurs, right?" Martin looked at him and shrugged.

"I am not entirely sure. There are many who could explain the subject better than I can. In simplest terms the energy expended somehow was able to pass through cracks in the space between the two worlds. The impact was lessened by the crossing however in most cases was still quite devastating."

Martin patted Eric's hand. "I know lad. It is terrible. During the Great War many of the things Sahae did while fighting against each other must have spilled over into the human world as well. There is no telling how much collateral damage was caused back then. The scholars discovered portals that had appeared here and there in Sahae that connected to the human world. Each group that passed through reported he same discovery. Humans were living in every corner of the land. Some were still primitive and easily destroyed or cowed but most had advanced to a point where they were able to kill Sahae that attacked them. We discovered how much the world had changed and over the next few years, many of our kind were lost to the wars with man. There was a resurgence of enmity towards humanity and large hosts of Sahae were sent through the gates regularly to attempt to quell mankind."

Eric looked at Martin in horror. "What do you mean quell?"

Martin looked at him sadly. "Quell? To return them to the more manageable number they had been before. There was a movement among the more traditional. They said that we had been lax in our stewardship of this world. We had failed to control the pest population and now it was swelling to dangerous levels. This group was led by two of the three strongest houses. Their word was law in Sahae. They came up with a plan that amounted to nothing short of annihilation of the human race."

Eric looked back at him, stunned even through the spell holding his emotions in check. "Why? Why would they want to kill us?" Martin looked at the table, not meeting Eric's gaze.

"I do not know lad. I suspect it was fear. Sahae had always feared the human race. The way they bred so quickly, how they would spread over the land and dispersed so quickly if not controlled. The sudden discovery that all their fears had come true drove them to drastic action. They did their best to control human expansion, they tried to discourage and even destroy the advancement of technology.

Sometimes they were successful. After hundreds of years the whole of Sahae was faced with a difficult truth. We were losing the war. Humans continued to advance, continued to expand. What was worse, technology had become dangerously advanced." Martin absently played with his cup.

"Sections of Sahae were badly damaged in what you call your first world war. However, no one was prepared for the absolute devastation that accompanied your second world war. A grand host was gathered to fight back. The wisest of our kind decided we should attack the most technologically advanced stronghold of humanity. So they went through a gate into Germany. The fighting was horrific from what I hear however the host did massive damage to the human strongholds."

Eric leaned forward in his seat. "You're telling me that the Sahae helped take down Nazi Germany? Seriously?" Martin nodded as he sipped his tea. Setting down the mug, he continued.

"At the time, the advancements in technology were greatest there and seen as some of the most dangerous. The host lost many in their assaults but they were quickly able to decimate the technological abilities of the enemy. Man reflects the great bombing raids during the war as instrumental in removing Germany's ability to make war. The devastation of the area was no small thing, I saw the weak reflection of it in Sahae and the damage there was massive. Still, the host of Sahae destroyed more in their short campaign than man had done cumulatively to that point. In no time, the tide had turned and the bombs stopped falling in that area. The Sahae thought that they had been given a respite that is until the Great Blight."

Eric looked at Martin in confusion. "What was the difference between the bombings that had already come through the cracks between the worlds and this new blight?" Martin looked at Eric, grief etched on his small face.

"The first blight of this kind was not discovered until later, as it hit in a desolate area of the Sahae, but this was not true for the Great Blight. A great crater of devastation and destruction struck a highly populated and ancient area of the Sahae. The loss of life was on a scale not seen since the Great War of the Sahae. A second Blight caught the survivors fleeing and set the Sahae into widespread panic. Had the human war not ended shortly thereafter, had they dropped any more of these giant bombs, it is hard to say how far the chaos would have spread."

Eric looked at Martin and felt horror again trying to claw its way through the spell that fought to keep it at bay. "The Great Blights, they were caused by atomic bombs weren't they?" Martin nodded grimly.

"Yes. The Sahae were thrown into upheaval, as many elder Sahae and entire families were wiped out in the destruction. Out of the ashes, factions arose, two of which began battling for dominance. The names do not translate well; the closest would be the Dalana and the Garos. The Dalana wanted to destroy humanity using forbidden magic—destructive weaves that would throw the human world into an early ice age or decimate the continents with fire. The Garos wanted to use guile and subterfuge to guide humanity to a more benign state. The two sides worked together at first, waiting to see which side would be more successful. The clashes of human and Sahae were couched in conflicts falsely told in your history books.

"Most of the subterfuge that the Garos sowed soon spun out of control. The direct approach of the Dalana fared no better. There were, however, two great successes. From the Dalana came a clever strategist that drew humans into fighting away from their seats of power and into the wild lands. Here, his followers were able to decimate their human adversary with impunity. He fought his battles in the far shadow of the Great Blight and his rampage took the lives of many humans.

"The other success was a Garos who spun the concept of honor and loyalty into a great web of intrigue. He caused the humans to create great alliances of peace and brotherhood. It didn't seem to matter to the humans that these alliances of peace caused more deaths than they prevented. The idea of nobility outshone the actions of nobility. Neither faction proved better than the other, and both were overshadowed by the appearance of other blights as other humans gained the power of the great bomb."

"Fearing the humans would destroy us and themselves, a third faction quietly set up a great ritual that it was believed would destroy the connection between the worlds of man and Sahae, this time for good. The magic was disrupted at the last moment by members of the other movements, each for different reasons. The Dalana wanted to continue their campaign and destroy the humans; the Garos wanted time to guide their charges to a better path.

"The effect was wholly unexpected and devastating. The third faction was obliterated, along with the leaders of the Garos and Dalana factions and many of their followers. Magic spewed out into the gap between our worlds, making wild storms appear on both sides. Hurricanes the likes of which had never been seen appeared in the human world. The storms in Sahae were violent and uncontrollable manifestations of magic. Instead of the power dissipating over time, it has remained constant, leaving a trail of destruction in both worlds."

Martin took a deep drink from his tea and then refilled the cup from a flask out of his pocket. "It was at this time that your father came back to the human world. He slipped through a little known gate to study the disruption from this side. For many years, he traveled through the human world, seeking refuge in old Sahae strongholds of power to regain his strength. Even for one as powerful as he, the constant exposure to the creations of man was a great drain on him.

"In the first days, it was easier, as the only metal that truly hurt us was iron. As time passed, the development of steel, electricity and other technology has made it truly taxing for most of our kind to live in the modern human world. He suffered greatly to conduct his study, coming close to death on several occasions. "

"After lengthy research, your father concluded that the power would not dissipate until channeled into a direction. Instead, it would simply build until it overflowed and disruptions would appear on each side of the puncture. Think of it like a container that keeps building up pressure. First you have cracks that appear. Eventually if you do not find a way to relieve the strain the entire thing will explode."

Eric fought against the lethargy he was coming to associate with the geas and interrupted. "So why not just complete the ritual and separate the worlds? It doesn't sound like the Sahae and humans should be anywhere near each other. Separating the worlds would at least make sure both sides are safe and could do their own thing, right?"

Martin looked uncomfortable at this. "Well lad, it is strange you should say that. I offered forth something close to that opinion during one of my more heated arguments with your father over this subject. I really cannot pretend to understand your father's genius. He was able to simplify it for me thusly. He believed, strongly, I should add, that if you were to successfully sever the connection between worlds, it would have cataclysmic results. He theorized that the two sides balanced each other, and that the damage that had been done needed to be repaired.

"Using his knowledge of magic lore, which was unparalleled even among our kind, he devised a ritual to stem the surging power. It was done in secret, with the help of many powerful ancient beings, and in the end he was able to set up a spell that bled the power from the rift. The toll this took on him was enormous; nonetheless, he used what he had learned to formulate a new spell. He believed this new ritual would be able to remove the energy and restore the connections between worlds. However, it was not something that he could do himself. He would need much more power than he possessed to complete the ritual safely. "

He returned to Sahae, and called a Great Council, as was his right as the scion of an ancient house. With great passion, he told the assembled hosts of Sahae what he had learned. His discovery set off a firestorm of disagreement."

Eric leaned forward and rested his elbows on the table cupping his chin in one hand. "Why? You would think they would be happy that someone had discovered a solution." Martin waved his hand irritably as he continued.

"Well as with all things that are simple there are those that need to unnecessarily complicate it. The remnants of the Dalana and Garos wanted to harness the great energy for their own ends. One wanted to use the power to wipe the human world clear and send the survivors back into the trees. The other side wanted to use the spell to enforce peace on the humans once and for all, giving the Sahae an endless labor pool of slaves. Some others even argued for the severing of the realms.

"Your father denounced those that would turn his research to their own ends. For months, he tried to convince them to see reason. He explained that to try and fight the humans would throw the worlds into a war that neither side would win. His reasoning was that if two Great Blights had so decimated the Sahae that multiple Blights set off during an all-out war could mean the destruction of everyone in both worlds. To those that would enslave the human race he pointed out that there were many who were aware of the Sahae and they would not sit idly by while their race was shackled. To the final group he tried, in vain, to explain that if the worlds were severed, there was a good chance one or both would be destroyed."

Eric took a drink from his mug. "So I take it that he didn't have a lot of success. Wait a minute. He argued with them for months? Man, I thought Congress took a long time to do nothing." Martin looked at him in confusion at the reference. Eric was about to explain when the small man waved him to silence.

"None of his arguments made much head way. Most believed he was too young to be taken seriously, others could not accept the validity of what he was saying because it differed too much from their own views."

"The arrogance from all the Sahae, each sure of his or her own position without any knowledge to back it up, sickened your father. Having lived among the humans, he had seen they were 'as noble,' his words mind you, not mine, 'if not more noble than the Sahae.'"

"When the elders demanded he tell them how to harness the power, he refused and called them fools. They flew into a rage and against all convention and law, they violated the free passage of the gathering and your father was seized and imprisoned."

"At first, I thought it would be all right. I figured your father was working an angle. The factions started trying to figure out the problem on their own, but your father was brilliant and had an insight that no one could match. He was also one of the few powerful Sahae who dared to put himself at risk to do the proper observations. When it was clear that he would not give the information willingly, the factions decided to torture it out of him. After a week he was near death and they were forced to stop, lest he die before the information was shared." Martin took a deep drink from his mug, his eyes growing more distant.

"It was then that I was able to sneak him out of the prison and to the human world. I took him to an ancient safehold to heal. It took many years for him to regain his full strength and during that time we had to move frequently to avoid capture. When your father was finally able to fake a return to Sahae, the pursuit took up after him there. I was forced to leave him to keep up the ruse and fool his pursuers. It was while I was gone, a mere few years, that your father met your mother." A wry smile appeared on the small blue face.

"Your father had worn many disguises in his travels among humans and had become quite comfortable interacting with them. He altered his appearance to pass the most intense inspection by the most learned of humans and was at ease among them, something I still have not managed to accomplish. He met your mother while staying in a cabin near Grand Lake, high in the Rocky Mountains of Colorado. She and her friends had gone there to celebrate their graduation from college, and he told me he felt something akin to a wound the first time he saw her."

"Against all reason and good judgment, he introduced himself to her one day near the marina. He claimed when their eyes met it was as if they had recognized someone they had always known. He courted her in the ancient and honorable way for two years before revealing himself to her. "

"By this time, I had returned and strongly advised him against this, as he was putting their welfare at risk. In the end, he could not be dissuaded and she took the news better than I expected. She told him it was as if he was telling her head a secret that her heart already knew. Rather than turning her away from him, this final truth cemented their bond."

Martin took a heavy drink from his tea and pulled out his pipe. Tamping it down, he rose and got a brand from the stove and returned to his seat. He puffed away for a few moments on the stem before returning to his narrative. "Geas or not, this next part will be hard to hear and harder to tell. So I ask you, lad, to try and stay calm. I . . . I was not for your parents' union." Eric felt a small flame of anger in his chest, but remembering what Uncle Martin had asked, pushed it down and tried to focus on what he was saying.

"It was not that I did not love your mother. She was a lovely woman and always terribly kind to me. No . . . It was tradition and history that were fighting in my head and heart with what your father had chosen to do. We had one of our worst fights when he told me of his decision to tell your mother the truth."

Martin paused and tears filled the edges of his eyes as he continued. "The union between a Sahae and a human is considered unclean. Humans are considered to be beneath us and the thought of uniting with one is as ludicrous to our kind as one of you marrying a horse. However, it happened in our past and the results were half-breed children who are considered Abominations."

The fire flared up again in Eric's chest and with no small effort he forced it back down. *An abomination? Is that what I am?*

"There are stories of these unions many times in the history of the Sahae. Sometimes the couple would try and hide in Sahae, other times here in the human world. The end result was always the same. The Sahae hunt them down and kill them. Any offspring they produced were slain, and any place that sheltered them was decimated." Eric shuddered.

"Your father knew this and yet he could not keep himself from being with your mother. Even after he told her the entire truth, she embraced him and they were wed. It went beyond sanity! Though I disagreed with your father, once he had made his choice, I stood by him. I had thrown my lot in with his years before when I helped him escape, and for better or worse, the path was set before us. As he put it, 'they can only kill you once.'"

Martin rose, gathered the kettle, and poured more water into their cups before dropping more of the grass-like tea into the steaming water. He finally sat back down and forced his eyes up to meet Eric's. "It all became so complicated so quickly. Your father and mother were surprised by how soon she became pregnant. And you arrived and were a wee blessing. Your father was so proud that he seemed to swell to twice his size. However, after that he began to take my warnings to heart and he and I planned contingencies for protecting you and your mother. Between the two of us, we made sure that money, property, and what magic we had were spread to provide a network of safe houses. This place is the greatest of them, very much like the last one you stayed at, as fate would have it."

Eric looked around the kitchen with a different set of eyes and realized that this room did not evoke any memories from him.

Martin pushed Eric's mug of tea over and continued. "There were such happy times after that. Your father spent every free moment he had with you and your mother, when he was not working on some new research that he had started. I do not know what he was up to, but I can tell you that for him to have spent any time away from the two of you, it must have been very important. He tasked me with watching over you and your mother while he was gone, and I found myself more than happy to oblige. You were quite the engaging little one."

At this, Martin rose from the table and went to another room, returning shortly with a framed painting. "Here . . . I should have gotten this straight away." Eric looked down at the portrait and saw Martin, a baby, and two faces he recognized from his dreams. "These are your parents, Eric. And more than anything, you need to know that they loved you very much."

Eric felt part of himself fighting to break through the numb detachment. For an instant, he wanted to scream his pain and lash out around him, then as quick as that it was there, it was gone, subdued by the geas. Leaning the portrait against the table, Eric met his Uncle's eyes. "So what happened?"

From the look on his face, it was obvious that this was the question Martin dreaded. Rising, he lit his pipe again from a brand out of the stove and puffed away for a moment before answering.

"It was March. The winter was still strong in the world and you had been unwell. Your father and mother had been forced to take you into a larger city to a hospital.

"I remained behind, looking for some magical means for us to cure you, though I admit we had already tried most everything we knew. Your mother insisted that we get you to a doctor and your father took her to the best hospital in the area.

"You were admitted and spent a week there recovering from a rather nasty virus. From my understanding, they had to feed you through a tube and kept you sedated the whole time. Your father was forced to leave you and return here as the massive technology surrounding you was damaging him and he thought you and your mother would be safe enough.

"At the end of the week, he returned to collect you, leaving me outside of town. He was on his way back with you and your mother when you were attacked. Human minions of the Sahae, apparently hired guns, set upon you as you left the hospital. Your father was weakened from the technology, you see, and it was up to your mother to drive you all to safety. She managed to evade pursuit until the outskirts of the city.

"Your father had just begun to regain his strength when a large host of Sahae attacked the vehicle. In the ensuing chaos the car left the road and crashed. From what I could tell, your father managed to get you out of the car before it exploded. However, he went back for your mother and . . . the car . . . he and your mother were incinerated."

Eric felt hollowness join the numbness inside him and for once he pushed toward it, glad for the lack of emotion inside him. Martin seemed to be fighting to control himself, a battle he appeared to be losing. Watching Eric with tears streaming down his face and pipe shaking in his trembling hands he continued. "The Sahae tried to take you. Thankfully, the first to attack were the lesser kin, and I slew them in droves. I had arrived too late to save your parents, but I was quick enough to save you." Martin's eyes grew distant as he fell back into the memory. "There were so many of them, I knew that I would never be able to protect you on my own. I can fight, however the sheer numbers meant that eventually I would be overwhelmed and they would have you.

"Your father and I had talked about almost every contingency and though I was cut off from our safeholds by powerful magic, I knew somewhere you would be safe. Taking you away from the site of the crash, I was hounded at every turn by Sahae who wanted you. I took you to a specially selected orphanage that was surrounded on all sides by high power lines, businesses and technology.

"It took everything I had to get you to the door and ring the bell . . . I left you there to lead the chase away. I had planned to return to you, however I was forced to fight and the wounds, coupled with exposure to high levels of technology, almost put me into the long sleep. I had to retreat to a nearby bolt hole where I spent years re-covering my strength."

"I knew you were out there and once I was fully recovered, I started to search for you. Things had changed so much in such a short time. The place I had left you was closed shortly after you ar-rived there. It took years of research to track you to the children's home you were staying in. I was working out how to approach you when I suddenly found you had been spirited away. It took more time to track you here. "

Martin smiled ruefully."I had thought to use a slower approach to meeting you, but then you started sending out bolts of power that could have attracted every Sahae in the area. I knew I must act and get you to safety."

Setting his pipe aside Martin fixed Eric with a serious gaze. "You cannot survive as you are right now. Even fully trained and as powerful as your father, you would be hard pressed to survive a hunting pack. It is imperative that you be taught to protect yourself and learn how to hide from the other Sahae. If they find you, make no mistake, they will kill you."

Martin sighed and sat back in his chair. He swept his hands through his hair and rubbed his face vigorously. "Look Eric, I know this is a lot to take in. What I am talking about strains the levels of credulity you have, even with what you have seen already. All I can tell you is that I am on your side and I am honor-bound to make sure you learn what you need to know so that you can survive."

Eric rose from the table and walked to the other side of the room. Even with the calming effect of the geas pushing his emotions down, his mind was still fighting to sift through everything he had been told.

"Martin, what are the Greens going to think? They're going to call the cops, who in turn will think I'm a runaway. Not only am I going to be in trouble, but I'll have the cops looking for me."

Martin smiled and waved a hand to calm him. "Your father was quite a master of magic. His was a talent not often seen. I helped him make this place and I barely understand half of what he did. He crafted a pocket where he could spend a lifetime with you and your mother. That is the beauty of this particular safehold. One of its particular powers is that time passes differently here. For us, every day we are here we only age a few hours. In the world we left behind for every day that passes only seconds pass." Martin smiled at Eric's look of disbelief.

"Your father wanted to not only be able to watch you grow; he wanted to be able to train and prepare you for anything either world could throw at you."

Eric looked at him in stunned silence. "Eric, we could spend the next hundred years here, training you in what you need to know, but the real world will not even know you are gone. And make no mistake when I tell you this. Right now, you would not last a week out there if they found you. If you do not learn to control your powers, you may be stuck here forever."

7

HITTING THE GYM

ERIC WAS GETTING really tired of the taste of his own blood. Every time he thought he was starting to understand what Martin was trying to teach him, some part of it would slip away. In a normal classroom setting, this would mean minor embarrassment or extra homework. In Martin's world, it had more painful consequences.

"Again," Martin said from across of the room.

For the last hour, Martin had been teaching Eric how to dodge, which seemed like a stupid thing to learn. Eric had, of course, made the mistake of telling Martin this and he suspected that quip was making this lesson far harder than it needed to be. Martin loved to make a point, especially when he thought it would help Eric learn something. Currently, the only thing Eric felt he was learning was that he had a long way to go before he was ever going to get out of this place. Well, that and how to properly apply an ice pack.

Two days after their arrival, Martin had removed the geas from Eric. The dangers of him losing his temper and giving away their location were overruled by the need for him to learn in his normal state. The end result had been a mixed bag as far as Eric was concerned. It was too easy to get frustrated or angry when you had no idea what someone was talking about half the time.

Martin was a harsh taskmaster. His instructions came once and were not repeated. If Eric failed to listen to a detail or forgot something, there were consequences, painful consequences. The result was a collection of bruises, bumps, and cuts all over his body. Pulling himself up off the floor, Eric squared his feet and put his hands to his sides, assuming the "at rest" pose Martin had taught him.

"As I have told you too many times to count now, Eric, the idea here is to have your body and mind working together, not against each other. You will instinctively want to put your entire body into dodging, however, that is not always necessary. "

"By training your mind, you will be able to determine what the body needs to do so that it can avoid almost any object. Ready? Here we go."

Eric tensed as Martin brought his arm up and threw a wooden croquet ball at him underhanded. Without thinking about it, he stayed in place, only moving when Martin threw another ball overhand directly at him. As he was trying to re-center himself, Martin threw four more croquet balls in rapid succession. Eric panicked as the air seemed to fill with projectiles and tried to leap out of the way causing two of the balls to hit him, one in the back which struck really hard.

"You hyperactive pixie! What are you trying to do, kill me?" Eric burst up off the floor and winged a ball back at Martin, who caught it effortlessly. The frustration he had been feeling all day burst through when instead of trying to calm him down, Martin threw the ball right back at him. Without missing a beat, Eric leaped forward, caught the ball, and threw it back all in one fluid motion. The movement was so quick that he actually managed to hit Martin in the ear.

The two of them stood there for a moment in shock, staring at each other. Martin recovered first, rubbing his ear and smiling wryly. "Well now, that was certainly unexpected. Perhaps I am going about this the wrong way. Maybe you need to be emotional to do a good job. It may be that your emotions can even help you tap into the Way."

Eric replayed the last few moments in his head and realized that there was some truth to what Martin was saying. He had been angry. To be honest, since Martin had removed the geas, he had been running on low-level anger the whole time. Martin's admonishments about his anger causing spikes of power that any Sahae might follow, coupled with his personal quest to control his temper, had kept him at a low boil.

This time, his self-control had utterly failed and he had been furious. When he thought of all the times, just today, that he had failed against one of Martin's tasks, there were definite commonalities.

Moments of panic, doubt and fear that caused him to lose his concentration with disastrous results. This time though, he had been so angry that there had been a moment of clarity. Granted, he had been focused on making Martin eat a croquet ball, but that had allowed him to avoid locking up. Something that Martin said registered with Eric.

"The way? I've heard you mumbling about that, but what does it mean? Some special technique I'm supposed to be using?"

Martin laughed and hopped down off the raised platform he was standing on and sat on the edge of it. "No, boyo. Not the way. The Way. The path of power. In human terms, you might call it magic."

Eric's eyes lit up. "Like real magic? So I should be able to make a shield of force in front of myself or summon a warrior to fight for me?"

The look on Martin's face was a mix of incredulity and horror. "Where would you get a daft idea like that?"

Eric looked a bit uncertain and shrugged his shoulders. "Well, when I was younger there were these pencil and paper games we played with dice. And there are, you know, movies and stuff."

Martin slapped his palm into the center of his forehead. "Such nonsense stuffed into that head of yours that I must overcome! No flashy parlor tricks will save you when a fellow is trying to bean you with a wood ball. Summon a warrior to fight for you? What utter bollox!" As usual, when he went off on a rant, Martin's accent began to drift all over the spectrum. When he paused to take a breath, Eric jumped in to try and defend his questions.

"Look, how am I supposed to know? This is all new to me. Besides, you said that hybrids could sometimes do things that Sahae can't. And how am I going to learn if I don't ask questions?" Eric was irritated and he starting speaking faster and faster until the elder Sahae swept his hand down with finality.

"Enough! Eric, you would try the patience of a bloody rock!"

Martin's eyes blazed bright blue for a moment before settling back to normal. "You ask questions without thinking. The way to wisdom is to think before you ask the question and never waste time by asking questions you could answer yourself." He stalked to the far side of the room, but as he neared the door Martin's steps slowed. He stopped with his hand on the door handle. Without turning, he spoke.

"I . . . I am sorry lad. That was uncalled for. You are right to be asking questions. And it is not your fault that your rearing lacked the most rudimentary understanding of magic. That fault is mine. And I fear that guilt is causing me to lash out at you." As Martin turned around, Eric was shocked to see tears in his eyes.

"The past few years have been a strain on me and I had not thought about how different you would be when I found you. Some part of me still expected that wee baby who giggled whenever I told him bedtime stories. When I think of all the parts of your life that I have missed, I . . . well, I should have been there for you, lad. I am sorry."

Eric recovered quickly and crossed the room to place his hand on Martin's shoulder. "Uncle . . . I know you came for me as soon as you could. I can't tell you what your finding me means, well aside from the whole not being dead thing. You've told me things that I'd given up hope of ever knowing. Things about my parents, about who I am, and about why I ended up where I did..."

Martin looked up at him, trying to discern the boy's authenticity. For a moment, they locked eyes before Martin looked away. "It seems that we are both going to need some time to adjust to all of this, lad. Take some time to yourself for practice and we can talk more tonight at dinner. I can tell you more about your parents, if you would like."

Eric grinned at Martin both over the promise of the stories and some valuable time alone. "Yeah, Uncle Martin, I'd like that." After Martin left the room, Eric approached the practice dummy and began going through the first few basic fighting stances that Martin had taught him.

It was hard to judge time here like he was used to, his watch had stopped working when they got here and there were no windows. Based on the routine, Eric estimated he had been away from his home for almost a month. Despite Martin's assurance that for every day they were here a few seconds passed back home, it was disconcerting. Perhaps his uncle was telling him what he wanted to hear. It did not really matter though, since he had no idea how to get out of here and Martin was not going to let him leave until he was ready.

The first night, Martin had shown Eric to an amazing room almost four times the size of his bedroom at home. The door was made of a huge single piece of oak that opened into a room dominated by a gargantuan, four-poster king-sized bed. The bed, also made of oak, had the softest mattress Eric had ever slept on. In the morning, he had explored the room a bit and found a bathroom off the bedroom with a tub the size of a small in-ground pool.

After his bath, he had dried himself on an oversized white cotton towel that was so soft it almost felt wet when he picked it up. In his room, he found his dirty clothes missing and a set of new clothes laid out for him. The clothes took some getting used to. The pants were simple enough to figure out, with a drawstring that crisscrossed at the front. He put them on and pulled the string tight and tied it like a shoelace. The shirt was a simple t-shirt and his shoes had been replaced by the same soft slippers that Martin wore, minus the points on the end. After dressing, he had left the room to find his way back to the kitchen where Martin was waiting with a steaming pot of porridge.

After breakfast, he had asked Martin about something that had occurred to him while he was playing with the controls and filling the tub. He noticed that nothing in this place was made of metal. Everything that would have normally been metal was made of the same stone as the stove in the kitchen. Martin nodded at the question and chased his food with a large swig of tea before answering.

"Well lad, there are many kinds of metal that do not bother the Sahae. However, iron and the different blends of it have detrimental effects on our health."

"Each type of metal has a different impact level depending on the Sahae you encounter. For the lesser, the touch of a cold iron nail is enough to bring sickness or even death, whereas some of the greater can tolerate metal well enough to handle it on a regular basis."

"It is, as a matter of fact, one of the reasons that many Sahae think the human race is driven to build using so much metal. The first homes were warded by metal clasps, metal nails in the frames, metal fences and gates and even metal roof ornaments and tiles. When we made this hold, your father wanted to give your mother as many of the creature comforts as he could so the two of us set about creating many of the things that are here in the house. The stove took us a full week to form out of a solid block of stone." Eric looked at the stove in an entirely new light after that day.

Once their food settled, Martin had announced that they were going to begin Eric's training. He had shown Eric to the gym, which was down the hall from his bedroom. Easily the size of the school gym at home, it had a collection of dummies, heavy bags, ropes, obstacles and things whose use Eric could not even begin to figure out. The first few days had passed in a blur of sore muscles, bruises and blood. Martin pressed him every day and Eric was surprised at how quickly he was able to improve his physical performance.

He ran until he felt like he was going to puke and after almost no rest was forced to run again. Martin showed him basic forms of fighting and defense and something about them seemed familiar to Eric. It took a few weeks for him to truly understand what Martin was trying to do. He wanted to see how much Eric knew and how much he needed to learn. Until the breakthrough today with the croquet ball, he had begun to wonder if he was doomed to an eternity of failure.

Walking over to a table near the wall, he poured himself a cup of water from the clay pitcher and sat down with his back to the wall. Closing his eyes, he held the cool glass against his forehead, relishing the feeling against his overheated skin. He found his thoughts going back to Seaverville.

I wonder if anything sensed me enough to come to town. I would hate to think that something hurt the Greens, or Matt, or anyone looking for me. Then again, if what Martin says is true, I could spend years here and still be back on the same day to deal with anything that was looking for me.

He found himself questioning what his future held. Martin had sat him down and had a long talk with him about what would happen once he could handle his powers. None of the options sounded appealing, at least not now that he had found a home. If Martin had showed up while he was still in the orphanage, he would have jumped at any of the choices and never looked back. The most obvious and painful truth he had to face still remained an unresolved question. Should he disappear? While he could stay and continue his life with the Greens, doing that would put them and everyone else in town at risk. Martin had been adamant in his thoughts on the subject.

"Eric, there are some hard truths to be dealt with. It is possible that you might be able to control your powers and live the rest of your days in Seaverville. In many ways, it is a very defensible position. All that technology makes it hard for most Sahae to even visit the town."

Looking at his uncle with a pained expression, Eric spoke. "Is it worth it? Would it be worth it if I were happy for a day? A year? Twenty years? I could live my entire lifetime and then have everyone I know and love killed because of me. Or it could happen five minutes after I get home."

"That is true, lad. Life is full of choices. Luckily, it is not a choice you have to make today, or for some time to come. First we must finish your training and you have quite a ways to go. There will be plenty of time to discuss this once we have a firmer grasp of your abilities."

Martin was right. At the rate he was going, he could at least take solace in the fact that his inability to master skills left him plenty of time to plan his future. The thought of leaving Seaverville hurt more than he ever thought it could.

As much as he had told himself he did not need a home, parents or the Norman Rockwell ideal, he realized now that it had all been a lie. That need had been locked deep inside him like a monster in a cage. The monster had been unleashed and there was no putting it back in the box. Rage swept through him and leaping to his feet he smashed the practice dummy to bits before he regained control of himself. Breathing heavily, he leaned back against the wall and closed his eyes.

This is so unfair. When do I get to actually be happy? Is there a reason the universe has to dump on my head every single time I've got a glimmer of hope? No, it's not bad enough that I'm an orphan. I finally find a home just in time to find out I'm a half-breed freak that's marked for death by an entire race. And if I ever learn to control my powers, the best thing I can do for everyone I know and love is to leave? Seriously?!

He threw himself forward into a wild series of moves that sent him tearing through the remaining practice dummies. Standing amid their shattered remains, he finally felt the last of the rage drain from him, leaving him empty. Sinking to the floor, he fought back tears of frustration. As much as he hated to admit it, Martin had a valid point. Even if he ever finished training, going home might not be an option.

Returning put the entire town at risk. Whenever the subject crossed his mind he recalled the stories that Martin had told him, stories that haunted him. Places that had harbored Abominations, god, he hated that term, had suffered horribly. They were wiped off the map or their inhabitants had mysteriously disappeared. Their only crime had been harboring a half-breed, or hybrid, as he preferred to call himself.

The right thing to do, the noble thing, was to hurt the Greens and everyone else to keep them safe. Let them think they had failed and that he did not want to be part of their world. It would be very easy for him to make it impossible for them to keep him. Even the perfect Greens had their limits. Getting sent back to the orphanage would be very simple and very painful. Maintaining a facade of disdain would be no more difficult than his facade of cheerfulness had been when he was younger.

Once he was back at the orphanage he could disappear; just another statistic. No one would bother looking for him; they never really do for teenaged orphan runaways. Well, maybe Mrs. Clark would. Or he could arrange for early graduation from high school and get to college early. That would give him all the independence and anonymity he would need. School had always been easy. When he was living at the orphanage he had taken every class he could and currently had more credits than anyone in even the junior class. Without all the AP courses he was taking he could probably have graduated this year, so if he switched over it would be possible to get out early.

The actual thought of leaving Seaverville filled him with such anguish that he had trouble breathing. He had never been happy when he was returned to the orphanage, but even the last time was a sliver of pain in comparison to this. Standing up, he brushed himself off and grabbed a broom to sweep up the mess. The simple task helped him to clear his mind.

His heart and head were at odds at what to do. His head told him that it only made sense to get away from everyone. He only put them at risk by being there. His heart just wanted to go home. It might be childish, selfish, and unreasonable, but that was why he was so angry. It was not fair when he finally found a place where he fit in, where he was starting to feel like just another kid, that it all would be taken away. With his guard down, there had come a moment here and there where he had almost felt like he could relax and settle in. Then the universe stepped in and kicked him right in the face.

Tossing the broom in the corner, he began setting up new practice dummies. It was just all too much to think about right now. For now, he had to focus on trying to learn as much as he could. If he trained hard enough, maybe, just maybe, he would be strong enough to go home. Placing the last dummy in position, he shook out his arms and legs and prepared to start practicing again.

8

LEARNING THE WAY

A FEW DAYS later, Martin closed up the gym while the boy went off to soak his aching muscles in a hot bath. It was astounding how well the boy had taken to the training. When they first started, the lad had shown a natural gift for physical combat, something he had at first attributed to Eric having been forced to fight from a young age. *Sometimes a harsh upbringing can be a blessing in teaching one how to survive.*

But his abilities went well beyond the life experience; the boy was one of those rare cases, someone who had the natural aptitude for combat infused into every fiber of his being. It had become painfully apparent that as skilled as he was at physical combat, he was woefully inadequate in the Way. Martin had been beginning to fear that Eric was an Abomination that was only able to randomly tap the Way, albeit quite powerfully. The incident with the croquet balls had given him hopeful insight to the contrary.

Once the boy had mastered his body, his mind would follow and then they would know for sure. The first two months of training had hardened the boy's muscle and greatly improved his already superior physical condition. His mental state and his confidence were what Martin had to deal with now. And it appeared that the boy had his father's famous temper.

If Martin was not careful in teaching the boy control, he would have an obvious flaw for his enemies to exploit. The problem was the only progress they had made was when the lad lost his temper. Just this afternoon, Eric had spectacularly lost his temper. It had begun innocently enough. Towards the end of the session, Martin had continued pushing Eric to try reaching out to the Way.

"What's the point? This is stupid! I keep trying and failing and you just say, 'again!' Like saying 'again' one more time is going to magically make it happen. It's like being trapped in a cage with a reject from a bad Kung Fu movie. It's crazy!"

Martin had simply raised an eyebrow at Eric. "Well, it is possible that you are no more than an unteachable Abomination . . ."

As soon as the word left his mouth, the boy exploded into action. Turning with a wordless howl, Eric had grabbed him and thrown him across the gym. Martin had been caught flat-footed, not only by the speed of the attack but also by the sight of Eric's eyes. They had gone a brilliant, luminous red, just like his father's would when enraged, and Eric had spoken a word of power that Martin had never told him.

"Eshajek!" The booming power catapulted Martin into the ceiling before releasing him to smash to the ground. When he woke, sometime later, he found Eric standing over him with a look of abject horror on his face. "Martin! Are you okay? I'm so sorry, I don't know what happened. I just . . ."

Martin held up a hand for silence and rose from the floor. Apprehension grew in Eric's eyes as he waited for retaliation from his Uncle. He seemed surprised when all Martin did was chuckle.

"That was unprecedented, my boy. Simply astounding! You not only used the Way, you also used a Word of Power without any training. That is exactly the kind of thing I would expect from your father's son." Martin paused, looking unsettled. "Well, this definitely proves that you can, and must, be trained in the Way. Properly trained, you will be an asset to those around you rather than a danger."

He had Eric try multiple times to recapture the Way, but it was obvious that the original effort had drained him, so he sent the boy off to soak in the bath. As he closed the door to the gym, he grimaced. *He may just have a fighting chance after all. But how do I train someone whose abilities I do not fully understand?* He had downplayed how upset he had been by the experience, letting Eric think he was embarrassed by being caught unaware. The reality was that he was prepared to give his life to train the boy if necessary and had gone into this with his eyes wide open.

The simple, terrifying fact was that Eric should not have known that Word of Power. The words were a closely-guarded secret among those that had mastered the Way. To have an unskilled novice use them not only put the user at risk, it also could cause massive devastation. For Eric to be able to pull a word from nowhere and use it so effectively against Martin opened up all sorts of unpleasant thoughts.

What if the old ones were right? What if the mixture of our two races makes beings that are unstoppable engines of destruction? Will Eric truly be able to control what he does or am I simply arming him with additional abilities to destroy?

Martin suddenly felt a great weight settle on him. If the boy were to become a force for destruction he would truly be responsible for evils far greater than he was currently accused. He sat for some time, drinking tea and thinking about the boy before coming to a decision.

I threw my lot in with his father long ago, and that loyalty now belongs to the boy. For better or worse, the path has been chosen. From what I have learned of him so far, he has the heart of his mother and the will of his father. I cannot imagine a world where he would become a force for destruction, even with all the years I have lived.

Feeling somewhat better, he headed to bed. The next day, Martin began using a new training model, making Eric emotional. At first, he tried a myriad of emotional responses; however he found that anger and fear had the best results. Fear was hit or miss, mostly because deep down the boy seemed to trust him. Anger yielded better results.

When the boy lost his temper, he was able to sharpen his focus enough to call upon the Way. It allowed them to take the first step towards harnessing his power, though it came with an obvious weakness. Once Eric had learned to reach out to the Way and tap it without anger, Martin planned to redouble his efforts to teach him to control his temper and still call upon the power whenever he needed it.

At the moment, Eric was neck-deep in an ice-cold bathtub trying to remember the words of a simple warmth spell Martin had told him. He had been at it for some time and his lips were beginning to turn blue. Rather than let him out of the tub, Martin decided to take the training to the next level.

"If you cannot focus enough to call upon what you need under pressure, then you will die in the real world. It is as simple as that. You think the water is uncomfortable, boy? This pales in comparison to what the Sahae will do to you if they find you out in the open! They will take no pity on an Abomination!"

Eric glared at Martin. "I hate that word!" His chattering teeth turned the scathing comment into something a bit more comical. "Abomination. What a crock! Science has a name for what I am. When you take two things that normally don't go together and combine them to make something that has the best traits of both, it's called a hybrid."

Martin glanced down at Eric dismissively before turning away. "Make sure to explain that to them as they are ripping you limb from limb." He felt the tension growing and decided to take one last pot shot. "From your description, I would expect a 'hybrid,'" he commented snidely, pausing to make air quotes with his fingers, "to be able to master a simple warmth spell. So either put up or shut up."

Eric went silent for a moment and then chanted the spell of warmth with such power that the water in the pool exploded into steam. With a "Yipe!" he came bounding out of the now empty tub, his skin the color of a well-cooked lobster.

"Ow, ow, ow, ow, ow! Oh, that hurts, oh, ow," Eric pranced in a circle while Martin, too overcome with laughter at his antics to assist him, looked on helplessly.

When Martin finally got his breath back, he muttered a phrase of healing and the red skin dissipated and red blotches appeared on his own skin. Eric stopped jumping around and turned towards him.

"That's better. Hey! Uncle Martin, what happened to your face? Did the steam catch you too?" Martin sat down heavily on the bench near the wall and shook his head.

"No lad, I took most of your hurt from you. It is a dangerous spell, as it does not so much heal the recipient it simply removes the injury done to them and visits it on that caster. You can share the burden of a friend with neither one of you suffering the full effects. It also helps to speed the healing a bit, although it does take more out of you than some of the other spells."

Gingerly moving to the side, he motioned for Eric to sit. After taking a moment to center himself, he continued. "Control, boy; you are seriously lacking in control. Using your emotions to tap into your ability was a mistake. I see that now. We will have to try a different way. It will take longer, however today illustrates how dangerous and unpredictable your abilities are. There is already an inherent danger in what we do. Magic is primal and, in many cases, capricious, especially given the current state of our two worlds.

"Your lack of control using the simplest of spells reflects how hard it is going to be to teach you anything harder until you have mastered our own emotions. Trying a spell as powerful as the healing transfer can lead to serious injury and even death, and there is also the danger of small bits of you being transferred in the process if it is done wrong." He saw a look of horror cross Eric's face and his accent took on a bit of brogue as he continued with a sardonic grin. "No danger of that with what I cast. I have done this before, you know."

Eric smiled in relief and then his face clouded. "So the power surge between the two worlds is impacting magic no matter where it is cast?" Martin looked at him in confusion at the subject change before making the intuitive leap.

"If by power surge you mean the paradoxical backlash of unfocused magical energies that threaten to tear the very fabric of existence apart, then yes, it has a very long reach. The spell that your father managed to put in place was never meant to last as long as it has.

"The fact that it is still in place at all stands as a monument to his superior intellect. Still, the overflow around the edges of the spell has caused it to deteriorate over the years. This in turn damages most powerful spells that are built to last. For example, I have had to check the wards regularly since we arrived. A few of them have required reinforcing since we got here. Part of that is might be caused by you. It has long been theorized that . . . hybrids can disrupt magic simply with their presence.

"The same is said to be true of technology, although I do not think, in this case, that the random destabilization is being caused by either you or technology. Based on their initial condition when we arrived and the repairs I have made, I would say there is a growing danger of power surges, as you put it, getting the best of most of the wards in the coming years. The stronger the magic, as we have in here, the more likely it is to be impacted by the magical chaos out there. When we created this place, the magic was much more stable, otherwise I doubt we would have put such strong wards in place. There are numerous smaller ones that would have worked as well, granted they do not give the time distortion that is invaluable to us right now. Still, once you are trained, this place would be best abandoned. It takes far too much effort to keep it stable."

Eric looked around the gym and felt a twinge of sadness. The time he had spent here with Uncle Martin had already made this place feel like a home. Not like the Greens', where some part of him always felt afraid, like it could all be taken away from him again in just an instant. No, here he felt truly comfortable, like he belonged in a way that he did not have to explain to anyone. It was as much his home as it was Martin's. It was the first time he could really say that about any place. Clearing his throat, he caught Uncle Martin's attention.

"So, if I chose not to return to the Greens', what would I do?" The unspoken fear that his Uncle would wash his hands of him once he had fulfilled his obligation to train him hung in the air. Martin seemed to read between the lines and gave Eric a warm smile.

"Well lad, there is an endless stream of possibilities. Granted, most of them follow the same basic form, but the substance that form takes would be entirely up to you. First off, we would have to address the human authorities."

"After all, you have to be able to move around freely. After we sorted that out, it would be a simple matter of finishing your primary education. Then, if you wanted to follow in your mother's footsteps, you could choose whichever secondary school, I believe they call them colleges, and course of study that you want. I, of course, will continue to school you in the finer points of the Way."

Eric looked surprised and relieved at this and Martin grinned at him devilishly. "Oh yes, it is going to take at least a decade or two to get you where you need to be, if you continue to be an excellent student. Most Sahae spent at least a century learning to control and master their power. Given the limited lifespan of humans, we had best accelerate your path. Even once you are proficient, I will need to instruct you on nuance for decades to come."

Eric let out the breath he had not realized he was holding. Some part of him had feared that this was just another temporary situation, one of so many that had been part of his life for as long as he could remember. Now it dawned on him that Martin was not going to disappear and that gave him more comfort than he thought possible. This little blue man was family, more family than he had known his entire life, and it was a new and wonderful feeling. After having spent so much time with Martin, he realized that he did not want to imagine a world in which he could not have both Martin and the Greens in his life.

9

THE DANGERS OF MAGIC

THE NEXT DAY, as Martin finished breakfast, he felt the wards flare and a strong spike in the Way. Startled, he closed his eyes, extended his senses, and felt no further stirring. With the ease of one who had been navigating the magical currents for centuries, he traced the disturbance to Eric's room. Leaving the pot on the table, he hurried down the hallway. As he entered the boy's room, he saw that there was a thin layer of dust everywhere. Looking askance at Eric, he watched the boy's face flush crimson.

"I . . . ah . . . I had a little problem with the water pitcher."

Martin glanced at the room and realized the item that was missing was in fact the large ceramic water pitcher. Raising an eyebrow he fixed a stern gaze on Eric. "And what, pray tell, was the nature of this problem?" Eric ran his hands through his hair and took a deep breath.

"Well, I got tired of having to wash my face with cold water every morning, so I decided to heat the water in the pitcher, just a little." Martin rolled his eyes and brushed a bit of dust off the nearby chest of drawers.

"You did this without examining the pitcher or even giving a thought to whether or not the vessel that is full of water every time you wake might have an enchantment on it?" Martin could see from the boy's chagrined expression that his arrow had found the mark.

"Eric." Martin cleared a chair of dust with a flourish of his hand before sitting. "I cannot stress enough how dangerous that was. Magic is connected in complicated ways that can have unexpected and violent reactions if interacted with improperly." In the dust on the floor, Martin drew three circles, one at each point of a rough triangle whose edges overlapped.

"This first center circle represents the vessel you interacted with. As you see, it sits adjacent to the other circles that hold it in place. To imbue it with the refilling spell, and please keep in mind this is the simplest layman example I can give with my limited teaching knowledge, you must gently lay your dweomer, your enchantment, into the center of one of the adjoining circles. Now, let us say this cup, placed in the other exterior circle, represents the cooling enchantment placed on the vessel. The original casting would have balanced the spell by, in effect, moving some of the circle to the other side. Therefore, when you attempted to heat the water, it altered that balance and all three circles came apart."

Eric thought about this for a moment, nodding. "Wait," Eric said. "Does that mean that if a person was enchanted and you tried to remove an enchantment, the same thing could happen?"

Martin nodded solemnly and Eric's expression turned to one of horror. "To a certain extent, yes, though it would be rare for someone to burst. All people have some power in them and most objects do not. Even those that are imbued have much less resistance than a sentient being. However, it is easy to overbalance a spell with less volatile, but none the less disastrous, results. Most spells placed on creatures have a way of removing them easily without magic."

Eric's eyes lit up in understanding. "Like a back door in a computer program!"

Martin looked at him in confusion. "I am not sure what you mean half the time. Let me give you a point of context that we both understand. In the old stories, your ancestors told of the sleeping girl being awoken by a kiss. That is a good example, though overly simplistic. Barring using a known trigger to remove a spell, which few casters will readily tell you about, there are specific ways to counter a spell. First, you must be aware of the spell. This requires detailed examination of what is there and then further exploration, non-invasively of course, to see if there are any nasty surprises hidden in the enchantment. "

Martin caught Eric's gaze and held it. "It is absolutely vital, Eric, that you take the time to do this before you even think about attempting to work magic on anyone or anything. Granted, this step goes out the window in a combat situation, but beyond that, it must be inviolate. Otherwise, you can end up doing more harm than good."

Eric sat on the edge of the bed brushing even more dust onto the floor. "How can I be sure that I have found every aspect of a dweomer though?"

Martin sighed. "You cannot, Eric. In the end, it will be up to your skill, experience, and intuition to guide you. Magic is, at times, as much about intuition as it is about structure. It is important to approach each situation with the utmost caution, and to trust your instincts."

They sat in silence for a moment while Martin collected his thoughts. "As to how a being could be affected, the main difference is that a living being has been touched by the Way. The energy of life in each creature resists alteration on a primal level. Now, this is greatly reduced if you can find the true name of a subject. In most cases, the resistance you will face when trying to exert your will onto another will be quite taxing.

"For example, your decimated water pitcher. I am familiar with the magic used to create it as I am, in fact, its creator. I laid complex layering spells on it to resist breakage, remain at a nice, cool, drinkable temperature, and to refill whenever it was emptied or each day. This is, by the way, a pitcher of drinking water and not, in fact, for washing your face. There is a basin in the water closet that is for that function that I shall show you after we finish speaking."

Eric looked embarrassed; Martin pretended not to notice and continued. "Now, with a complex, if straightforward, enchantment such as this, you can unbalance the object fairly easily. It is entirely my fault for being lax in my instruction. I should have warned you not to practice magic on any of the objects here unless you had my permission. Once you have destroyed an object by magic, it is very hard, however not impossible, to recover it."

Martin closed his eyes and began speaking too softly for Eric to hear. A faint blue nimbus surrounded his hands and began to brighten with each passing moment. Soon the light became too bright to bear and Eric was forced to avert his eyes, throwing an elbow up and covering his face. When he could almost see the bone of his arm, he heard the sound of sliding debris accompanied by a loud snap. The light vanished and he lowered his arms, blinking tears out of his eyes. A rather wan-looking Martin sat before him with the restored pitcher in his hands.

"You see," Martin said weakly. "In this case I must admit I cheated a bit, as I know the true name of this object as well. However, you can see how much of me this took to restore. That, Eric, is a very important lesson. To restore takes far more than to create which, in turn, takes far more energy than to destroy . . . Restoring an object can drain you of all your life essence, so you must be very careful if you ever attempt something like this. There must be a very important reason to do so."

Eric reached out and steadied Martin as he swayed a bit on his chair. "You could have just told me, Uncle Martin. Why risk doing it when it is so dangerous?" Martin took a deep breath and sat up straight in his chair, fixing Eric to the spot with the strength of his gaze.

"It was necessary! I have to teach you what you need to know so that you do not kill yourself because of some nonsense you heard of as a child about magic. This is a serious pursuit with serious consequences. It is up to you to make the right choices for yourself and those around you when you use the Way. That will be the lesson for today, I think. I need to rest and you have much to think about. Do not practice any more magic until we are back together. Also, please do not experiment with magic unless we are together and you have received my permission to do so."

Martin reclaimed the drinking glass from the floor. He slowly rose and moved over to the table, setting both the pitcher and the glass back on the tray.

Motioning Eric to follow him, he led him into the bathroom and showed him how to use the sink there. It was located in a recess Eric had overlooked. As Martin walked back out to the bedroom, Eric caught his arm.

"Uncle, I don't understand the Way very well yet, I know that. I'm confused. Sometimes I can do things and I've got no idea how I do them. I've seen the surprise on your face, like the day I knocked you into the ceiling. You were afraid, not of me necessarily, but of what I'd done. Other times, like today, I do something that is monumentally stupid. Well, at least it is clearly stupid once you explain it to me. The thing is, I'm having a lot of trouble getting my mind around this. Why can I just wing some things and others nearly kill me?"

Here it was at last. The moment he had been dreading. It was time for them to discuss the very fears that Martin had been keeping to himself the entire time. Sighing, Martin motioned Eric to sit on the bed. Taking a seat next to him, he took a moment to think about how he wanted to phrase his news.

"Eric, I...well, I have thought about this conversation many times since that day and I can think of no nice way to say this." Eric grinned and elbowed him.

"Well, if you can't say something nice come sit next to me."

Martin smiled despite himself. *How like his mother he is, so able to set one at ease with a simple silly joke.* Wiping the smile from his face, he became serious. "Eric, I know that you do not like the word 'Abomination.' You prefer the term 'hybrid.' However, this is the time that I must stop and explain to you why my kind calls

94

hybrids by this name." Eric's eyes took on a gleam which Martin had learned to associate with his near insatiable desire for knowledge.

"You see, lad, the combination of races can be unpredictable. Our history, and yours for that matter, is full of stories describing these offspring. To put it in perspective for you, think of Greek and Roman history. The offspring of the gods? The gods were Sahae that were trapped here when the path between worlds was closed. Rather than go into hiding, they set themselves up atop an unscalable mountain and convinced your forefathers that they were divine.

"Their dalliances with the human population produced many children. Some were able to pass as human. They were well-liked for all the help they could give their brethren even while they were envied. Other offspring were horrific, even monstrous. Think of the Harpies, the Gorgon, the Minotaur, and lest I forget, the Titans. Somehow, the humans got the story screwed up, with the Titans being the forefathers of the gods, silly as that is. In truth, they were Abominations that tired of their parents shunning them. The cruelty of the father turned the son into more of a monster than he appeared on the outside. Well, son and daughter. In the end, the battles laid waste to whole swaths of land and left many Sahae and Abomination dead."

Eric tensed every time he said the word and Martin decided it was time to address it. "Lad, you must realize that a word has no power over you. Rather than let it anger you, let it roll off your back. Giving any opponent such an obvious hole in your armor will lead to your destruction. It is just a word. You must see yourself as something better and the words of the world will be like ash flying upon the wind." He saw Eric consider his words and continued. "There is no way of knowing what powers any Abomination will have. I have heard of those that could start fires with their mind, others whose touch killed by transmuting flesh, like Medusa or that fellow who could turn people to gold. They fill all the extremes from a subtle ability to charm while speaking to exuding acid from their skin."

Eric looked at him questioningly. "So what are you saying? I'm going to become a monster? Or a god?"

Martin grimaced and shook his head. "No, well, not really. The problem is that you have already exhibited abilities far beyond things I have ever heard tales of. Your ability to know and use a word of power is unlike anything I have ever heard."

Martin ran his hands through his hair and leaned back against the bedpost. "Look, I am making this up as I go. First off, I do not think you are a monster or will ever become one. I am your family and I am on your side. I love you and will stand with you until the end. I am simply trying to explain to you the dangerous area of magic that we have entered. Your being aware of your possible abilities increases the danger many times over. It is imperative that you stop all experimentation with magic. Unless I am with you and we discuss it. The fact of the matter is that I have no idea what might happen. You could set the bed on fire or you could accidentally blow yourself to pieces." He raised his hand at the boy's terrified expression. "Yes, I am trying to scare you a bit. However, I seriously do not have the faintest idea where your powers lie."

Eric became thoughtful for a moment. "Uncle, I…wonder if my nightmares might be related to my power?"

Martin looked at the boy in shock. "Your nightmares?" Eric nodded.

"I've had them for as long as I can remember. Most of the doctors I saw said that it was night terrors brought on by a traumatic event in my childhood. Since no one knew anything about my past, they just kept trying to draw it out of me. They didn't have a lot of luck." Over the next few minutes, Eric told his uncle what he remembered of his dreams, most of which were things he recalled from his dream notebook.

Martin looked at Eric quizzically. "This last dream you had, you said that the creature said its name was Elder? And he killed the woman that you now believe was another Abomination?" Eric's eyes hardened a bit at the use of the word but he nodded.

"Gadzooks. It is worse than I thought. If He is loose on the world of men, you are in even greater danger than I had imagined." Rising, he began to pace back and forth near the bed.

"What is it, Uncle? Do you think that it is more than a dream?" Martin stopped and faced him, nodding, and watched the color drain from the boy's face.

"You mean this creature, Elder, he actually pulled that woman's heart out? Simply because she was like me?"

Martin nodded grimly. "Yes. You seem to have the power to project yourself while you sleep. Whether you are drawn to other Abominations, to other of Sahae blood or if you could go anywhere I do not know. The full extent of your powers will take time to discover. That, however, is not the worst of it. It may confuse you that after telling me so little about your dream, I can tell you with certainty that it was real. You see, I know that particular Sahae, he was never mentioned around you as a child so you would have no way of knowing who he is. He is a great and powerful old one, perhaps one of the oldest left of our kind that will walk between the worlds. His mastery of the Way is unparalleled, as is his resistance to technology. He is by far the greatest threat to you; if he ever learns of your existence, he will single-mindedly pursue you until he personally obliterates you from the world."

Eric watched him with growing horror and confusion. "Why the hell would he do that? Does he just hate every Abomination so much that he has to seek and destroy them all?"

Martin shrugged and nodded. "While it is true that he will destroy any Abomination that he finds, with you it is bit more personal. Perhaps that is why you were able to see him…You asked me to tell you about your parents, well it seems the time has come to tell you about your father's sire. You are in danger not just because you are an Abomination in his eyes. You are in danger because you are also a humiliation to him. Eric…Elder is your grandfather."

10

STEW AGAIN?

ERIC TOOK THE lid off the stew pot and had to cover his mouth to keep from puking. *I never thought the smell of stew could smell worse to me than an open sewer.* Taking a moment, he managed to breathe through his mouth and the bout of nausea passed. It was getting much harder to deal with the food here. Other than the first few meals, which they had eaten out of Martin's supplies, they had been eating the same thing for what he calculated was almost a year. It was horrible, and it was beginning to take a toll on Eric. The everyday physical and mental training regimens required fuel, and the only fuel they had was porridge and stew.

He had eaten lakes of porridge and oceans of stew and couldn't stomach anymore. He was fighting a losing battle. Eventually, he was not going to be able to keep either of them down, yet Martin did not seem to grasp the issue when he brought it up. Growing up, he had known what it was like to be hungry. He had never had a problem eating anything, from the simplest fare to the most complicated dish. Food was food. Or so he thought. Now there was no doubt in his mind that if there was a hell, it had a stew and porridge pot in its kitchen.

The safehold did not have much in the pantry to doctor up the morning porridge, but it was bland enough to choke down. The stew, however, was the same every day. It was hearty, with thick gravy, carrots, onions, celery, potatoes, large chunks of meat and other vegetables that Eric had not yet identified. To be fair, it was the kind of stew that people would pay top dollar for anywhere that had an annual snowfall. It offered all the food groups and helped fill a belly, especially one regularly emptied by hard labor. At the moment it was all Eric could do to ladle a new bowl full and begin choking it down. As he dutifully choked down what seemed like his millionth bowl, he found his thoughts wandering back to Seaverville and he caught himself wondering what everyone was doing.

Same thing they were doing about twenty minutes before I left. It was hard to wrap his mind around the fact that while so much time had passed for him, so little had passed for those he left behind. He had been at this for about a year, at least according to the marks he had made at the beginning of each day on the wall of his room. It was unfair to miss people so much and then realize they did not miss him at all. Granted, they were all frozen in time, but the selfish part of him yearned to be missed and felt as if the universe was slighting him again.

Martin glanced up from his bowl and caught Eric's eye. "What is it, lad? Homesick?"

Eric started in his chair, wondering if Martin could read his mind before realizing that with as long as his uncle had lived he had probably seen the signs many times before. "Yeah, I guess I am, Uncle Martin. I know it seems silly, but it would be nice to know that people missed me. That they noticed I was gone and wondered where I was. I've spent so much of my life not really having that and now that I finally have people who might miss me, they don't even know that I'm gone." Eric expected Martin to dismiss him yet he nodded and looked quite serious.

"That is something I can relate to. You live as long as I have and it is like you are living our current situation, just in reverse. I would return with very little time having passed and an old friend would be dead and the man before me would be his great-grandson, all grown.

Take yourself as an example . . . I last saw a babe, just a wee little thing, and here you are, nearly grown to manhood in the blink of an eye. The world can be cruel and unfeeling in the passage of time, my boy. Never do forget that. If there is one thing that I wish I could impart to you it would be this, keep close to you all the things that you hold dear, for the moment you dismiss them, they may be gone forever."

Eric sat at the table, mechanically spooning the revolting stew into his mouth while he thought about this. As lonely as he felt, he was overjoyed to have found Uncle Martin.

Simply having the small blue man around had helped much of his anxiety disappear. Taking a break, he pushed the bowl aside, trying to distract himself from a rising wave of nausea. "Uncle Martin?"

"Yes, lad what is it?"

Eric drummed his fingers on the table as he tried to think of what he wanted to say next. "You told me about Elder, well what you know of him, anyway. I was wondering, what can you tell me about my mother?"

Martin seemed to have been expecting this question, as he simply put his spoon down and pushed his chair back a little. "Well lad, now that is a lengthy tale. I do not know everything about her, though I had a bit of checking done on her when I began my search for you."

Eric's eyes lit up in interest. "Really? What did you find out?"

Martin grinned despite himself at the lad's obvious interest. "Well, I had to cast a fairly wide net to try and find you, so I hired a few private investigators to dig up what they could. One of these fellows went back and tried to check on your parents. The poor man found nothing on your father, no surprise there as we went to great lengths to make sure there was nothing to find. He had a bit more luck with your mother. Her full name, well, her maiden name was Antonia Diane Rosenta.

"She was born in Seattle, Washington, which is where your maternal grandparents met. Your grandfather was a carpenter and your grandmother was a homemaker who had a reputation for making a mean apple cobbler. Your grandfather finished his apprenticeship and moved to Portland to take a position with a company there. They bought a house and your mother received her primary education as well as college education in Portland. From what I understand, you get your love of literature from her."

Eric smiled at this, grabbed his bowl and began shoveling food back into his mouth, using the story as a good distraction to pack down the food. "So is she who I get my affinity for tinkering from?"

Martin shook his head. "I never really saw her tinkering, but then again, she knew how detrimental technology was to our kind so perhaps she only did it when we were not around." Eric refilled his bowl and sat back down, eager for more information.

"It seems that her parents passed shortly after she did. As they had no known living relatives, their home was sold and their estate liquidated by the state. I am sad to say that there are no mementos that I know of from that part of your life. Your mother did have some things that she put in storage; however, I doubt they are still there."

Easing back in his chair, Eric dropped his bowl on the table, trying desperately to ignore his stomach. The nausea was almost unbearable, so he focused on Uncle Martin, pushing it out of his mind. "Well, that is more than I knew before; still, it would be nice to at least be able to see what my grandparents looked like."

At this, Martin smiled. "I can actually help you with that, lad. I have no pictures of them, but I have seen a few." Raising his hands, Martin began to pull upon the Way. Before Eric's astonished eyes, a section of the air changed to reflect two older people smiling, like a blown up picture. The image sharpened and became clear enough that he almost expected to see them move. He could see himself reflected in both of them.

Little things, like how one of his ears was a little crooked, he could see the same thing on his grandfather. And the odd little thing with the edge of his nose being slightly turned, right there on his grandmother's face. He turned to Martin, the question sticking in his throat. Martin seemed to understand as Eric felt him pull upon the Way and the picture expanded. Next to his grandparents he now saw his parents standing, smiling happily. Here the family resemblance was most striking. His hair, his eyes, and the way he stood, all if it right here in front of him.

Almost as an afterthought, Martin expanded the image further and Eric saw two incredibly beautiful, thin people standing on the far side of his parents. The man was familiar, the frightening countenance of Elder.

The woman took his breath away, with a gentleness about her that tore at his heartstrings. He stood for a long time just staring, his eyes started to tear up and he realized he had forgotten to blink. Turning to Martin, he saw his uncle looking back at him somberly.

"Ah, lad, I feel I have caused you heartache where I simply meant to enlighten."

Eric shook his head and wiped his eyes with the back of his hands. "No, Uncle, this is wonderful. I went from not even knowing what my parents looked like, or even knowing who my grandparents were, to being able to see all of them. I can't tell you how much this means to me."

Martin cleared his throat and pulled out his pipe, fussing with it. "Well lad, now that you have seen them, I will teach you a spell to recreate their likenesses whenever you want." Eric smiled, nausea gone. Martin waved his hand and released the Way and the image faded from the air.

"Uncle Martin, can you tell me more about my father's family? And, hey, what was my dad's name? You have mentioned him a ton of times and never said his name."

Martin shuddered and put his pipe away, pulling his flask out in its place and taking a long drink from it. "Well, that is a much more difficult story. Let us first address the issue of your father. I mentioned that he was imprisoned and tortured and that I spirited him away. What I did not go into was the extent of his crimes against the High Court."

"His refusal to cooperate caused such an uproar that your father was banished, even as he languished in a cell, a great spell was cast that erased his name from use."

"It is something done rarely in Sahae society as it takes several powerful Sahae to cast, normally three such as would sit on a Council of Judgment. "

"It is a fate worse than death in the Sahae world and caused a bit of trouble later in life as even in the human world, as no true name could be given for others to use."

Eric stared at his uncle in disbelief. "So you're telling me that you can't tell me his name because a spell was cast to prevent you? So what did my mom call him? 'Hey you?'" Eric smiled a bit at that last part until he caught sight of the look on Martin's face.

"Actually, your mother normally called him pet names, some of which were quite entertaining as I recall." Martin gave an evil grin. "It was a huge handicap in interacting with both Sahae and humans, as it was intended to be. It was a way for the powerful to punish someone without actually having to exile them. Instead, it served as a nameless reminder to the masses of what could happen if you stepped out of line." Eric shook his head in disbelief.

"So you can't write it down? Or spell it? Or anything?" Martin shook his head. "Lad, I cannot even remember what it was and I knew your father longer than most. As I said, it is a very powerful spell, cast by at least three powerful Sahae. And one of those that agreed to the sentence and then helped in the casting was his own father, your grandsire." Eric gave Martin another look of disbelief, causing him to chuckle humorlessly.

"As we have discussed your grandsire, sorry, your grandfather, is a being of great power that, as far as I know, rarely leaves the Sahae realm. His wife, as you saw, was a creature of unsurpassed beauty and grace. She was lost shortly after your father attained independence, what you would call 'becoming an adult.' She was a casualty of a blight that occurred nearby. Your father and grandfather took her loss very hard, each in his own way. She had always been a bit of a peacekeeper between them, you see, and her loss caused a rift between them that was never repaired.

"Your father, being an inquisitive fellow, wanted to know why. He was interested in finding the cause of her death and making sure it did not happen to anyone else. His father, on the other hand, was only interested in revenge. To his mind, anything short of oceans of blood would not atone for the loss of his love."

"The two had a bitter argument over the matter; your grandsire called your father a coward and your father called him a savage."

He took another deep drink from the flask. "Your father severed all contact with him and you must know that although he is related to you by blood, he would never consider you part of his family. He is an old Sahae and holds to a strict code of conduct. He would consider it his solemn duty to destroy you and anyone that ever knew of your existence. His actions towards his own son show that he has little space in his heart for love, or pity. Granted, when they parted it was with heated, hurtful words. It was this bitter split between them that was the setting for their final meeting. Your father calling your grandfather a fool in front of the assembled Sahae drove the final wedge between them, in my opinion."

Eric grew cold thinking of this, that his own grandfather would hunt him down; kill him, if he knew of his existence. It seemed surreal. *Though no more surreal than being in a time bubble learning to fight from a little blue man.* With difficulty, he forced himself to ladle out another bowel of stew. Each mouthful was a torturous effort, his roiling stomach fighting with his knowledge that he had to eat. Martin looked on in amusement as Eric choked down the stew.

"You know, if the gruel is more palatable I could just make that instead." Eric looked up at him in surprise and then shook his head.

"No, this stew has meat and vegetables in it. As tired as I am of eating it, I know better than to eat fiber non-stop. Now if you wanted to talk about ordering takeout, I'm all for that."

Martin pursed his lips and tried to change the subject before they began an argument neither would win. "I thought tomorrow we would begin to work on your magic theory."

Eric perked up at this and gave Martin his undivided attention, which is exactly what Martin had expected. "Theory?" Eric managed to say around a mouthful of stew.

Martin looked at him in disgust. "Ugh, close your mouth and no talking while you chew. Good lord, that sight is enough to put a fellow off eating entirely." He waited while Eric wiped his mouth and then continued. "Magic theory is a very dangerous area of study. When it comes to the Way, most initiates like you, are taught to access their power under the strictest of regimens."

"Ritual and practice are used to help them to achieve the highest level of concentration, thereby ensuring the safe and successful access of the Way. However, once they have become accomplished, it is important to show them how to improvise certain uses of the Way to become more proficient. You have shown a remarkable aptitude and I feel that it will best serve you to follow a more . . . hybrid form of training."

He paused and barely failed to suppress a smile at his play on words. "So tomorrow, in addition to your physical regimen and supervised casting, we will begin to discuss the more intricate aspects of spell work. I would take the opportunity to warn you that any experimentation could be fatal, however I believe we have already covered that topic." At this comment, Eric looked up with a slightly haunted look on his face and nodded hurriedly.

"Good, well if you do not mind I will leave the clean-up to you this evening, as I am a bit drained from the day's lessons. Remember that once you are done with the stew pot you need simply put the lid back on it and return it to the hook so it will be ready for the day tomorrow. No cleaning it out and, it goes without saying, no magic. Clear?"

Eric nodded again, a bit stiffly now. "Yes, Uncle Martin, you made your point. There's no need to beat a dead horse."

Martin paused and looked at Eric with a trace of a smile on his face. "How much like your father you are at times. Goodnight, Eric." Rising from the table, he left his own bowl behind and headed down to his room. Eric managed to shovel four more bowls of stew down his throat before his taste buds rebelled.

It was official, the food here was going to kill him long before any Sahae got anywhere near him. He recalled one week the kids at the orphanage had to eat spaghetti morning, noon and night due to a food shortage. At the time, it had seemed like torture. Compared to a year of eating porridge for breakfast and stew for lunch and dinner, it was a nostalgic memory. Eric was ready to kill for a bit of bread. Hell, liver and onions would be a nice change of pace. Maybe some broccoli or lima beans. *God, it's so wrong that my mouth is watering at the thought of lima beans.*

He dumped the bowls in the sink then grabbed the stew pot, slapped the lid on it, and hung it from the hook near the stove. Moving back to the sink, he filled it with soapy water and cleaned the dinnerware. The physical activity was a welcome respite from his thoughts of food. Until he left this place, there was no possibility of getting anything different.

According to Uncle Martin, he had only set up a few spells for cooking. His father had set everything else up so that Eric's mother would be able to cook whatever she liked. Unfortunately, he had not envisioned the safehold being used without her and thus all the enchantments had become useless upon his mother's death. *One more kick in the teeth from the universe; not only do I lose my mom, but I'm sentenced to a purgatory of training eating only porridge and stew.*

Stashing the dishes, he headed back to his room. It had become a nightly ritual to run through all the physical and mental practice forms and then take a bath before bed. The routine not only helped settle his nerves, it helped settle his stomach. As he sank into the tub, he thought about his dreams.

After he had revealed them to his uncle, they had discussed his dreams at length. Martin's theory that he was able to project himself while sleeping was actually a relief; no one liked the idea of being crazy. Having his uncle confirm that the dreams were real had opened a floodgate of memories.

That very night when he had gone to sleep he had dreamed a re-play of Elder killing Tilly in the alley. It was horrible to relive, but the dream did not hold the same power over him that it once had. Granted, he still woke upset, but he did not wake up and not remember why. And other dreams came back to him night after night; things he was never able to remember suddenly sprang, unbidden, from his subconscious mind into his dreams.

It was phenomenal to know that not only did he have this power but that he was not, in fact, mentally damaged. His shrinks would be thrilled if they could see him now. Discussing his dreams with his uncle, using the Way to recreate them as best he could, he confirmed that his dreams were, in fact, multiple visions. The visions of other people and places were hard to identify, however Martin had recognized places he said were in Sahae. Other places meant nothing to either of them. The more he practiced, the more he was able to pull out of his head. It was as if the Way helped to pull the foggy memories to the front of his mind.

When he asked Martin why he had not had any new visions since they arrived, he had laughed. "I told you, lad. For every day that passes here, only a few seconds passes back there. So in the few minutes that have passed likely little has occurred that would interest you."

Eric had felt foolish for having asked such an obvious question, but instead of teasing him, Martin had used it as a jumping off point into their discussion of magic. In the end, his talks with Martin made him realize that it was not that he could not remember his visions, more that he had not wanted, or needed, to recall them. It was like a defense mechanism and now that he realized what the dreams meant, he found he was able to remember a lot more about them. Especially the last dream.

Tilly. Her name had been Tilly Crayes. She had been a total monster herself, but she still did not deserve what she got. The casual way that Elder had killed her chilled him to the bone.

The new knowledge let him sleep; really sleep soundly, for the first time. While he had never felt tired due to his lack of sleep, he now woke up charged with energy every day. It was amazing how much more he was able to do with the extra sleep and conditioning.

As he slid out of the tub and prepared for bed, he stretched the last of the knots out of his muscles. Sliding beneath the sheets, he found his mind wandering to visions of baloney sandwiches and popcorn. With an effort he banished thoughts of food and slowly slipped off to sleep. As consciousness fled he wondered if the magic of the kitchen would work have for him if he had actually known how to cook.

11

FOOD FIGHT

AFTER ALL OF their time in the safehold Martin was finally starting to see the progress he had been hoping for. In fact, one part of Eric's training was going so well that the boy was now working without instruction from Martin at all. The last few months of training had honed Eric's martial skills to the point where he could hold his own against Martin in their daily sparring. The bruises had begun to pile up even though Martin suspected that the boy was holding back. Despite his small size Martin was an accomplished fighter, yet still the lad fought him to a standstill.

Beyond the skills Martin had taught him the boy had learned to use almost every weapon in the armory. A few still puzzled him and he lacked mastery of any of them, however he was far from the untrained lad who had first entered the safehold.

With a few more months of practice Martin would not be surprised to see the boy master more than one of the weapons. It was a rare thing for one to be so powerful in the Way and also be a skilled fighter. Among the Sahae one normally focused on mastering the mind or the body. Doing both was not unheard of; it simply took a long time to accomplish. And it was rare for any Sahae to work so hard to become a recognized master in both the Way and physical combat. One was normally more than enough to earn a Sahae respect. Eric's progress gave Martin hope that one day his student would be able to survive in the real world.

Even though I hate to think of it we will one day have to leave the safety of this safehold. I fear our first test of Eric's skills will be in a trial by fire. A fight to the death to save himself from some Sahae bent on killing him simply for what he is.

Martin took comfort that the boy's martial abilities were progressing well. It was gratifying to see the boy getting better every day, knowing he had helped put his feet on the path. Still, his magical abilities were far behind where Martin would like to see them.

The current focus was the use of Eric's magical skills in real-world situations. It was imperative that the boy learn to use the Way when in pain, when afraid, when surprised and in any other conceivable situation. Martin had put the boy through all manner of misery just to test his abilities. So far the results were promising however Martin did not dare take any progress for granted. Instead, he focused on pushing the boy every day.

Using the Way was not unlike using a muscle. You had to train, to build up your endurance and to use proper form. In the end the only way to get better was to constantly practice using your powers. It had also required that the complexity and danger of their magic sparring be continuously escalated. Recently, they had reached the point where he was afraid that they might damage the safehold's protection wards. After realizing that the wards would not take the abuse of their dueling Martin had come up with a different course of study.

Martin had set Eric the task of doing an escalated exercise with the Way. It was designed to help him expand his ability to tap into his power until he finally reached his limit. Thus far the boy had not reached a plateau, which was beginning to concern Martin. Though he was still training the boy already had more power available to him than many members of the greater Sahae houses.

Because of this he decided it was time to teach Eric something about the subtlety of magic. It would not do to have someone with such a well spring of power be contented to simply overcharge his spells. Instead, he focused him on using less power each time to do the same tasks. By refining his casting Martin had shown Eric how to use about half the power he had used before.

In addition, he had tasked the boy with trying to discover a 'sleeper spell' he had hidden somewhere in the safehold. The task should have taken the boy a few days at the least. After all, Martin had used all of his guile to construct and hide the spell. The boy had confounded him by finding the spell in record time.

Then Eric had examined and dismantled the spell in almost less time than it had taken Martin to create it. The boy was lagging behind in his magical studies in comparison to his martial skills and yet he was still mastering in months what would take others years, even decades, to do.

This only accentuated the flaws the boy grappled with. After all his training, Eric still struggled to control his temper. It bordered on the absurd at times. Despite all their work on the problem, their progress was depressingly slow. Nothing that he had tried seemed to thicken the boy's skin at all. It might very well be that he would never find a way to calm him down. Even when the boy knew full well what he was doing, Martin was able to get him to lose his temper, often in spectacular fashion.

He is his father's son . . . and his grandfather's. He comes by the temper honestly. I just hope he learns to control it better than either of them. Between the issues with Eric's temper and a few other holes in his education, Martin feared they were going to be here a lot longer than Eric wanted. Now it seemed that the boy had decided to rebel against, of all things, his diet. They were sitting at the table in the kitchen when Eric issued his ultimatum.

"I can't take it anymore. I'm done. Finished. Finito." Glaring across the table at Martin, he forcefully slammed the lid back atop the stew pot. "If we stay here much longer I'm going to die. Starve to death. Loose this mortal coil. I need to get out of here and find a pizza or some salad. Hell, I would eat a bowl of black eyed peas or lima beans right now!"

The last was delivered with such disgust and horror that Martin could only assume it was something used to torture children in the human world. Looking at his charge, he calmly tried to placate him.

"Eric, I have told you, it would be dangerous and consume an enormous amount of my strength to go out and get food. I am not sure if I could maintain the safehold long enough for us to exit and re-enter."

"You are not nearly done with your studies. What you suggest could leave us vulnerable, exposed, and in a situation fraught with danger. Sending you out into the world right now would be like dropping you naked into a den of wolves."

Eric chopped his hand down between them. "No! No more discussion. No more delays. I've shown you what I can do. I more than hold my own in the physical sparring and I can more often than not fight you to a standstill in the magic ring as well. Just today didn't you say that you expected the sleeper spell to keep me busy for days?"

Martin nodded. "Yes, and I am overjoyed at your progress. However, you still lack the proper discipline to survive. You have not yet developed the kind of self-control that is necessary. This little outburst proves my point. Out there, you cannot lose your temper. Not once. Not ever. Your temper flares and it is like turning on the Rat Signal."

Eric laughed despite his anger. "Bat Signal, not Rat Signal. And quit trying to change the subject. You know that the chance of a Sa-hae being anywhere near enough to see a slip is iffy at best. You yourself took months to find me and you were specifically looking for me. And I have been a lot better with keeping my temper."

Martin stood and walked to the sink, then turned and fixed Eric with a severe glare. "Had you been giving off power like you were before I brought you here, I would have had very little trouble finding you. It was like following a pillar of flame on a moonless night." Taking a deep breath, he released the tension that had been building in his frame during the argument and slumped back against the counter.

"Eric, you are not ready," he said, enunciating each word. "There is no doubt in my mind that you think you are. Confidence is a great thing, until it gets you killed. We cannot leave here until you are ready. Not today, not tomorrow, not next week. If you leave the safehold now it is not just you that dies. It is the Greens, your friends . . . and me." Eric stopped short, the angry retort that had been in his throat lodged in place.

Martin gave a small smile. "Hey, I may be a little blue 'shrimp' as you put it, but I can still fight. And I will stand between you and danger while I still draw breath. There is no one and nothing in this world or the next that will hurt you without going through me. There are, unfortunately, many things out there that will tear through me like wet tissue paper. So yes, when I tell you that you are not ready there is a bit of self-preservation in that. Make no mistake lad, I would prefer to be lucky enough to die before you. Having to live through the deaths of your parents, I could not bear witness to your death as well. I lost you once. I beg you not to throw away all that we have done because the food here offends your delicate palate."

The last was said with just enough humor to remove the edge and Eric found himself smiling abashedly. They sat in silence for a moment and then Eric reached over and took the lid from the stew pot. He set the lid aside and ladled two heaping bowls of stew out and sat down at his place. With a grimace of abject horror, he began shoveling the food into his mouth. "You know," he said after the first bite had cleared his mouth. "Once we get out of here . . . I have never been a picky eater, but I can think of two things that are going to be off my menu permanently."

Martin grinned at him in understanding. "I agree, lad. Let this also be a lesson that when planning a safehold, one must think of more than safety; you never knows when long-term comfort will come into play." Eric nodded and seemed to seriously think about this before he began eating again. He started and stopped eating multiple times, finally setting his bowl down and leaning back.

"So, Uncle Martin, my grandsire, or Dad's dad or Grandfather Spooky Britches, whatever. You said that he and Dad had a big falling out about how to deal with Grandma's death."

Martin set his spoon down. There goes my appetite. Here again was another conversation he had been dreading. The more Eric found out about his father, the more he wanted to know. "As usual, that is a huge oversimplification, if generally correct. Both of them were dealing with their grief in their own way. Your father always wanted to quantify things. To him, the world, both worlds really, were logical; you just had to figure out the pattern."

Eric nodded. "The more I learn about the Way, the more I agree with him. There are constants in everything; the trick is figuring them out so you can see the big picture and how all of them fit together."

Martin stared at him for a moment before shaking his head ruefully. "It is frightening to me sometimes how much you sound like your father, lad. He used to say nearly the same thing. In his mind, the entire problem, the death of his mother, was simply a lack of knowledge. If he could find out why it happened, they could make sure it did not happen again. Simple as that, though in truth the reality almost never is. Your grandfather, of course, saw it a bit differently. In his mind, the 'how' was not nearly as important as the 'who.'

"To Elder, it was obvious that the problem was caused by humans and so he should just keep killing them and eventually the one that was responsible would die. If that meant killing every man, woman, and child, then he would do just that. I had more than one conversation with your father on this subject, normally late at night over more than a few drinks. To him, the very idea that his father would simply smash and destroy like a savage was mystifying. In the end, it would not bring your grandmother back, if anything it would just lead to more deaths. However, in trying to convince your grandfather of that, he only drove him further away."

Martin felt his mind slip back to those days, he could almost hear his friend's voice ringing in his ears and a lump formed in his throat. He suddenly felt very old and overwhelmed, sitting here with Eric. How was he to be expected to train this lad, to protect him, to show him how to survive?

At least I got him into the safehold; here, at least, we are safe.

Eric shifted in his seat as he finished his food. When he finished the first bowl he managed almost two more before pushing the bowl away. He seemed to be in considerable distress and he sat quietly for a long time. Martin rose and put the lid back on the pot and washed the dinnerware. Sitting back down he looked at the boy who still seemed a bit green.

"Thanks for cleaning up Uncle Martin. And I can't tell you what it means, you telling me about the family. You know that I appreciate everything you've done to keep me safe and everything you've taught me. Also, I really do understand what you're saying when you talk about responsibility. There are a lot of people depending on me. And not just to be a good person and do the right thing. I also have to be strong enough to defend them. I've got to be in control of myself and my skills so that if trouble does come, I can deal with it. I get that, I really do. That's dealing with the reality I live in and I get it. But here's some reality that you have to deal with, no disrespect intended. The time is coming, soon, where I will not be able to eat this food. I physically WILL NOT be able to eat it. When that day comes, you'll have to accept that wherever we are in my training, we'll have to leave. To use your words, it would be a shame to do all this work and then have me die of starvation."

Eric looked at Martin solemnly for a moment and then rose from the table. As he stared after him, Martin gave a quiet sigh and began to contemplate what steps to take to fix the holes in his student's education before they ran out of time.

12

OUT OF THE SAFEHOLD

THE FIRE IN the fireplace cycled through a myriad of colors before settling into an unnatural deep blue. With a grinding noise, the hearth expanded to gargantuan proportions. Two figures stepped from the flames and into the Greens' living room. Eric looked around the room, amazed that it looked exactly as it had when they left. *Guess Uncle Martin was right on the money with his calculations on how much time has passed.* His uncle grasped his arm and halted him in front of the fire.

"I still think this is a mistake, lad. There is no guarantee that any Sahae that were attracted to this area have left. They could spend a decade just wandering around looking for another whiff of power."

Eric looked at his uncle in exasperation and put up a hand to quiet him. "I know, I know, Uncle Martin. It would be better to stay locked up in our hideaway. It would be better be able to train for an eternity. You've so much more to teach me. We've gone over and over this. The one thing we can't get past is that I can't take one more minute in that place. It's stifling. No sunlight, no fresh air, and worst of all, only porridge and stew to eat."

Martin looked a bit offended at this last part. "I did my best, lad. There was not much call for me to cook and the only things your mother ever let me prepare was porridge and stew. She said it was hard to screw them up." Eric shuddered at the mention of stew and cut Martin off.

"Regardless, there's a real danger of me going out of my mind under those conditions. We've been at this for over a year, and I've got a pretty good handle on it."

Martin nodded, showing his irritation. "Yes, you have come an amazing distance since we first entered the safehold. Physically you are in astounding shape now from what you were when we left. Also, I will allow that this town provides a certain amount of protection based on the uncomfortable levels of technology present. However, I must still object to the timing." Martin looked back at the portal behind them.

"You are just beginning to get a full understanding of the Way. Now, more than ever, you should be focusing somewhere away from distractions rather than seeking them out."

Eric sighed and put his hand on Martin's shoulder. "Look, I know you're worried. So am I. I know the risk I'm taking here, not just with myself but with everyone I love, you included." Martin kept looking at the portal but Eric saw the glint of tears in his eyes. "The truth of it is that no matter how much I train, I'll never truly be ready in your eyes. There is a part of you that wants to lock me away and keep me safe. I just can't live like that." Martin tried to object but Eric kept going. "Either I start living my life or the Sahae might as well come for me now. I need to learn to live in the real world and right now is as good a time as any."

Martin stiffened at Eric's tone and replied tightly, "You have no idea what you are talking about. If you had a true understanding of what we face, you would grab some food and have me take you back to safety."

Eric shook his head and sighed. "We've been over this and over this. If this is truly my call, then this is what I want to do." Eric set down the bag he was holding and looked around the room. It looked exactly as it did when they left. At most, a half hour had passed. Martin had explained that for every day they were in the safehold they only aged a few hours and only a few seconds passed in the real world. There had always been a part of him that had doubted this; worried that too much time had passed for his plan to work.

As it stood now, it seemed that everything was as it should be. Moving through the house, he stowed his bag inside his trunk. It contained all the personal items his parents had left in the safehold and he did not want to have to explain to his foster parents where they had come from. When he rejoined his uncle in the living room, he found Martin pacing impatiently in front of the fireplace.

"Very well, Eric, I can see you are as stubborn as your father and mother combined. If you are truly determined to proceed and that is your final word, then I will close the passageway to the safe-hold."

Eric looked at the portal and then nodded firmly, his jaw set. He barely felt a ripple in the Way as Martin released the portal and the fireplace shrank back to its normal size. Martin moved to Eric and jumped up on the chair opposite Mrs. Green so he could look the boy in the eye.

"I will remain close. I have a small dwelling in the woods near the bluff. Here, let me show you." Taking a small amount of the Way, he formed it into an aerial view of the town and indicated his dwelling. Eric had not been there before, but knew where it was. As he watched, Martin zoomed in on the park at the edge of town and swiftly followed the path to a strange rock. Once he was sure Eric knew where to go, he dismissed the power.

"If you get in trouble, do not fight, just run. Whatever is after you will not hesitate to kill those around you; but it will also not stay to attend to others in lieu of chasing you. Remember, your strength against your pursuers is that they cannot follow you into areas of high technology. This is the best way to get away. Do not get over-confident and let them corner you anywhere, as they can easily take advantage of one of your great weaknesses . . . and starve you out." The last he said with a wry bit of humor.

Eric hesitated and then embraced his uncle. It was awkward, as he had to stoop as he would for a child. Martin stiffened at first before relaxing and accepting the hug, clapping the boy on the back.

"Do not let me rile you, lad. I am simply worried about your safety. No amount of training will save you if the Sahae catch you.

When I leave, the spell on Mrs. Green will break and she will wake up thinking she simply took a nap. I warn you again, Eric, if things go badly, do not stay to try and defend anyone. Run and do not stop. I will find you if the need arises, but do not wait for me. Your best defense is to outsmart and elude any pursuit. Do not make any rash decisions and for both our sakes, keep your temper in check. Understood?"

Eric wiped a grin off his face and nodded solemnly. "Absolutely, Uncle Martin, you can count on me." Martin looked at the boy for a moment before nodding and walking to the door. Taking a leather glove out of his pocket, he put it on before grasping and turning the handle.

Confusion crossed Eric's face before he stopped to think about it. The doorknob in this house was quite old, probably original to the structure, and made of iron. It only made sense that if Martin had to travel in the human world, he would have gloves to help him navigate through some of the pitfalls, like iron doorknobs.

Stopping in the doorway, Martin fixed Eric with a long look, then nodded goodbye. He muttered the words to release the spell on Mrs. Green and closed the door behind him. From the living room, Eric heard Mrs. Green stir and felt a deep sense of relief. *Here we go.*

"Eric? Was that the door? Are you just getting in?" Mrs. Green looked up at him in sleepy confusion before looking at her watch in horror. "Is it really almost six? Oh, my. I must have fallen asleep." Eric followed her as she walked into the kitchen and started cooking dinner. He sighed with relief and sat back down at the table to finish the homework he had started so many months before.

After admonishing Eric for not waking her, Mrs. Green became a culinary whirlwind. In short order, she produced a succulent-smelling meal that had Eric's stomach noticeably growling. The smell of meat cooking was almost too much to bear. By the time Mr. Green came in the door, there were steaks on the table accompanied by mashed potatoes and green beans.

Mr. Green gave his wife a kiss on the cheek and settled heavily into his chair, giving a contented sigh once he was off his feet. As Eric stowed his homework in his bag, he was amazed at how easy it was to step back into his life. After so much time away, he had been worried about being out of practice with his normal routine.

If the Greens' noticed anything odd about his behavior, they did not say anything. After four helpings of dinner, a truly stuffed Eric sat back in his seat and relaxed into a food coma. He thought he had truly gotten away with it until after the dessert plates had been cleared. Mr. Green gave him a solemn look.

"Eric, may I speak to you in the office, please?"

The home office was off the kitchen at the back of the house. This ensured that Mr. Green could work with the least amount of distraction and that any late nights he had did not disturb anyone else in the house. Eric had seen the office during his initial tour but had only been there twice since. Once, to discuss his fighting at school and another time to go over the course study Mr. Green felt he needed to be on track for college.

Eric followed Mr. Green with his heart in his throat and sat in the over-stuffed green leather chair on the visitor's side of the desk. Mr. Green settled into his office chair, the well-worn leather letting out a small squeak of protest. For a moment, Mr. Green just looked at Eric. Then he sighed.

"Eric . . . I think you and I need to have a serious talk."

Eric felt his hands go damp and his mind started to race. Sometime during dinner he must have slipped up and Mr. Green was on to him. He remembered the contingencies Martin had spoken about and was going over the details in his mind as Mr. Green continued.

"I got a call from Mrs. Blair, the guidance counselor, today. She told me that there was a rumor going around school; a wild rumor that you beat up half the senior class today on your way to school."

Eric snapped to attention, his mind sifting through the details. They did not know. He had totally forgotten about Moose and the fight. It was not surprising, the fight was over a year ago for him, but to the Greens and everyone else, it just happened.

Putting on a slightly guilty expression, Eric nodded, causing Mr. Green's eyebrows to shoot up in shock. "Well, not the entire senior class. It was just this guy they call Moose and two other guys."

Mr. Green sat back heavily in his chair and looked a bit more tired. "I see," he said. "So, can you tell me what caused this altercation and what occurred?"

His foster father had slipped into his lawyer voice and Eric found himself quickly filling in the details. He left out his mental slip and instead went from the first punch to the end result but Mr. Green did not press him on the issue.

"So, if I am getting the timeline correct, you didn't engage the boys before the fight? You were accosted, assaulted and then defended yourself in such a way as to not cause any permanent damage to your assailants?"

Eric could see why Mr. Green was so successful; even outside a courtroom he had a way of carrying a conversation to get the information that he needed. Eric nodded. "Yes, but I've got no excuse for the fight."

Mr. Green seemed startled by that. "Eric, from what you're describing to me, you've no reason to be sorry. You were attacked by boys not only older than you, but bigger as well. Not only did you manage to defend yourself and your friend, but you did so without seriously injuring anyone. That, I'd say, shows immense self-control. I'm very proud of how you handled yourself."

This was not the way Eric had expected the conversation to go and it must have shown on his face. Mr. Green smiled and reached across the desk to clasp his forearm. "I told you, son, I will always ask you for your side of things. You made the best of a bad situation. In life, sometimes that is all we can hope for."

Tears welled in his eyes and Eric quickly looked away. Mr. Green leaned back in his chair again and they sat in silence for a few moments. Everything that he had gone through over the last year swelled up and threatened to overwhelm him. He came so close to breaking and blurting out everything to Mr. Green. Thankfully, he realized how ludicrous it would sound.

The two sat quietly for a bit until Mrs. Green called them out. Eric appreciated him not trying to push conversation into the silence. Later, as he settled into his bed in the familiar surroundings of his room, Eric again questioned if this was a mistake. Snuggling deeper beneath the covers, he was still trying to decide when he fell asleep.

13

MARTIN

MARTIN MOVED AWAY from the house, cursing himself for a fool. If he had made a few simple alterations when they were casting up the safehold, he could have made it possible for anyone to cook anything. Instead, the spells had been keyed for Antonia. With her death, they became useless. Had it not been for him adding a few spells for his former favorite foods, they would not have been able to use the safehold at all.

And now here they were out in the world, an old Sahae and a young Abomination, that is, a hybrid, with nowhere near enough training. For all he knew, the entire area was swarming with hostile Sahae looking to rip both of them apart. Pulling slowly from the Way, so as to keep his exposure to a minimum, he cast layered masking spells that would hide him from all but the strongest of his kind.

While he was not the most powerful practitioner, he had made more strides in stealth magic than most. *When your life depends on passing unnoticed, you either get good or you die.* Feeling more confident now that he was concealed, he moved away from town and entered the woods. Although he had built up a rather high tolerance to technology over the years, it was still a relief to move away from it and enter the unspoiled wilds.

As the darkness of the woods settled around him, he gave a gentle sigh and eased his awareness back into the space around him. It was liberating to be out of town and, though he had trouble admitting it, even to himself, to be out of the safehold. Though he could have kept the space active indefinitely, the constant renewing of the wards had exhausted him. That, coupled with his long training sessions with the boy, had drained him more than he liked to admit.

The area north of town was bordered by a high bluff that provided a natural boundary. Taking the path west, he scouted through the woods, finding no trace of any Sahae. He stopped only briefly at his small dwelling, to assure that it was undisturbed, before heading off into the surrounding night.

He sensed that the fey light he had sent out as a decoy before they entered the safehold was still racing towards the far end of the state, though it was starting to fade. *Hopefully that led anyone away from here; however I will rest better once I have checked the area.* He moved around the perimeter of the town and was amazed to see that the technologies swept out in every direction. There were towers and such built far outside of town that made no sense to him. He could only assume the city planners were either insane or planning for an expansion that was beyond his comprehension.

It was very late and he was more than exhausted, which is why he could almost be excused for nearly walking into the midst of some water Sahae near the river. He was able to withdraw just in time and was relieved when his wards successfully hid him from their view. He was amazed to see so many Sahae living in water so near a high concentration of technology. As he watched, a pair of young males played in the water near the shore while an adult couple watched from nearby.

Further out in the water, he saw a few other family groups swimming around. Moving to a higher vantage point, he watched as the couple called the boys back from the shore and moved upstream. Trailing behind them, he tracked them to a branch on the far side of the river that flowed back into an unincorporated area of woods. He watched them until they disappeared from sight.

Sitting there in the dark, his mind flew back to his youth and a place very much like this in Sahae. In a terraced ocean that flowed out from a central water spout, giant waterways spanned hundreds of feet allowing travel between the terraces. Thousands of Water Sahae lived here together in loose communities. It was not unusual for visitors to linger for hours, admiring the beauty of the spray twisting into mesmerizing ever-changing shapes.

Turning to the south, he swung in a wide circle around town. Far to the west, he found an unusually high concentration of Sahae. While that itself was not alarming, their presence did indicate that a gate must be nearby.

There was a surprising diversity to the Sahae and they were far out into the forest. *The boy may need to give up his old life regardless of his wishes if they get too close. It is like he is near some bloody vacation destination.*

Taking his time to make sure he was not followed, Martin took a circuitous route back to his house. Finally satisfied that he had no pursuers, he slipped through his wards and moved up to a large stone. He removed the glamour and his home appeared in place of the stone. The dwelling itself was two stories with a thatched roof, not unlike an old cottage from the Emerald Isle.

Martin had spent a great deal of time on the Isle in the old days and felt a certain affinity for the place. He had created this house from memories of multiple homes he had lived in when he was younger. The bottom level was made up of a simple kitchen, living room and bathroom. The upper level held a single loft for sleeping, accessible by a rough timber staircase that wrapped along one wall. Stepping inside the door, he hung his cloak, damp from traveling through the woods, on a hook and built up a fire. Putting the kettle on, he found a ripe apple which he savored one slice at a time. After what seemed like an eternity of the same food day in and day out, the apple tasted better than anything he had ever eaten.

He had just finished the last of the apple when the kettle began its low whistle and he jumped to grab it from the hook. The fire had taken the damp from the air and he felt a chill he had not even been aware of ease from his bones. Pouring hot water over his tea he watched the steam rise into the air and settled wearily back into his chair. He could not remember the last time he had been this exhausted. The last year had been challenging and the future held more uncertainty than anything else. He stirred his tea and took a deep drink, willing some of the tension out of his shoulders.

It was surprising to find the water Sahae near town. It was also interesting that so many Sahae were living in relative peace with the humans in the area. Perhaps he had been away too long and Sahae had changed. The level of integration was astonishing.

Before, this kind of tolerance would have been abhorrent and unheard of by Sahae. Had he been spotted he doubted their new-found tolerance would have extended to him. Recognition by any Sahae was a death sentence. He was lucky he had not given himself away; at least he was fairly confident his magic had kept him hidden. No matter what changes had occurred in his absence, there would be no welcome for a blood traitor. Still, it had been good to see his kind, even if they could not see him.

Blast, I am getting maudlin in my old age. Next I will be lamenting my misspent youth. Turning the mug in his hands, he took another sip. As much as he did not want to admit it, he missed his people. His crime, though done out of love, was no less unforgivable. And no less true, for those that accused him were right in saying he had betrayed his own kind.

It had all started out with the best intentions. He remembered the day so vividly. He had been home visiting friends when he heard of Eric's father's return. He had met him for dinner and listened in abject horror as his friend described his theory—the end of all things, unless they could repair the rift between worlds. Martin was not so deluded as to think he actually grasped even a portion of what his friend told him, but he got the gist of it. As far as his rather learned friend was concerned, there was no doubt what needed to be done and if it was not done, both worlds were in danger of being destroyed.

Martin had therefore been appalled when he had seen him taken into custody. As if that outrage had not been enough, word had reached him that his friend was being tortured and might not survive. No amount of appealing to reason had helped, and his shock had been complete when he discovered that the person who authorized the violation of safe passage and the torture was his friend's own father.

Seeing his friend's father rail against his own son, with the light of madness shining in his eyes, had set Martin on his path. Against all reason and logic, he had concocted his rescue plan. No one suspected him; he had a well-deserved reputation of neutrality.

Unless it involved wine, women, or song, he was rarely interested. He had surprised and overpowered the guards outside his friend's cell, severely injuring both of them.

Witnesses had seen him leaving the area with a small cart, where he had hidden his friend. When the escape was discovered, pursuit had not been far behind. At the forefront was Martin's own family, who had thought to catch him and make him see reason. However, by then it was too late. There was no choice left to him, for to change his mind was to doom his friend to imprisonment or death. He had accepted the responsibility of helping his friend, even though it cost him everything. His family, his place in the world of Sahae, even his life was forfeit if he was ever captured.

He had tried to reconnect with his family a few times since then. The last after he had left Eric's father in the human world had been an utter disaster. They had shunned him, accused him of being made. There was simply no convincing them that there was any reason to defy the Court. For them, if the Court said it was wrong, it was wrong. With a sigh, Martin drank down the last of his tea and rinsed his mug. Placing it on the shelf he turned his weary feet towards the bathroom. When he had killed Felinor he had crossed a line that he could never step back over. His family would never forgive him for what he had done. No understanding could come for a kin-slayer. It did not matter to them that Felinor would have killed the boy, his brother was just doing what the Court said was law. No matter what he did, they would never understand why he took such radical steps to help a friend, one that, in their opinion, was so obviously wrong

As he washed up, he thought about what his friend had said. If the damage to the connection between worlds was not repaired, then eventually all things on both sides will cease to exist. The Sahae Court had vehemently disagreed with the conclusion, even though none of them bothered to do the leg work that was necessary to form an informed position. The official Sahae decision was that the power building up needed to be put to one of two uses: either eliminate the humans or enslave them once and for all.

Walking up the stairs, he remembered the look on his sister's face when he had tried to talk to her. It was before the boy, before he had lost everyone. He had thought perhaps to try and heal the rift. She had looked at him like he was a madman and fled in fear. Since then, he had avoided all of his kind as he had today. As far as he knew, the price on his head was still enough to tempt even close friends into turning him in, much less a bunch of silly water sylphs.

One of the first things he had done after creating his dwelling was to encircle it with wards to keep away both human and Sahae. As he climbed into bed, he stretched out his awareness and gently explored his defenses. They were all in place and undisturbed. Slipping beneath the covers, he relaxed against the cool pillow and pulled the blanket up to his chin. The last thought that crossed his mind was the laughing camaraderie of the water Sahae he had seen at play in the night. As consciousness fled, a single tear slid down the side of his face.

14

BACK TO THE GRIND

ERIC WOKE TO the smell of frying bacon, which made his stomach growl like a cave bear. Flipping himself out of bed, he hit the bathroom and got ready in record time. Hopping down the last few stairs, he had his shoes on even before entering the kitchen. Mrs. Green had set an enormous breakfast out, including a large platter of bacon. Eric grabbed a few strips as he sat down and stuffed them in his mouth.

"Make up a plate, Eric," Mrs. Green admonished. "Mr. Green will be out directly, however there is no need for a starving man to stand on ceremony." The last she said with a twinkle in her eye; even after shoving the bacon in his mouth and chewing, Eric's stomach had continued to voice its complaints. Pausing she turned back and looked at him for a moment. "I swear Eric it is like you have sprouted a few inches over night! Well we better make sure we get you enough food to keep you growing."

If you only knew the half of it. I'm glad I dressed in baggy clothes, at least she didn't notice the extra muscle I put on 'overnight.'

Smiling, he shoveled huge helpings onto his plate and began eating. By the time Mr. Green appeared at the table, Eric had polished off most of the bacon. Mrs. Green saved about ten slices before he got them all, and a good helping of the eggs and potatoes. Mr. Green looked on in astonishment as Eric finished his third serving and began working through the platter of sweet rolls Mrs. Green placed before him. Finally he slowed down, settled back, and savored his third sweet roll under Mr. Green's amused gaze.

"Feel better?" he asked.

Eric grinned in return, grabbed a fourth sweet roll, and dropped it onto his plate. "I think I'm almost not hungry, but not quite full. That has got to be the best meal I've ever eaten in my life."

Mr. Green laughed and Mrs. Green blushed at the praise as she sat down with her coffee. "Oh, it's just the normal breakfast I always make. I do appreciate the compliment, though." She paused and glanced at Mr. Green before continuing. "So Eric, I hear that you have been having some trouble with a few of the older boys at school." Eric glanced between them and then nodded. Mrs. Green set her coffee down firmly and locked eyes with him.

"Now, I'm not going to ask all the details, I know you and Mr. Green have already spoken about this. But, if you have any issues that get out of hand I want you to be sure to come to us, okay?" Tears gleamed at the corners of her eyes. "We . . . we're your family and if someone has a problem with you, then they have a problem with us all!"

She spoke the last with such vehemence that it actually made the hairs on the back of his neck stand up. He pushed the part of sweet roll his was chewing past the growing lump in his throat. "I appreciate that, it's nice to know that you're here for me. The thing is…I really don't understand why it happened. I hope now that I've stood up to them they'll leave me alone."

Eric stared down at his plate and Mr. Green subtly shook his head at his wife. When Eric looked up, Mrs. Green smiled at him and patted his hand. "Well, if you think it is settled, then I will try not to worry about it. You don't look any the worse for wear, thankfully." Eric gave her a lopsided grin and grabbed another sweet roll off the plate, scooped up his bag and headed out the door.

AS SOON AS the door closed behind him, Mrs. Green sighed and turned to her husband. "Edward, what is really going on?"

Mr. Green gave her a wry smile and took a bite from his sweet roll. He washed it down with a bit of coffee and set both down.

"Well, Claire, as far as I can tell, our boy is a bit of a scrapper. It appears that Dave Mackenzie, you know, Jesse's son? Well, it seems like Eric has gotten onto his bad side."

"That explains it," she said with a smile. "A few of the ladies down at the beauty parlor mentioned that that Mackenzie boy was a real piece of work. He was dating Emily Randall, Penny and John's girl? Well, if she was making eyes at Eric, not that I think the boy would even notice, mind you, that would get him in deep. Maybe Dave noticed, and decided to make an example of Eric. To keep the other boys away from Emily."

Mr. Green frowned and nodded. "Mrs. Green, I would say that you have the makings of a first class investigator." Taking a long drink from his coffee, he grinned at her. "It seems that Dave did decide to point a few boys in Eric's direction. From what I understand, Eric made short work of them. No surprise really, when you consider how long he has been in the foster system. I expect he has had to learn to take care of himself."

Mrs. Green's eyes started to tear up again and he hurried on. "When Dave got frustrated, he somehow enlisted this Moose kid, the state wrestling champ? Eric was ambushed by Moose and two other boys when he was walking with Matt and though he took his licks, he managed to whip all three of them." The last bit he said with a bit of pride, trying to hide a smile.

Mrs. Green looked at him in annoyance. "Edward! You're not encouraging that boy to fight are you?" He thought for a few moments before answering, pausing to take another bite of sweet roll and sip of coffee.

"Am I encouraging him? No. I truly think the whole event upset the boy. He was worried, if you can believe it, that he could have hurt them. Hurt them! When they ganged up on him like a bunch of cowards! I would rather he didn't have to fight, but I can't help being proud of him. Not only for the obvious fighting prowess required to disable three opponents, although that is impressive."

"But to be able to do it without seriously injuring them shows either extreme luck or excellent skill and control. Based on what I have learned of his past tussles, I'm of the opinion it is the latter."

He paused to take another drink of his coffee before continuing. "You know that I'm a firm believer in law and order, Claire. However, we must never forget that there is a thin veneer of civility over a million years of savagery. A man must know how to protect himself and those which he holds dear. I'm just glad that Eric knows how to handle himself."

Mrs. Green sat for a moment in silence before she spoke. "I know it's silly. I just hoped that he would have an easier road. After all he has been through. What was it that Dorothy Clark said? He'd been placed in over fifteen homes since he was an infant and none 'were able' to keep him. It seems like bad luck and hardship have followed him since he was born. I'd just hoped things would be simpler . . . better...for him here."

As she spoke, she cleared the dishes from the table and placed them in the sink. Mr. Green rose from his chair and came up behind her, enfolding her in a hug.

"I like to think that he has a better life here than he has known before, Claire. We love him and accept him for who he is and encourage him to become whoever he wants to be. I don't think he has known that since he lost his parents, although he was likely too young to remember them. Heck, if you get down to it, scrapping with boys over a girl is probably one of the most normal of life's experiences."

Mrs. Green let the last dish slip into the sink and turned in his arms to rest her head against his chest. "I suppose you're right, Edward. I just, well, I just want him to be happy."

Edward held her, the embrace comforting them both. "So do I, my love. So do I."

15

HERE COMES THE DARK

ON THE WESTERN outskirts of Seaverville, where the forest re-claimed the land, darkness began to form. It began as a sinister fog on the unsullied grass near the walking park and thickened quickly. Roiling like black smoke it churned violently, overcoming a small copse of elm trees. Bursting loose of the trees, the malevolent cloud moved toward the lights of town. Streaking up the walking path it expanded to cover the crushed limestone. At the irons of the park gate, it crashed to a halt, unable to pass through the metal barrier. Angry hissing filled the air and the inky fog separated, sliding up and down the edge of the park before coming back together near the park exit. The darkness faded and in its place appeared a strange group of men.

Had anyone been present, a group of four hairy men dressed in ragged skins suddenly appearing out of the wildly unnatural fog bank would have been enough to cause alarm. But it was the men themselves that would have terrified any onlooker into outright flight. Upon closer scrutiny it would have become apparent that the-se were not men at all. Instead of four men, there were in fact eight creatures, each with one foot and one arm, with the noses of dogs. Moving in pairs and hopping around, they left tracks in the loose limestone that looked like normal human footprints. The creatures moved with shocking swiftness, tracing the perimeter of the park in frustration, growling and hissing as they found the entire park was ringed with an iron chain connecting post to post, with the grand iron gate in the center, shut tight.

To most park visitors, the closed gate and the knee-high fence were simply a decorative feature that marked the edges of the park. The gate was shut simply to let them know that the park was closed for the night, which they were expected to honor instead of simply stepping over the chain to enter the park.

To the half-men, the iron chain marked an impenetrable barrier. It turned the beasts back and kept them at a distance. Racing back and forth, the creatures began to make a low, awful sound in their throats. It was horrid to hear, like a wolf howl mixed with the choir of hell, haunting and horrifying at the same time.

As their cries pierced the air it was as if someone flipped a switch and every other nocturnal animal sound stopped. The strange creatures quieted as a figure appeared from the darkness of the forest. Stepping onto the path, his features were illuminated in the moonlight. Long black hair, so black it was almost blue, fell carelessly past his shoulders. Eyes the color of darkest emerald glinted dangerously beneath a furrowed brow. He wore a tuxedo of archaic design, complete with black bow tie, cummerbund and matching spats. He held an ornate walking stick and had a top hat perched atop his head. Well over six feet tall, his trim, wiry muscles made the fabric of his clothing bulge as he strode purposefully down the path.

As he approached the creatures, his angry glare sent them crashing down on the ground to their bellies, whimpering. Moving past them, he hopped lightly over the iron chain again and again while continuing to glower at the prone figures. Stalking up to the dog men, he stopped in front of them and raised his left hand, holding his elaborate cane over them. The creatures keened and babbled as they prostrated themselves before the figure.

"Master," one of the largest of the creatures whined. "We have lost the scent. The cursed metal is everywhere and we sense worse further into the human settlement."

The figure glanced at the creatures and sighed in exasperation. "By the nine layers of color! You Pi Nereske are useless! I look for a simple bit of fun, a lark, to take my mind off the horrible time I have been having in this mind-numbingly boring place. Yet, instead of finding me some sport, you blather at me with excuses for your weakness and incompetence."

Moving closer to the pack, he raised his hand and his voice took on an unpleasant intensity. "If you mongrels cannot pass a simple iron chain, you are of little use to me. Return to your dens to think about how you will overcome your deficiencies and succeed next time!"

Muttering a word under his breath, he outlined the creatures with fire and their howls cut through the night. He watched them writhe in pain with a smile on his face for a few moments before losing interest. With a wave of his hand they disappeared, their cries cut off mid-scream. Glancing around, the figure frowned in irritation. "Delamar! Where are you? Insufferable creature! I demand your presence at once!"

With a soft pop a tiny figure appeared in the air near his face. Dark, leathery skin covered it from head to claw. Atop its head were small, curved horns while behind it, a long, barb-tipped tail cut back and forth through the air in fear and frustration. Red eyes gleamed to slits as it swooped near, its tail tracing a lazy circle. It looked like a horrible child's doll with bat wings.

"Yes, Lord Eishao?"

Imperceptibly raising the hand with the cane, Eishao caused the creature to shrink back in fear. "Mind your manners, you little twit, or I shall seal you in a block of ice for the next few decades." Delamar shrieked in protest and began to exalt the prowess of the Great Lord Eishao. After a few minutes, when the little bastard started to repeat himself, he waved it to silence.

"Very well, you irritating gnat, you are magnanimously forgiven for your insolence. Now, as my dogs are apparently going to be of no use to me, I am going to send you into this hamlet to scout. See if you have any more luck than they did ferreting out whatever it is that is using so much power around here. When you find it, you may return. I would suggest not taking too long, as the toxic levels of technology around here could be quite deadly to one as small as you."

Delamar looked as if he were about to protest then seemed to change his mind and bowed low. "As you say, my master. I shall not fail you."

Eishao looked at him in genuine amusement. "Of course you will not fail me, Delamar. Because if you do, the idea of being encased in a block of ice for all eternity will begin to seem like a vacation in comparison to what I shall do to you." Turning on his heel, Eishao walked back into the forest.

DELAMAR WAITED FOR a few moments before disappearing again, letting his mind wander to how he would like to see Eishao suffer a lingering death on a rack of iron spikes. Again, he cursed his fate at falling in with the insufferable egomaniac. It had been several centuries ago that Delamar had been forced to serve Lord Eishao. Even calling him that made his skin crawl. It had been a time of great change in the world.

Back then, just as now, the monkeys had been spreading across the land at an alarming rate. In their wake had followed the bane of his existence, technology. Delamar had been living quite well in the backwards hamlets of the Russian steppes. The locals were still poor enough that they did not have the luxury of much metal in their lives, which suited him fine. He was able to enter any home and take what he wanted. It had been necessary for him to actually limit his stealing lest he become too fat to fly. Then that blasted peddler had come.

To this day, Delamar cursed the name Nicolai Broshkiaf. The fat, jolly little man had rolled his cart into the backwater village one day and destroyed Delamar's happy existence. It had started with blasted cooking pots; cheap, affordable pots. Then nails, enough nails to rebuild homes and make them secure from the elements and from Delamar. Within a few years, the entire area was full of metal and Delamar was close to starving.

Then had come the fateful day when he was hit by an iron arrowhead meant for a bird he, himself, was trying to catch and eat. Nicolai had seen him and spread his tale of a flying demon far and wide. So well-liked was the cherubic monkey that the entire town had come after Delamar. He was pursued for days and forced to flee to the forest. Weakened by the arrowhead he had been unable to remove, he had been close to being caught when Eishao appeared.

He had rescued Delamar that day, with the condition that Delamar swear an oath of fealty to serve him for all time. Had the situation not been so desperate, he never would have agreed. There were still times when he thought it might have been better to let the villagers have him than to suffer the continued indignities of serving Eishao.

Lifting off from the ground, he slowly spiraled up into their air to begin his scouting duties. Once aloft, he dropped his invisibility. Humans rarely looked up at night and if they did, he would only be visible against the moon or other lights. He moved over the city, giving a wide berth to high power lines and the other massive quantities of metal and technology that pervaded this wretched hamlet. After almost flying into some metal lines in the dark, he decided to take the coward's way out and retreated to an old warehouse near the waterfront to rest.

The building was ancient, probably one of the oldest in the city, with very little in the way of either metal or technology in it. To his delight, he found an old pigeon coop on the roof that was filled to capacity. After a rather enjoyable decimation of the local bird population, he hunkered down inside the coop and fell into a contentedly deep sleep.

Irritating rays of sunlight brought him back to awareness. Unlike many of the shadow born, the light did not cause him pain or injury. It was, however, to one that reveled in the cool bliss of night, damnably bright. Slipping out of his blood and feather-soaked bed, Delamar took a few minutes to clean himself up. If he was summoned back before the master, he knew that a stray feather would reveal his less-than-diligent search for his lord's quarry.

Giving himself a final once over, he was satisfied that he was clean. He turned himself invisible and leaped into the air. From the sky, this tiny hamlet revealed itself to be quite large. "Bloody apes always did sprawl out as far as they could," he muttered to himself. Seeing that his search would take longer than he had first envisioned, he started a slow, lazy spiral using his roost from the night before as a starting point.

The high concentration of technology had his head splitting by the time the sun was at its zenith. Despite the pain, he only allowed himself a short break before taking to the air again. The master had been quite certain the quarry was here or had been here recently. The magic had flared only briefly, but once the master was on a hunt he rarely turned aside.

By late afternoon, his wings felt like lead and his strength had begun to fail. Alighting on a low tree branch, he rested his body and found some solace in the shade. He shuddered to think of what Eishao would do to him for failing to find any sign of his quarry. It never seemed to matter to the arrogant git that a task he set might be impossible; he only wanted results. Leaning back against the trunk of the tree, he let his nails dig in and dozed a bit.

An angry blast of noise that sounded very much like an angry human mob brought him awake in a panic. Looking all around he relaxed when he realized the cacophony was just a large number of children walking by the tree, apparently on their way home from school. Stretching, he glared at the mini apes in irritation and was about to take to the air again when he spotted her.

Lithe and strikingly beautiful, she had blond hair that ran half down her back and the most piercing blue eyes. Delamar felt his heart leap with joy. *Oh I am saved. Even if I do not find the source of the magic, I can tell the master about her. She is perfect, exactly the kind of human he likes to play with.*

As she passed, he dropped from his branch and perched gently on the backpack she was wearing. The added weight barely seemed to faze her; she adjusted the bag slightly and kept walking.

She did not even pause in her conversation with her female friend, a dark-haired girl with an unusually large amount of freckles. "No, Becky," the fair one said. "He and I are ancient history. Dave was nice when we were younger, he really was, but somewhere along the line, he just became a jerk. I think about the time he hit puberty." The one called Becky laughed, causing the beauty to smile. "After going out with him as long as I did, I think I know him better than anyone, and even I only got to see the real him towards the end. At first he was so nice, so romantic, but he kept trying to go further and further when we were alone. No matter how much I told him I wasn't ready, he just kept at it. I guess he figured he could wear me down. Eventually, I had enough and told him off. We had a horrible fight and he called me all sorts of nasty things."

Tossing her hair angrily back over her shoulder she almost knocked Delamar from his perch. "I figured we were through, but the next thing I knew I was showered with flowers and he was taking me out, apologizing for what he had said. It was so confusing. He said he would change, that it would be different this time. And I was stupid enough to believe him. God, I was such an idiot. In the end he managed to keep sweet-talking me until he got exactly what he wanted."

A tear slid down her face where the other girl could not see it and she quickly wiped it away. "After we went all the way, every-thing changed. Then whenever we were alone, which he wanted to be all the time, he started trying to get me out of my clothes. I told him that I expected to be respected and treated right and he laughed at me. The way he figured it, once I gave it up to him, I should be ready to go anytime, anywhere he wanted. He told me I was being a tease and I needed to learn to please my man. When I told him that wasn't going to happen, he got pissed and I got a really good look at who Mr. Perfect really was. Let me tell you, he's nothing like he lets on in public."

Her friend squinted hard, making her eyes nearly disappear. "Oh, Emily…that sucks. I mean you were such a good couple and he is so hot. So…you don't miss him at all?"

Emily snorted. "No way! Prince Charming is actually a toad. Just a walking bag of hormones that turns into a jackhole the minute he doesn't get what he wants. He has spent so much of his life just getting whatever he wants he doesn't have a coping mechanism for being told no. When we were going out at first it was great, but that wasn't him. That was who he thought I wanted him to be, and he was right. I wanted someone that was thoughtful, smart, romantic—"

Becky interrupted her. "He was romantic! What about the flowers?" Emily laughed.

"Flowers are just flowers. As a matter of fact, they're a cop out at best. Guys see flower ads so they go get flowers, usually after they've done something wrong." Becky gave her a confused look.

"Think about all those times I got flowers. Each time was because Dave had been an idiot in some way. He was trying to buy his way back into my good graces. It would have been romantic if he had bought the flowers for no reason, just because he was thinking of me. With him though, flowers always came with strings. Usually tied to my zipper." Becky giggled at this and they turned the corner from school heading up the hill.

"If I ever do . . . that . . . again, it's going to be with someone that matters." Emily looked back at Becky defiantly, as if daring her friend to contradict her.

Becky sighed. "At least you've had a boyfriend. I've never even been kissed, much less had sex."

Emily shushed her friend and pulled her forward, away from the crowd and any wandering ears. "Good god, Becky, say it louder, why don't you? I'm sure my parents didn't quite hear you."

Becky looked horrified and Delamar barely suppressed a laugh at the goofy contortions her face made while she tried to look serious. "Sorry! Sorry, I'll be quieter." The two walked on in silence for a moment before Becky glanced over at Emily. "So…do you think maybe that you might want to . . . you know . . . with Eric?"

Emily looked at her for a moment and then shrugged. "I don't know. I mean I think Eric is hot, I could just get lost in those beautiful green eyes of his. And don't even get me started on those dimples! Uh! But whenever I try to get time with him he does a quick fade. I thought he was afraid of Dave, but after that whole thing with him and Moose, I doubt Dave even fazes him. God! It's so frustrating. Boys are so stupid sometimes. There's Dave, who can't take a hint and leave me alone and Eric, who can't take a hint and ask me out."

The two of them turned down a bright, well-lit street and Delamar was abruptly knocked off the backpack as if struck by a lightning bolt. His painful exit yanked the backpack hard enough to make Emily stumble. Turning in anger, she glared behind her as Becky looked at her in shock.

"What's the matter, Emily?"

Emily looked at Becky with a puzzled expression, her anger fading. "I swear it felt like someone just grabbed my backpack and yanked back on it. I half expected to see Dave standing here."

The two girls scanned the area and saw nothing that could provide anyone a suitable hiding place. Shrugging, they continued down the sidewalk, chatting. Delamar shifted in the small bush he had landed inside, grateful for the camouflage. Whatever had hit him had left him completely defenseless and if not for his luck landing in this bush, he would have been totally exposed. Once he was alone, he carefully extracted himself from the branches.

He felt weak in a way he could barely explain and glanced around searching for a cause. On a post nearby was a sign close to where he had felt the assault. The lettering read CALL BEFORE DIGGING: BURIED FIBER OPTIC LINE. Delamar felt the power coming out of the ground and emptied the remains of his pigeon meal onto the grass. He had been so distracted by the humans' prattling that he had not even noticed the danger. Taking to the air, he barely managed to maintain his invisibility long enough to get back to his lair atop the old warehouse. Collapsing in a dark corner of the coop, he shuddered uncontrollably as consciousness slipped away.

When he awoke, his world was pain. Fire burned his skin and a crushing force held him. He was still so weakened from his ordeal that he lacked even the strength to scream. The fire abruptly cut off and he saw the face of his master leering down at him.

"What, Delamar, no pleas for mercy? No excuses? This is most unprecedented. Is it possible you have actually grown a backbone in my absence?" Eishao stepped closer and examined him before frowning. "Blast, you appear to have gone and gotten yourself injured." Muttering a few words, Eishao passed his hand over the creature and gave a hiss of pain. "Powerful technology did this. What was it? Where have you been?"

Delamar swallowed and tried to speak, however he could not force the words past his throat. With an irritated grunt, Eishao sent a blue nimbus into Delamar and the pain he had been feeling lessened.

"Thank you, master. I was unable to find the source of the magic, however I continued to search. I was struck down while riding on a backpack of a rather interesting girl. I did not see a sign indicating something called 'BURIED FIBER OPTIC.' The blasted technology nearly did me in and I fear I will not be able to scout for you for some time."

Eishao's face contorted in rage and he half raised the cane before he stopped. "Wait, what girl? What was so interesting about her?"

Delamar hid his relief well and solemnly recounted to his master the description of the girl watching as a familiar evil glint begin to appear in his master's eyes.

"Well," Eishao said, smiling. "At least one of my servants knows how to obey. You may not have found the initial diversion I asked for, however this one sounds like it will be even better. You may rest now, Delamar. I shall not call on you for one week while you recover."

Delamar kept his head bent so his master would not see his smile of triumph. He had never had such an abundance of free time. It might even be enough for him to find a way of breaking free of his master's control.

"Thank you, master," he said as Eishao turned and swept from the room. Burying his head underneath his wing, Delamar let his conscious mind retreat and fell into a healing sleep.

16

MOOSE CROSSING

MATT WAS WAITING just inside the tree line as Eric approached through the shortcut. Catching sight of him, Matt motioned him to stay back. Eric slid up next to Matt instead and peered through the trees. Standing there, larger than life, was Donny 'Moose' Calig, and he did not look happy. Feeling a minor flare of frustration, Eric brushed past Matt, who made a vain, if valiant, attempt to stop him. Moose caught sight of Eric exiting the path and squared up his feet.

"Hey, Green. I want to talk to you."

Eric changed his course slightly, stopping just outside of Moose's reach, a fact not lost on either of them. "Yeah, what do you want?" This direct approach seemed to put Moose off a bit, but he recovered quickly.

"I hear that you're bragging about how you beat me down. That I'm some sort of pushover that just lies down."

Eric's eyes hardened into a glare so forceful that Moose took an involuntary step back. "So what? Are you looking for a rematch, Moose? The sun was in your eyes, you need a do over? That kind of thing?" Eric could see that he was making Moose mad, and part of him was doing it on purpose. He was through putting up with this kind of stupidity. Dropping his weight slightly onto his back leg, he nodded at Moose. "Okay, let's go."

Moose visibly paled and put his hands up in protest. "Slow your roll there, man. I'm just here to talk, not to fight."

Eric stepped back to a safer distance, wary of another ambush. Glancing around, he saw that other than Matt, who was still hiding in the trees, they appeared to be alone.

Moose sighed. "Look man, I think we need to sort some things out here, because I'm starting to think I got some bad info. If it turns out that the facts check out, we can dance again."

Eric was honestly confused by this turn of events and the expression must have shown on his face, because Moose seemed to relax a bit. "So, the way the story came down to me, you were saying stuff about me, what a punk I was. Now straight up, I want you to tell me if that is true or not."

Eric fixed Moose with a very direct stare and spoke levelly. "I never said anything about you to anyone. As a matter of fact until we fought I hadn't said anything about you at all. Whoever told you that is a liar. If you had taken the time to ask me this before you grabbed me and punched me in the face we probably would not have had a fight at all."

Moose's cheeks reddened and he nodded, looking down at his feet. "Yeah, that was kind of stupid. When Dave said you were talking smack, I was surprised, I mean you and I hardly know each other. But when Diane Graber said she heard the same thing, I figured it was legit." Turning to the woods, Eric waved for Matt to join them.

"Diane Graber? I don't know her."

Matt was close enough that he caught the last part. "Diane Graber? How could you miss her? You can see her from space!" Eric winced at the description, knowing that, in true Matt form, he must have said something similar directly to Diane Graber, tact not being in his social toolbox.

Moose laughed at Matt's comment and nodded. "Yeah, that's her."

Eric glanced at Matt. "She told Moose that I'd been saying I could take him. She backed Dave up, spreading the same rumor he was. I don't get it. I didn't even know who she was before now. Why would she be spreading lies about me?"

"Duh, because she has a huge thing for Dave!" Matt smacked himself in the forehead. "He once threatened to beat me bloody for saying something mean about her, mostly just as an excuse to beat on me, mind you, and she has worshiped him ever since."

Moose glared at Matt, an angry look growing on his face. "Are you telling me that I got played? Your bud here hasn't been talking shit about me?"

Matt gaped at Moose with honest surprise. "Captain Tolerance over here? The man doesn't even rip on Dave, and god knows that dick has earned it." Turning, he fixed Eric with a mock serious expression. "Come to think of it, Eric, you might be just a little too pure. What does someone have to do to get on your bad side?"

Eric laughed despite himself and clapped Matt on the shoulder. "Normally messing with a skinny asthmatic does wonders. Seriously though, you've got to pick your battles. I learned a long time ago that it's too hard to fight everyone all the time. If you did, you'd always be fighting, because there has never been a shortage of jerks in life."

Looking between the two of them Moose seemed to come to a decision. He stepped forward and extended a hand to Eric. After hesitating a moment, Eric took Moose's hand and shook it.

Moose held his grip for a moment and looked right into Eric's eyes. "Look, I'm sorry for jumping you. I should've talked with you first and I was totally in the wrong. I hope you'll accept my apology." Eric didn't break eye contact and nodded his understanding, shaking Moose's hand in return.

"Okay, Moose. I accept. Glad to know we're cool."

Matt, of course, could not keep from chiming in. "So does this mean that Dave is going to have a beating in his future?"

Moose looked uncomfortable for a second. "Guess it would only be right, huh? After all, his jerking me around caused this, so he might as well reap the reward." Matt was grinning at Moose as if he had just told him that he had won a lifetime supply of beef jerky. Looking between the two of them Eric shook his head. Moose looked at him quizzically.

"It's not worth it, Moose. He's not worth it. I read in the paper the other day that you're looking at college and scholarships, the last thing you need is to get into a fight with someone who will run screaming to his daddy."

Matt looked rather impressed at the derogatory tone Eric took. Moose just looked surprised. "I didn't think anyone even read the paper anymore." Eric grinned.

"I get bored sometimes. Besides, the subject came up when I talked with my foster father about our fight. He was surprised that you'd take the chance of fighting with so many schools looking at you right now."

Looking sheepish, Moose nodded. "Yeah, it was a real bone-head move on my part. That's part of what pisses me off. I could've really screwed myself all because Dave wanted to mess with you." Matt grinned at Moose and spoke in a low, conspiratorial tone.

"Well, lucky for you, Moose, you just happen to be talking to one of the most underhanded, sneaky members of our town. What say you and I put our heads together after school today and come up with a horrible, yet legal, way of taking Mr. Fancy Pants down a few pegs?"

Moose grinned wickedly. "That sounds like a plan, Matt. It'll have to wait until after my workout, say around six? I'll meet you at your house, if that is okay?" Matt nodded and smiled in return.

"Oh, yeah! This is going to be so good. He is going to rue the day he screwed with you, man—full on, full frontal ruing!"

Laughing, Moose waved as he headed off down the street. Matt ran back to the trees to grab their backpacks. Coming back out, he tossed Eric's to him and they started strolling down the path.

"Heck of a day there, Matt. You go from hiding in terror to making friends with one of the toughest guys in town," Eric commented.

"Well, since I was already friends with the toughest guy in town, I must be a magnet for badassery," Matt replied. "Now that you two are firmly ensconced on the same good side, the dark days of Dave are numbered."

Eric smiled, but said nothing as he again felt a sense of surrealism. It was maddening to have gone through so much with Uncle Martin and not be able to talk to anyone about it. Keeping the two series of events straight was giving him a headache. In retrospect, he should probably have been more concerned about the fallout from the fight. Or concerned at all, he had not even seen the thing with Moose coming. In the end, it had gone far better than he ever would have been able to imagine. Still, it was time to get his head back in the game before he did something that might arouse suspicion.

As he and Matt, who had kept up a rambling, one-sided dialogue during the entire walk, approached the school, he could feel a palpable sense of anticipation from the student body. As he drew closer to where Moose was standing with a few of his friends, he noticed a collective holding of breath. Walking by, he nodded to Moose, who nodded back and put out his fist for a friendly bump. Eric bumped fists without slowing and the crowd let out an audible gasp of surprise. He caught snippets of conversations as he walked to his locker.

"Did NOT see that coming."

"What are they, best buds now?"

"Did you see how casual that was? No drama at all."

"How freaking cool was that?"

"Dave is going to freak when he hears about this."

Opening his locker, his good mood soured immediately. Someone had broken into it and dumped what smelled like manure onto the entire contents. Luckily, he had cleaned almost everything out recently, so there were only a few textbooks and an old jacket in there.

The smell hit him like a blow to the face and his eyes watered. Stepping back, he fought his gag reflex as others in the hall took notice of the smell and turned to find the source.

Well, at least it's not beef stew, he thought wryly. He could tell that those watching were waiting for him to explode. A day before, in their world time, he would have done just that. But, he had had over a year with Uncle Martin to work on his temper and it was not so easily triggered. Stepping back a few feet, he nodded towards his locker, meeting the eyes of one of the girls in the hallway.

"School stinks," he deadpanned.

There was about a three-second delay and then the girl and the students around her burst into laughter. Mr. Garretson, the science teacher, came over to see to the commotion and gagged audibly when the smell caught him.

"Good Lord, Eric. What is that smell? Oh my goodness, what happened to your locker?!" Without waiting for an answer, he hurried to his classroom and Eric heard him calling the office over the intercom system. A few minutes later, Mr. Campbell, the principal, arrived with the janitor to survey the damage.

"Well sir, the lock is shelled," the janitor, Mr. Dien, decreed. "It looks like someone jimmied it with a screwdriver. Even after we clean it, the smell is going to last for weeks. Everything inside is a loss, four textbooks and the coat." He looked at Eric in apology, as if the damage was somehow his fault. Donning a pair of rubber gloves, he began carefully placing the offending items in a heavy plastic trash bag.

Mr. Campbell looked irritated and motioned for Eric to follow him. "Eric, please accompany me to my office."

Eric groaned internally and followed along. Mr. Campbell led him all the way into his office and closed the door behind him. He sat behind his desk and motioned for Eric to sit down. Once Eric was seated, Mr. Campbell sat for a few moments, watching him, before he spoke.

"Eric, I know that it can be difficult to start a new school. I also know you have attended a lot of schools. I want you to know that we at Seaverville Community School take the safety and well-being of our students just as seriously, if not more so, than the larger schools you have attended. We have a strict 'no bullying' policy and we'll get to the bottom of who did this to your locker."

Eric sat confused for a full second before he realized that Mr. Campbell had brought him in as the victim to be consoled. Barely missing a beat, he nodded back solemnly.

"I appreciate that, Mr. Campbell, but do you think there is really any way that you will catch whoever did it?"

Mr. Campbell nodded emphatically. "Yes, indeed. I think you'll be surprised how swiftly justice will be served in this particular situation. You have my word on that, Eric. And you have my sincerest apologies that this has happened to you." Patting him on the shoulder, Mr. Campbell asked him to wait for a few minutes and stepped out of the office.

Curious, Eric quietly rose and peeked out the door into the main office area. He saw the faculty gathered around one of the roll away TV/DVD sets that the teachers used in class to show videos. The janitor had just put a DVD in and was pressing 'play' when Eric glanced out the door and snuck a peek at the television screen. He saw a view of the hallway from above.

Holy crap. They have the place wired with video cameras. That's good to know before I go streaking down a hall. Or getting into a fight on campus.

As he watched, they fast-forwarded and the oversized timestamp showed the early hours before school. The video showed people, mostly teachers, passing by his locker. Finally they slowed the video and rewound to replay a section and he saw Dave Mackenzie and one of his cronies. They popped the locker with disturbing ease and doused the interior with something from a few spray bottles before closing it up and moving down the hall.

Mr. Campbell said something quietly and left the office. Eric moved back to his seat. A few minutes later, Mr. Campbell was back with Dave in tow. Dave was pale and panicky. Mr. Campbell directed him to the seat next to Eric, and Dave sat down heavily.

"In all my years as an administrator, David, I've never seen such willful disregard for school property, private property, personal safety and well-being! You should know that I am seriously considering suspension and possible expulsion for your behavior!"

For the first time since they met Eric actually felt sorry for Dave. The horrified expression on Dave's face spoke volumes.

"David, do you realize the seriousness of this? Suspension could disqualify you for scholarships and grants. And if you are expelled, you would have to find a school with open enrollment. The closest one is hours away from here, I can tell you that. Or perhaps you would prefer to get a G.E.D. at the local learning annex?"

Dave squirmed in his chair under the relentless verbal assault. He apparently was not used to being in a situation where anyone talked to him like this. "Mr. Campbell! I . . . it was stupid, I know. I just . . . I had to get him back for kicking my . . . ." Dave stopped himself too late and a look of horror crossed his face.

"What do you mean, 'kicking?' Kicking your what? Have you boys been fighting? Eric? What is he talking about?"

Eric saw the opportunity to take Dave out, and it would be so easy. One small nudge and he would be gone. Expulsion. A senior ambushing an underclassman and then damaging his locker? Easy sell. But, that would mean implicating Moose and that just did not sit well with Eric. Shaking his head, he arranged his face into an expression of disdain.

"Fighting? No way, Mr. Campbell. Dave is just mad that I beat him in a game of flag football we played at the park. It was mostly luck on my part, but I think Dave was getting a lot of ribbing from the guys."

Eric felt a little ridiculous, like a character from a bad after school special. But he could tell from the expression on Mr. Campbell's face that he was buying it. Not only that, some part of him realized that he was telling the principal exactly what he wanted to hear. Something that fit better into his view of the world than the truth did.

Dave glanced at him in shock for about half a beat but quickly recovered. "Yeah, they were riding me pretty hard. I got mad and just figured I would mess his locker up a little bit. It just got out of hand."

Mr. Campbell glanced back and forth between the boys, as if he were trying to gauge if the boys were being genuine. Before he could say anything his secretary called him to the outer office for a phone call.

As soon as he was out of the door, Dave turned and hissed at Eric. "What's your game, Green? Why the hell are you covering for me?"

Eric stared at him without expression and then shrugged. "It would get too many other people in trouble. You need to let this go. I don't see any reason for either one of us to waste any more time on this. It's up to you, though. You keep pushing and you might just succeed in getting yourself expelled." Mr. Campbell came back in and took his seat behind the desk.

"Well, David, I've just spoken with your father. He has assured me that he will take care of the cost of cleaning the locker and the replacement cost for all the articles that were destroyed including, Mr. Green's coat. He has also assured me that he feels that it would be better for all concerned for him to deal with you and in this one instance, I will agree. But, I've made him aware, and I'm making you aware, that if there is one more instance of tomfoolery from you before you graduate, you will be expelled. Is that clear?" Dave nodded and looked convincingly abashed.

"I've decided that as punishment for your misdeed, David, you'll remove your belongings from your locker and for the rest of the year use Eric's locker, the locker you ruined."

At this, a flash of anger passed across Dave's face. He masked it quickly and hung his head as Mr. Campbell went on. "Eric, I realize that you may want to forgive and forget, however I cannot allow this property damage to go unpunished. Now, unless the two of you have anything more to say, I want you to shake hands and get out of my office. And David? Remember what I said. I don't expect to see you back in here ever again."

The boys stood, and after an awkward handshake, left the office with Mr. Campbell trailing after them. He watched Dave empty his locker and carry its contents to Eric's newly cleaned, yet still fragrant, locker. After he placed his things in and closed the door, Mr. Campbell sent him back to class. The janitor showed up around that time with replacement textbooks for Eric.

Placing all but the one he needed in his new locker, he watched the janitor install a new lock. Handing Eric the combination, he waited for Eric to try it and make sure it opened correctly before heading down the hallway. Mr. Campbell gave Eric a slip to get into class and headed back to the office. Smiling in amusement, Eric headed to his next class. After that the rest of the day fairly flew by, and in no time he was stowing his books and getting ready to head home when he was startled by a sweet voice.

"So, it is true, you're my new locker mate. The property values in the area should go through the roof."

He could see her smile without even turning around and a part of him quailed in terror. He would know that voice anywhere. It was Emily Randall; cheerleader, class president, honor roll student, cutest girl in school and ex-girlfriend of Dave Mackenzie. Turning, he saw her in all her radiant glory. Her flowing blond hair fell to the middle of her back and shone like fire in the afternoon sunlight. Clear blue eyes with green flecks that drew him in like endless pools. Full, red lips with a slight upturn, as if she were always smiling. He felt his mind spin off into the atmosphere.

Panic swept over him and he felt his knees turn to jelly. He had totally forgotten that Dave's locker was right next to Emily's. Dave had traded away his assigned locker for this location at the beginning of the school year. He tried to talk and felt like his tongue was suddenly made of lead. She smiled at him before self-consciously touching her hair and tossing her books into her locker. After a few seconds, he managed a pathetic reply.

"Yeah, locker mates."

As the words left his mouth, he wished he could take them back. It sounded stupid even to him. Emily just turned and gave him a radiant smile that made him feel like his sneakers were melting into the ground.

"Hey, your face looks great. There's no sign of that big bruise from yesterday at all!" As she said this, she stepped closer and ran her fingers over the part of his face where Moose had hit him so long ago. Suddenly self-conscious, he felt his face flush.

Damn, of course she would notice that. He smiled at her in return, his mind absolutely blank. *Say something, idiot! Form a coherent response.*

"Well, I guess I'll see you tomorrow," she said.

He stood there like a slack-jawed fool, just watching her walk away and out the door and stayed standing until Matt, who had been watching the whole time, sauntered up behind him and bumped his shoulder.

"Hey, you might want to pick your tongue up off the floor. Someone might step on it and besides, who knows what is on this floor."

Eric glanced at Matt and gave him a weak smile.

"We're gonna need a crash cart, STAT! Good god, you got it bad, man," Matt said in mock horror. "Pull it together before you make a worse spectacle of yourself." Glancing around, Matt pulled Eric off into a side hallway. "Well, superhero, it looks like we just found your weakness. You're susceptible to girls. Who knew?"

Eric replayed the last few minutes in his head and groaned audibly. "God, I just made a huge fool out of myself."

Matt opened his mouth as if to argue with him and then closed it.

"Yes…yes you did. Still, I don't think anyone but Emily noticed and she seemed to like it. I honestly was wondering if you were going to respond or throw up on her shoes. I gave it fifty-fifty odds either way. So consider it a victory that you actually managed to talk to her." Pulling his backpack up tight on his back, Matt turned towards the door. "So, are you coming to the planning session?"

Eric looked up in confusion before remembering that Matt had plans with Moose this afternoon. Shaking his head, he leaned against the wall and slid down to the floor, watching Matt head towards the door. As bad as today had been, he was struck with the realization that there was an entire school year left for him to make a fool of himself in front of Emily Randall.

17

MARTIN WAKES

EMERGING FROM HIS slumber Martin had a nagging feeling that something was wrong. The cobwebs that filled his head were slow in clearing and he bashed his shin on the bed frame on his way down to the kitchen. It was not until after his first cup of glorious coffee that he glanced out the window and frowned. Using a small incantation, he grimaced and then swore.

The cantrip revealed that he had slept the entire night and day. Rising slowly from the table, he felt the muscles of his back spasm slightly and once again was reminded of his advancing years. *I am no longer a youngling to be taking on such an arduous task. If the fates were kinder, I would be relaxing in a gentle forest glen somewhere instead of traipsing through the human world.*

Pouring himself a second cup of coffee, he returned to the bedroom. Pulling on new garments, he took a moment before the mirror, smoothing his unruly locks before heading back to the kitchen for breakfast. He ate sausage, crackers and cheese until he felt like the seams of his clothes would burst. He sat at the table for a long time, allowing the warm, nutty scent of the coffee to push away the new wave of sleepiness brought on by being stuffed full.

It was possible, likely even, that he had gravely erred in bringing the boy back so soon. To be truthful, they could have spent decades training, and they should have. Sighing, he rubbed his forehead with the heel of his hand. The safehold was gone now. The magic was meant to be used once and the power expended had taxed him and Eric's father so badly that they had been nearly useless for a month. Alone, he had no chance of making such a retreat again. Rubbing his face again, he went back to staring at himself in the mirror hanging on the far wall.

Foolish or not, he had to admit that the decision to leave had not been entirely unappealing. Even when he had helped create the safehold, he had never planned on staying there, especially for an extended period of time.

The thought of being trapped in such a limited location for even the short duration of a human lifespan made him shudder. So when Eric had begun to chafe at the monotony of their existence, he had put up less of a fight than would have been seemly.

While the boy was lamenting Martin's limited skills as a chef, he had been sensing a larger, unspoken argument. It went far beyond his own limited ability to cook more than porridge and stew. Not that the boy did not have a point, he could not remember a greater meal than the one he had just eaten, which was entirely due to the monotony of his recent diet. It struck him how much he had in common with the lad. They were kindred spirits that could not stand to be contained in such a mediocre existence. It was understandable that his resistance to leaving had begun to crumble as he watched Eric master the skills he was teaching him.

Based on the initial analysis of the boy's skills and the first few weeks of training, he had feared they would be confined to the safehold forever. Overcoming the misinformation stuffed into the lad's brain had been one of their biggest hurdles. There was an unflagging desire in the human imagination to fill any gap in knowledge with a fantasy that fit their version of how the world should work. The nonsense that had come out of the lad's mouth had Martin shaking his head in disbelief one moment and teetering on the edge of rage the next. Flying carpets, throwing lightning bolts from his hands, and the idea that he could make a bag that would hold more than a large warehouse had been but a few of the wild ideas he had about using the Way.

It had taken Martin weeks to convince the boy that there were no magic potions, just some extracts that could be imbued with the Way to help in healing. They had finally had a breakthrough when Eric began to use science and technology, of all things, as a point of comparison. He compared the extract of a bulgar bush to something he called anti-itch cream and from there it seemed as if a dam burst inside the boy's awareness and he began making great strides in his understanding of things.

At first, he had been afraid that Eric was drawing false conclusions, mostly based on his own rather limited knowledge of technology. So he had the boy explain himself at length. As Martin had come to understand each comparison, he realized the boy was correct in his association. It also terrified him to see how far the human community had come since he last walked among them.

Quickly, it became apparent to him that science was well on its way to outstripping every aspect of the Way that he had ever used. Eric talked of technology that allowed a projectile to fly around the world in mere minutes. Hand held computers that could hold nearly every book ever written. Cameras that watched over almost all of humanity. It was chilling to hear the examples of advancements that had been made in the last decade. It made him wonder if similar changes had occurred with magic that he was simply unaware of, though he doubted it.

Science seemed a progressive study whereas the Way was intuitive. It depended more on the individual to discover new ways of doing things rather than all practitioners as a whole. He was astonished to see Eric make comparisons between two things that were so opposed to each other in the natural balance. The boy achieved an unprecedented grasp of not only compounds and mixtures, but he also showed intuitive leaps in tapping into and shaping the Way.

So profound was their progress that Martin found himself teaching Eric things that were well beyond some shadowborn individuals, even after decades of study. He had his father's drive, that one. At times he seemed to be even more driven, perhaps the influence of his human heritage. Martin had to carefully monitor the time Eric spent working and resting. It had become necessary for him to force rest on the lad as well as more than a little cajoling to get him to eat enough of the food available to keep his strength up.

There had even come a point where he threatened to geas the lad into eating if he did not take in more calories. Eric had finally relented and was a robust eater after that, if not an enthusiastic one. Food had only grown as an issue as time went on. It culminated in the rather unpleasant evening when Eric was unable to eat without complaining of overwhelming nausea.

When he began to vomit, Martin knew that there was no choice but to leaving the safehold. Although he had suggested the compromise of bringing loads of food through, the lad shot that idea down rather quickly.

Eric had pointed out, quite correctly, that the energy of bringing anything through the portal more than once would have taxed Martin to exhaustion. Rather than entering a potentially dangerous situation unable to maintain an adequate defense, the decision was made to exit the safehold immediately.

It had been a calculated risk, one that he had been argued vehemently against. Still, after his reconnaissance last night he felt a bit safer with their decision. Cleaning his plate, he put everything away and stepped outside. He closed his eyes and used the Way to feel for intruders nearby. A powerful shock went through him as his wards barely dispersed the searching tendrils of an active spell. The power behind it was horrifying. The complexity of the weave told Martin that a very old Sahae had cast it.

Quickly reinforcing his masking wards, he cast a simple spell that allowed him to track the other caster. The magic was emanating from west of his location, further from town. He quietly closed the door behind him and set off through the trees. It took very little time for him to reach his destination even though he forwent all magic other than his existing masking spells. What he found was in no way subtle. A large oak tree, nearly ten feet thick, far larger than those around it, stood in the midst of a thick web of spells.

The sheer number of enchantments that must have been laid since he had fallen asleep was staggering. The creature that dwelt within must be powerful indeed. Careful not to disturb the network of spells before him, he carefully began to withdraw. Once he put some distance between himself and the tree, he turned to quicken his retreat and saw a thin figure barring his path.

"Well now. This is a true treat! I have seen a few of the lesser of our brethren around here, however none like you. Obviously you are a Sahae of refinement."

Martin nodded with a casualness he did not feel. "I did not mean to disturb you. I was passing this area and could not help but feel the pull of your seeking spell," he said.

The gaunt figure grinned insolently. "Why yes, it was a bit gauche, however I was trying to track down a strange oddity that I felt in the Way earlier, and this is the fastest way to do that." The thin figure raised his left hand to his forehead and pretended to swoon. "Ah, where are my manners? We are already conversing and we have not done introductions. I am Lord Eishao, the houseless wanderer, orphan of the Great Blights, the scoundrel of the blessed night and kindred soul to Raganol. And you are?"

Martin paused as he took in this new information. Raganol was a well-known shadowborn; infamous for his indulgences among the humans to the point where most well thought of Sahae denied his existence. Looking slightly irritated, Lord Eishao again motioned for Martin to introduce himself.

"I am Vebanak, Lord Eishao," Martin lied. "I see that you are crafting yourself quite the domicile here. Are you newly settled to this area then?"

Eishao's expression changed to one of amusement and a snort of laughter escaped. "Settle? Here? Anywhere? No, my good fellow, I am simply taking a bit of diversion here. I was passing by a short time ago and felt the most peculiar disturbance in the Way. It was strangely powerful and yet quite primal and raw. I had suspected to find a strong, wild shadowborn out here, or perhaps an Abomination. However, so far I am hard-pressed to discover the source and the choking levels of technology around here are playing havoc with my efforts."

Easing himself back Eishao waved a hand and reformed a tree into a curved seat, losing half of its branches in the process. The display of raw power made Martin's heart sink. *He must be powerful to carelessly squander so much energy on something so unimportant. Obviously he is showing off, and enjoying himself quite a bit doing it. Yet how much of this is showing off and how much of it is having power to burn?*

"So Vebanak, what is it that you do? Are you perhaps a guardian of this area or, judging from the way you were trying to skulk away, are you hiding from them?"

At the imperceptible widening of Martin's eyes, Eishao clapped excitedly, like a small boy discovering a present. "Oh, happy day! A distraction! A puzzle! What a story you must have, Vebanak, to be hiding out here in the forest." Martin's face flushed and he glared at Eishao.

"I have no idea what you are talking about, sir. I merely do not like to socialize. It leads to conversations that tax my patience, such as this one." Martin turned and stalked off the path heading into the trees. Before he got ten feet away, Eishao appeared in his path again, leaning on a tree.

"Oh, Vebanak, quit being so pedantic. We have only just met. You cannot leave until I am ready to let you go." The way he said the last part, although he said it airily, made Martin's skin crawl. It was the matter-of-fact way in which it was delivered. As if Martin's wishes did not matter at all. His face flushed and he balled up his fists at his sides.

"So it is to be like that? Ye wish to fight, do ye?" As always when he was upset, Martin's accent slid into a rough brogue.

Eishao stared at him in shock and then clapped his hands again and danced in a circle. "A contest! Fisticuffs, as it were. I have not physically fought one of our kind in decades! Oh, what a treasure you are, Vebanak."

Eishao waved his hands and four posts sprung up from the ground, the hardened remains of buried trees. With another flourish vines wrapped around the posts until they formed the oddest boxing ring Martin had ever seen. He found himself in one corner and Eishao giving him a beatific smile from the far side. Two small shelves formed at the corners from the wood posts, with looked to take the place of stools in each corner. To his right he saw a bell form from a rock near the side of the ring. Eishao's expression became serious.

"Okay, rules now, Vebanak, rules. First, we may not use any magic. No touching the Way, no using tricks. Second, we fight until one of us yields, but no sandbagging. You must fight me as hard as you can. Third, the winner gets the prize of their choosing. Do you agree to these rules?"

Martin cursed himself for being a fool. Losing his temper, the very thing he had railed at the boy now for the last year, had landed him in a real mess. While the ring had been forming he had tried to slip away multiple times and had realized that he was in real trouble. The vines resisted every effort he made to try and slip through them. He was well and truly trapped.

Looking at Eishao all thoughts of escape vanished as he saw the determined look in his opponent's eyes. Settling into a fighting stance he took a deep breath. "I guess you have given me no choice." Raising his fists, he readied himself for battle.

18

DINNER AND ANXIETY

THE ATMOSPHERE IN the Green residence was light as they sat down to dinner. Though he was sure that both of them had already heard the story from the principal, Eric told the Greens about his day. At the mention of the damage to his locker, Mr. Green got a dangerous look in his eyes. By the time he heard about the principal's unique fix, he was smiling again.

"Well, Eric, it is good to know that Mr. Mackenzie is taking this seriously. We can go this weekend and get you a new coat to replace the one that was ruined."

Eric nodded and spooned a third helping of food onto his plate. "Yeah, that would be fine. It was a fall jacket anyway. I forgot it at school one of the warmer days and then just wore my winter coat back. I just kept forgetting to bring it home. I'm just glad they didn't make me pay for the books. I can only imagine how expensive that would have been."

Mrs. Green made a dismissive gesture and smiled at him. "They knew who was at fault, and hopefully this little episode smartens that David Mackenzie up. Imagine dumping fertilizer in someone's things! It's abhorrent!"

Mr. Green stifled a smile and tried to look solemn as he spoke to Eric. "So Eric, they moved your locker? Who are you next to now?"

"Oh, I'm on the end so I only have one person next to me. Emily Randall." Eric studied the pattern of his plate, trying to hide the embarrassment he felt. He missed the sharp look Mrs. Green gave her husband as she admonished him with a shake of her head. Instead of continuing, his foster father cleared his throat and took a drink of water.

Reaching across the table, Eric pulled the plate of fried chicken towards him and became lost in selecting another piece. Keeping his eyes on his plate, he shoveled food into his mouth until he felt the blood subside from his face. "Yep, it should make it real easy to get in and out of school now," he said with false enthusiasm.

Mrs. Green rose from the table. "Well, I am going to go get our dessert. I hope you saved room, Eric."

Eric nodded but refrained from answering, as his mouth was stuffed full from the bite he had just taken. Mr. Green stood up from the table and went into the kitchen to help her.

A FEW MINUTES later in the kitchen, Claire playfully slapped her husband on the upper arm. "Edward," she said softly. "The boy almost burst into flames he was blushing so hard."

Giving his wife a small grin he leaned back on the counter. "One of the pitfalls of having conversations with teenagers is that you will never know what comes out of their mouth. How was I to know that fate was conspiring to place the boy right next to the girl he likes? Although it makes sense I suppose if they had the boys switch lockers. David must be madder than a wet hen."

His wife gave him a stern look. "Well, you should be careful not to tease too much. You know how seriously they take these things at that age. You don't want to end up hurting his feelings."

Edward smiled and pecked her on the cheek before reaching into the refrigerator for a bowl of whipped cream. "Part of being a man is learning that you'll get teased about any girl you're sweet on. Why, back in the day, the boys used to bust my chops about being twisted around your little finger."

Claire blushed and looked at him coyly. "Did they now? And what did you say to them in response, Edward?" Mr. Green took her in his arms and gave her a sweet kiss before responding.

"Why, my dear, I told them that they were quite right and that sour grapes didn't suit them so they should go find a beautiful gal of their own."

IN THE DINING room, Eric found himself suddenly unable to eat his fifth helping. The reminder that Emily was in the locker right next to his had stolen his appetite. Every day until the end of school he was going to see her; maybe even multiple times a day. There would be endless opportunities for him to make a huge fool of himself. What little reputation he had would go flying out the window. Only this time, instead of just being on the outside looking in, he would be the laughingstock of the school. No matter how many books he read on the subject, he was still completely mystified about how to talk to women.

Granted, his experience with women was nearly zero. Back at his old school, he had not been popular. He had friends and went to his share of school dances, but the few girls that might have liked him seemed obsessed with the fact that he lived in an orphanage. At least, that was all they ever wanted to talk about when they were alone with him. It had made them angry when he did not want to open up more. Like he would want to discuss his crappy life with a relative stranger...

After a while, he just stopped trying to interact with the girls at his school. He was a bit braver on the rare occasions when he had talked to girls away from school. His only real success to date was one brief interaction at a summer camp he was sent to the year before. There was a girls' camp nearby, located at the opposite end of the lake. The lake separating the two locations had made for rather limited actual interaction between campers.

The exception was a yearly coed dance chaperoned by both sets of camp counselors. At the dance he had met a girl named Suzie Simmons. A fiery redhead with mischievous green eyes, she had walked out to the dock with him and they ended up kissing but were interrupted by two counselors before it could go any further. Then she was gone and the summer was over.

Eric decided he needed some real advice. And sadly, the best advisor he had available was Matt. The door to the kitchen opened and Mrs. Green came out carrying a warm blueberry pie. Mr. Green followed behind her with a bowl of fresh, homemade whipped cream.

Eric found he had regained enough of his appetite to partake. *Wonderful what having a plan does for the digestion.* After two helpings of dessert he pushed back from the table. "Would you guys be okay if I went over to Matt's for a while?"

The Greens shared a knowing glance over his head. "Sure, Eric," said Mr. Green, trying unsuccessfully to hide a smile. "Just make sure you get back before nine-thirty, it's still a school night after all." Eric cleared his plate and headed out the back door. It was not until after he knocked on Matt's front door that he remembered that Moose and Matt were supposed to be working out revenge on Dave tonight. He was relieved when Matt answered the door alone and ushered him down into the basement, or his "lair," as Matt liked to call it.

The house originally had an outside entrance to the basement. Sometime in the late seventies, the owners had added a garage. Due to the lot size they had been forced to incorporate the basement entrance inside the garage.

The opening was covered by a thick, heavy plywood rectangle set flush to the floor. It was so heavy that it could hold a car if you accidentally pulled forward too far. A workbench built along the back wall almost guaranteed that would never happen, although that appeared to have been added after the door was in place. It was so heavy that it had to be counterweighted on a pulley system. The end result was like an old drawbridge rising silently out of the floor. When they first started hanging out, Eric had nearly faced the fury of Matt's mother by taking the device apart and rebuilding it. After she saw how well it worked when he was done, she had been so happy she had given him all the malfunctioning items in the house to fix.

The first step was a bit of a drop, being almost three feet down, and led down to the rough stones of the original foundation. An old wooden door sat at the foot of the stairs. It had originally been an exterior door and had iron bands with rivets holding the wood together. Weathered, with a slightly rusty old iron doorknob, it swung inward silently. Eric had always thought it had the aged appearance of a dungeon door from one of the games they played and indeed, once you went through the door you were in a ten by ten room. On the far side of the room instead of a chest, though, there was the large form of Moose leaning over a card table. He smiled as Eric came in and waved him over.

"Hey, man. You have got to see this. Matt is a diabolical old soul." Eric stopped and waved just inside the door.

"Nope, sorry, I need to maintain plausible deniability." Matt laughed at this and nodded to Moose.

"Yeah Moose, cover it up, we want it to be a surprise after all." With an evil grin, Moose threw a tablecloth over the card table. "Well I'm gonna head home. I gotta go get some food. See you tomorrow." Moose slipped by them and shot up the stairs to the garage like a bullet from a gun.

"He's the only guy I know whose stomach growls as loud as yours," Matt said with a grin. "So, if you're not here to plan the counterattack—what do you need?"

Now that he was actually here, Eric had no idea what to say or what to ask. To forestall conversation, he flopped down in the overstuffed beanbag in the corner. Matt grabbed the other beanbag and dragged it over. True to form, he began rattling away without even waiting for Eric to gather his thoughts, which, in this case, was a comfort.

"You know, I wish I could tell you what I have planned for Dave. It's going to be epic! We're talking three to five years of intense therapy to get it ironed out of his shattered subconscious. He'll suspect me, but this time I'm going full stealth mode." Grinning, he kicked his feet out straight in front of him.

"There will be no proof. On top of all that, it's going to be one hundred percent legit. Nothing illegal and no rules broken. Bent perhaps, but no rule was hurt in the creation of this trauma." Matt looked up, caught sight of Eric's face and paused. "Dude? What gives? You look like you're about to blow chow or something." Matt grabbed a nearby bucket and shoved it near Eric, causing him to smile.

"I'm not going to hurl." Eric said pushing the bucket away.

"Good, man, because it's hard as hades to get the smell out. Concrete sucks odors in, you know? So, are you going to tell me how you ended up in your new locker?"

Eric took a deep breath, collecting his thoughts, and started from the beginning. As he got to the part about helping Dave avoid expulsion, Matt interrupted him. "What! You mean that you had that bullying puke dead to rights and you let him wriggle away? He would have been gone! What were you thinking?!" Eric was surprised at how angry Matt was.

"I honestly don't know." The two sat in silence as, for once, Matt struggled to control his temper. After a few minutes, Matt laughed.

"Well that's a switch. You, keeping your cool and me losing it. Pretty soon I'm going to be taking the football team out with a single punch." Eric grinned at that and the tension between them broke.

"Well, we've already established that you're a magnet for badassery. Some of it must be rubbing off on you." Matt laughed and gave Eric a playful shove.

"So, tell me, what happened next?" Eric told him the rest and by the end, Matt was grinning ear to ear.

"So let me get this straight. Mr. Stay Away From My Ex-

Girlfriend tries to keep you away. He fills your locker with crap and not only does he get caught doing it but he has to use the stinky locker and you get his locker. His locker. Right next to his ex-girlfriend? Oh man, this is rich. This is more than worth the price of admission."

Matt had tears running down his face and was holding his sides as he laughed. "Eric, you have got to be the luckiest guy I've ever met. You step in crap and literally come out smelling like roses. Oh my god, my sides . . ." Matt collapsed back into the beanbag and took a few moments to recover.

Once he could breathe again, Matt sat up and wiped the tears from his eyes. Gasping, he took a long drag off his inhaler and took some time to get his breathing under control. At last, he looked at Eric and smiled. "Okay man, sorry. Weezy is back in her deluxe apartment in the sky. Well, I guess it is good to know that the school has cameras watching our every move. Hello Big Brother. That being said I am going to have to totally rethink my plans for Dave. It is one thing to bend a few rules, it is quite another to do it on candid camera." Matt sat quietly for a second and then got a wide eyed look.

"Oh my...I gotta tell you, bro, you just gave me an even more epic idea than the one Moose and I had for Dave. Oh, it is going to be priceless." Matt grinned evilly and rubbed his hands together. "Now obviously since you didn't want to be in on the planning you weren't coming to see me about Dave. So tell me, what's the problem? You should be happy with how things went down, so what gives?"

Eric gave him a weak smile. "That's the problem. She stopped to say hi today and . . . you saw it. I froze, man. It was humiliating. I actually said something about being locker mates. Well, she said it first and I just repeated it like a moron."

Matt unsuccessfully tried to hide a smile. "Get you. No problem taking on a hulk like Moose. A girl, though? Yikes! Batten down the hatches!" Eric blushed furiously and started to get up. Matt realized he had pushed the wrong button and back pedaled quickly. "Relax! I'm just playing." Eric settled back into the bean bag sullenly. "It's not that big a deal. You just need to learn to chill a bit."

Eric held his head in his hands and when he looked up, for the first time, Matt saw fear in his friend's eyes. "What if I make a complete fool out of myself? I don't know how to talk to girls! She said 'hi' to me and I practically had an attack! What happens next? She asks me a question and I end up puking all over her?"

Matt cocked his head to the side and Eric knew he was getting a mental picture of that and stopped him before he could laugh. "I'm serious! I'm freaking out here!" Matt stared at him for a moment and then settled back, looking thoughtful. For once, he remained silent for more than five minutes, apparently lost deep in thought. Finally, he sat forward on his beanbag, elbows on his knees.

"This is your lucky day. I know that I don't get a lot of play in these parts, but there are a few ladies around here that appreciate a superior wit. So here is what you're going to do. First thing, girls sense fear. You have to be confident, in control. Second, you have to be cool. Not play it cool, but actually be cool. I would say be yourself, but I happen to know what a goofball you are in real life. Women want someone who is suave and romantic. You're supposed to ease her into getting to know the real you. You might get a little play in the meantime."

At this Eric, blushed so hard that he almost seemed to glow for a moment. Matt rubbed his eyes and the afterimage was gone. "Relax, I have it all figured out," Matt said. "Here is what we are going to do…"

19

EISHAO AND MARTIN

MARTIN HAD MADE a series of terrible mistakes. First and foremost was letting himself be caught sneaking around Eishao's tree. The second was not fleeing immediately upon seeing Eishao. Then there was actually thinking that he could take Eishao in a bout of boxing. He had always thought his martial prowess was fair, however, in comparison to Eishao, he was a novice. He had not lasted two rounds.

True, there was no permanent damage. After trouncing him soundly, Eishao had demanded as his prize that Vebanak, as Martin had told him his name was, join him for a meal. Though he was not currently in any mortal peril, he was in danger of being bored to death. So far, he had been subjected to hours of the most irritating conversation he had ever been forced to endure. It was like a new kind of torture, only one where the torturer was apparently oblivious to the damage they were doing.

The hour was growing late and Martin saw an opening to make his escape. As Eishao paused in his explanation of how he had been instrumental in causing the great San Francisco fire, Martin cleared his throat.

"I do hate to interrupt you, Lord Eishao, however I see the light is waning and I must still be about getting the supplies I had originally set out for."

Eishao looked at him in confusion for a split second before his face broke into a huge smile and he nodded. "Of course, dear Veba-nak, of course. You must be off to do your trivial errands and you have been gracious enough to share my company for so long. I had forgotten how wonderful it is to converse with a relative equal."

Martin kept a pleasant look on his face. *Conversations normally require both parties to speak, still, if agreeing gets me out of here and away from you, all the better.* Rising from the wooden bench formed from another full-sized tree, Martin gave a nod and began to walk towards the edge of the forest.

Glancing back over his shoulder, he saw Eishao give him a little wave and turn towards the door to his tree. As soon as he was past the edge of Eishao's wards, Martin cast a quick spell and disappeared from sight. A few minutes later he was leaving the trees and reentering the glade where his dwelling lay hidden.

He was inside the door preparing a cup of tea when he realized the worst mistake of all. Lord Eishao had gone to great pains to recognize every ritual, every little detail of etiquette that happened when two Sahae of fine houses met. However, of all the rituals that had been observed, the most important one, the ritual of inquiring about family and attempting to divine to what degree one was related, had gone unrecognized. Asking an unfamiliar equal these questions was second nature to the Sahae and forgetting to do so was considered the greatest of missteps. Having ignored that very important detail was a serious breach of protocol among their people which meant one of two things. Either Eishao was an idiot or he already knew who Martin was.

Even as the thought crossed his mind, he felt his wards bend and then shatter under an overwhelming magical assault. A strange, twisting feeling overcame him as he felt the Way move around him. Rushing to the door, he flung it open and ran outside. A mere handful of steps from the door, he slammed face-first into a clear, unforgiving barrier. It took him a few moments to recover and when he looked up he saw his blood smeared on the empty air.

Rising to his feet, he felt a growing sense of dread as he saw the light reflect off what looked like an endless curved wall of glass surrounding his home. It took him a moment to clear his head and realize the truth. Beyond the glass he could see enormous trees passing by and an enormous figure holding the glass bottle he was trapped inside. Eishao peered in at him in undisguised delight.

"Oh, Martin, you silly little fool! How absurd of you to think I would not recognized you. You are the great Martin Kinslayer, the Sahae that killed his own brother to save an Abomination. How your family loathes you! It was careless of you to remain near my home for so long. I spotted you skulking around long before I revealed myself to you. You were so busy trying to mask yourself you never felt the spells being layered over you to drain your strength. I simply had to delay your leaving long enough to give them time to take almost all of your power."

Martin realized that he did feel far weaker than he should, something he had foolishly attributed to his extended exertions. It suddenly got a lot darker and Martin realized that Eishao must have stepped inside somewhere, likely his tree. He saw the outside view steady as the bottle was set on a shelf. Eishao's leering visage took up the entire bottle as he gloated down at Martin.

"Oh, what a happy day this is. Not only are you an excellent diversion, you will also ensure the forgiveness of a mountain of my own transgressions in the past. Not only will the Great One reward me for bringing you to justice, your own family will heap accolades and treasures on my head. I may even be able to achieve unfettered access to a collection again. Oh joy! What a grand thing this is! Your death may be slow and agonizing, but know that you will bring joy and happiness to me, so it shall not be in vain!"

With that, Eishao threw a cloth over the bottle and Martin was shrouded in darkness. Martin wondered if this would be his final, fatal mistake.

20

SCHOOL DAZE

ERIC AND MATT got to school early, which was unheard of for them. Before the first bell rang, Eric had collected his books and was firmly ensconced in his first period classroom. After class, he made a point of asking Mrs. Garibaldi, his history teacher, for clarification on the assignment. This meant she had to give him a hall pass to excuse his being late to his next class.

By the time he reached his locker, Emily was already in her next class. As stupid as the plan had sounded last night, he was feeling pretty good about it this morning. At least he was until the end of second period when he was summoned to the office. He was surprised when he was directed not to the principal's office, but to Mrs. Blair, the guidance counselor.

She was on the phone when he came in, but she waved for him to sit, quickly finished on the phone, and beamed at him. "Eric, this should just take a minute and you'll be able to make it to your next class on time. I like to speak with everyone during their sophomore year to discuss their options in regard to college. This is just a quick visit so I can get you thinking about what you want to do, as well as provide you a little bit of information."

A few minutes later, Eric was lugging what felt like ten pounds of manila envelopes down the hallway to his locker. Mrs. Blair had apparently found information on every technical trade school and college with a high-tech program in the country. He was just opening his locker door when the bell rang. The stack was far too big to just be stuffed in his locker but he gave it a try. Just when he thought he was going to do it, the middle bulged out and papers and envelopes went in every direction. Cursing, he dropped to the floor and began grabbing them and stuffing them into the locker.

As he swung around to pick up another pile, he actually knocked heads with Emily, who was also down on the ground scooping envelopes up. He just managed to pull back enough so that he barely made contact, making what could have been a hard blow more of a gentle tap.

"Ow," Emily said, smiling, placing her hand on his bicep to steady herself. She kept her hand in place for longer than necessary before removing it to reach down towards the floor again.

"Oh, God, I'm so sorry! I didn't see you there." Eric felt the blood rushing into his face.

Emily laughed good-naturedly and kept picking up the envelopes. "No biggie. So, you had your first visit with Mrs. Blair, huh?" Eric smiled sheepishly and took the envelopes she handed to him.

"Yeah, she kind of overwhelmed me with information in the first five minutes." Emily raised an eyebrow at him.

"Five minutes? I barely got past the first minute before my eyes glazed over." Eric laughed in spite of himself and relaxed. Emily handed him the last envelope and left her hand resting on his just a few seconds longer than necessary. "So," she said. "I guess I'll see you next period."

Grabbing a book from her locker, she slammed it and raced down the hall to meet up with her friend. Both of them ducked around the corner and out of sight. Eric felt his heart skip a beat and he continued shoving the rest of his load in the locker. As he turned back around, he caught sight of Dave Mackenzie standing half in and half out of the library door glaring at him.

Eric gave him a jovial smile and waved. Dave twitched as if Eric had slapped him. Still glaring, he ducked back into the library. With a small grin, Eric tossed the last folder inside before slamming his locker. He was smiling like an idiot when he hit the locker room to change for gym class. Mr. Fellow, his gym teacher, was on his way out when Eric got to his gym locker.

"Speed it up, Green! We're playing volleyball, it's the first game of the inter-class elimination tournament and I want you there to anchor your team!"

Eric changed quickly and ran out onto the court. The class had already broken into five teams and Eric noticed that the rest of the class seemed to be a bit unbalanced. There were six girls on one team that were all starters on the varsity volleyball team.

Another team was made up of all senior jocks while the third and fourth were simply younger versions of the first two teams. His team, he could see, was what most of his class considered the losers.

There was Jan "Jbird" Weaver, a Goth girl who rarely, if ever, talked to anyone, much less played sports. Then there was Greg Tanner and Frank Martin, both of whom were good players but did not really get along with most of the jocks. Standing behind them, talking, were Tina Murphy and Teri Graber, best known for their work in the drama club.

Eric ran up and gave them all an easy smile, which even got him a smirk from Jan. "Hey guys, sorry I'm late. So, what are we doing?"

Jan stared up at him in disgust, nodding at the rest of the class. "Just waiting to get our teeth kicked in by the mecha Godzilla, Ken, and Barbie squads. I mean, seriously? How are these teams even remotely fair? They should just let us go shower now."

Eric glanced around the gym and shrugged. "Honestly? I think they've made a huge mistake. I know that you've got a wicked overhand spike; I've seen it in class. Well, usually when you're trying to break someone's nose on the other side of the net." Jan appeared shocked for a moment, as if she had not expected a response, much less for him to know anything about her.

Eric nodded at Greg and Frank and smiled. "These two have a standing issue with pretty much every jock in the school, on the grounds of the jocks being jerks to them all the time." The duo looked surprised at the derisive way he said 'jocks'. They overcame their shock and grinned at Eric.

"Too true, man," said Greg.

"I could do with bashing the ball into a few faces," said Frank at almost the same time.

Gesturing to Tina and Teri, Eric continued. "Those two are good at volleyball, better than some of the girls on the actual team.

Just because they would rather be in a play than play ball says nothing about their ability. So it seems to me that they've made some pretty large assumptions about everyone on the team."

Teri smiled, obviously flattered at the recognition. "And then they made the mistake of giving us you as a team captain," she said.

"What? Who said I was team captain?" Eric was sure his face reflected his surprise because they all laughed amiably.

"Well," said Tina. "You're the alpha male with the reputation for kicking upperclassmen butt left and right. What better leading man to take us to victory? Or at the very least keep us from being publicly humiliated?"

The rest of the group murmured in agreement at this. Mr. Fellow came by at that moment. "Who's your team captain?"

Before he could stop them, the team said in unison, "Green!" Moving off to the other teams, the gym teacher left Eric standing behind him, open-mouthed.

"What's the problem, Green?" Greg asked. "You seem like you have a pretty good handle on things."

Eric grinned and held his hands up in front of him. "Okay, I surrender. If you guys want me to be team captain, I'll be team captain. Only rule I can think of is work together and have fun."

"That's two things," Teri said.

"So we're actually going to do this," Jan asked "Seriously? What's the point?"

Eric could feel the goodwill of the team starting to slip and realized that if he did not do something, they very well could end up losing before they started.

"Think of it this way, Jan. Right now, every single one of those people is probably counting on you to lie down and quit. In their minds, there is no reason that we should be a threat to them. To them, this is a team full of outcasts that's already been beaten. They're not worrying about us, only sizing each other up. So it's up to you. We can hand them their victory on a silver platter or we can work as a team and crush their dreams."

Jan seemed to swell up in anger and for a moment Eric was afraid she might actually hit him. He had no idea what he would do if she did, especially since half of his training was reacting on instinct. She went stock still for a moment before giving him an evil smile. "What the heck, let's destroy their dreams and send them home to cry into their letterman jackets and designer clothes."

Turning, she slapped Greg on the shoulder in a show of camaraderie, taking him by surprise. As he surveyed the change in the group around him, Eric saw the independent players he had started with become a team before his eyes. Smiling, he pointed to their part of the court and led them forth into battle.

21

EISHAO'S IRRITATION

EISHAO WAS GETTING irritated. Once he set his mind to doing something, it was unusual for him to be vexed for very long at all; it was unheard of to be outright thwarted. When his minion had claimed the small human city to be a warren of hazards and pitfalls, he had attributed it simply to the fool's desire to escape punishment.

However, now that he had traveled through this cursed hamlet, he was forced to admit that the creature had been correct. The overabundance of technology that permeated the area was beyond uncomfortable. More than once in his explorations he had been forced to turn back as he found the way blocked by fiber optic lines, buried electrical wiring, and a huge cyber cafe that made him nauseous even at a distance.

There seemed to be no path that would take him further than the area adjacent to the school. The school itself was ensconced in a tangled labyrinth of technology that left little doubt in his mind that it was not accidental. No, it seemed far too complex a pattern to be pure happenstance. There was a hand guiding the deployment of these accursed human inventions; a hand which appeared to be intimately familiar with the strengths and weakness of his kind. Most of the lesser shadowborn would not have made it past the edge of town. Even many of the greater Sahae would not have been able to go half the distance he had travelled, something he took pleasure in. Over the years, he had forcibly exposed himself to more and more technology until he was sure he had one of the highest resistances of any of his kind.

Turning on his heel in disgust, he moved back to the edge of the historic building that faced the school. At one time, it appeared to have been a livery stable, however over the years it had been converted into shops on the ground floor and apartments above. It was the apartments that gave him respite, as they provided a break in the technological armor surrounding the town.

Someone had gutted and was in the process of renovating them.

Eishao had explored the space and found that while they might be destined for the same technology that pervaded the rest of the town, at the moment they were empty shells.

This provided him with a wonderful spot to watch over the comings and goings of the school children below. He found nothing to hold his interest other than the passing fancy of having his pets hunt a few of the more athletic children. That is, until he saw her leave the school. She was exactly as the sycophant, Delamar, had described her.

Flowing blond hair, far longer than what most human women wore in this modern time. It blazed under the sun, reflecting the light like molten fire. She stood tall for a human female, about five and a half feet, with the ample curves of a woman and the face of an angel. He found himself positively captivated and quite forgot his plan to follow her when she left the school. By the time he came back to himself, his quarry had disappeared out of view of his window. This unheard of mistake did nothing to diminish his exaltation at the discovery of this new, wondrous distraction.

Taking himself back out of the city, he retreated to his temporary abode to plot and plan. The shadows of the day lengthened and the tree went fully dark as the sun disappeared beyond the horizon. The darkness did not bother Eishao; it was his natural state of being. As that thought passed through his head, a wonderfully entertaining scheme unfolded to him. Grinning in a most horrible way, he moved through the tree, gathering items for a potent enchantment. His minions slipped as far away as they dared, lest they be caught in the power that surrounded him. Through the long hours of the night he worked. At the darkest point between the setting and rising of the sun he released the magic into the enchantment.

Slipping to a knee, he picked up the delicate item from the floor, gently blowing on it to clear dirt from its surface. It was an old plan; one might even call it cliché. *Well, if anyone dared to criticize me.* Calling forth a small light using the Way he held the object up , gazing on it with sheer appreciation.

Artfully crafted petals curled out from a gentle blue center that was made up of many small gems, giving form to the most unusual of flowers. Known in his homeland as a jeol blossom, it was very rare, having thrived in the area consumed by the first Great Blight.

It had been Eishao's favorite flower when he was young, what seemed to be a lifetime ago. For a moment, his mind drifted back to a simpler time. He could almost hear the voice of his mother singing the Way to bring forth their evening meal. His father would be busy with the end of the day's study; he had been a mighty user of the Way. His father's immense power and skill had done him no good when he had been caught in the Great Blight along with Eishao's mother, sisters and brothers.

His entire clan, his history, his past and his future were gone in the blink of an eye, snuffed out by arrogant monkeys who did not know their place. A small part of him realized that their loss had driven him mad, quite mad. Wandering the human world, he had been lucky enough to come upon the greatest of all Sahae, Raganol.

Before the tragedy, the Sahae had judged Raganol to be unbalanced and banished him to a dark prison. A few kindred souls had spirited him away from captivity and he had made his way to the world of man. Here he had established himself in different positions of power, using his extensive knowledge of the Way to sow chaos among the monkeys. It was Raganol who saved Eishao after he had torn his way through part of a small town outside of what was now called Nice, in the country of France.

Eishao had been exhausted from a mindless orgy of destruction. So many humans lay dead that he had nearly won his way free. In the end, it was the cursed metal that had brought him down. A bullet, the bane of all Sahae, shot by a coward that struck from a distance. It made no difference that he could do the same with the Way, he at least was a higher life form and therefore meant to prey upon them. The audacity of the monkeys to resist his slaughter of their putrid kind was simply another source of rage for him. The fools had bound him in chains and were arguing over whether to chop off his head and then burn him or just to burn him alive when Raganol had arrived.

He had slain the remainder of the humans with a spell such as Eishao had never seen or even considered possible. Not only did it strike the humans down, it made the already dead look as if they had been killed by the guns that humans were so fond of using.

Gathering Eishao to him, Raganol had spirited him away to a safehold and nursed him back to health. Though his physical wounds had healed quickly, his mental wounds took longer to tend. Raganol put up with his ranting and raving for almost a year. He kept him securely locked inside the safehold whenever he had to leave; eventually, Eishao burned through his rage and sat quietly in despair. It was then that Raganal began to speak to him of his future.

Eishao remembered that night as if it were yesterday. It was a dark evening, filled with energy from storms that rolled through the area. The safehold doors had boomed opened and then snapped shut and Eishao had known that Raganol was there. Before, he would have jumped up and rushed him, trying to win his way free, however this night he sat quietly at the main table. Raganol crossed to the other chair and sat down and begun speaking.

"The problem with the monkeys, my friend, is that they breed beyond counting. They rut and spread across the face of the world like a plague. The strongest among us can be brought down by them as they swarm. Their strength is in their numbers. In the past, we have kept them culled, a practice that I had perfected before the elders decided to stop me. One day, this lack of vision shall come back to haunt them. You must learn to be more subtle. I shall teach you..."

Raganol had started to train him slowly. He was wary that the new sedate compliance from Eishao might be a ruse designed to lull him into a false sense of security so that he could finally escape. Once he was sure of his new student, Raganol opened Eishao's eyes to how the world had changed. Beyond their ever-growing numbers, the humans had another great weapon, their thrice-damned technology. The Arts is what the learned humans called it, like some juvenile perversion of the Way.

Raganol taught him how to counter some of the technology with magic. He had also shown Eishao something even more fascinating, how to turn the humans against each other and then watch the fun. It had been the beginning of a wonderful relationship. In a short time, the two of them had wreaked unheard of havoc upon the human world.

In the end though, Raganol had proved to be too tame. His wish to play it safe continued to grate on Eishao until he could take it no longer and one day simply walked away and never went back. Since that time, he had delighted in pushing himself to his limits. Entire towns had been left vacant, countless innocents had been kidnapped and left to die in the wilderness or had been hunted down like the animals they were. And the things he did to the women...

Over the years he had been forced to deal with different agents of humanity searching for different killers, that were, in fact, him. The material he had collected after killing these agents told him that they suspected many of his crimes were perpetrated by their own kind. By what they called serial killers, multiple killers it would seem, preying on women all over the world. To them, the whims that moved him looked like different people doing the same thing for different reasons.

Their confusion was understandable. The randomness of his actions would only make sense to him. There were times when he honestly had become so bored with one of his prey that he would aban-
don the hunt. This he knew confused more than one human investigator in the past. It amused him that some of these females lived
their entire lives looking over their shoulders, waiting for him to
come out of the dark.

For him, it was about the fun and excitement. Sometimes, if he
lost interest in hunting someone, he stopped. Other times, he would
hunt them for weeks until he finally brought them down. In a few
cases, after they foolishly thought they were safe, he would swoop in
to deliver oblivion.

Some of the women he took the time to dally with, while most
he simply enjoyed terrifying. It almost always ended the same way.

They would flee, he would hunt them and they would fall. Still,
there was an art to baiting the trap for an animal, especially one as
wary as the human female. Some of them possessed an innate intuition that bordered on the mystical. He had many a quarry nearly in
the net, so to speak, when they would bolt for no apparent reason.

One of the few reasons the humans could track his activities at
all was the joel blossom. It was more than a bit arrogant of him to
continue to use the same lure. Soon, all the humans would need to do
is warn their kind off of ever touching the flower. They foolishly had
not, and from what he could tell from the files he collected over the
years, had no plans to do so. They thought to prevent others copying
his work, as if that were even possible. It amused him to think that
their cleverness actually made it easier for him to continue to kill
them.

The flower itself was unique, with petals that seemed to be
made of some sort of shimmering metal with a stigma of jewels. He
crafted it with a special set of spells layered delicately upon one another. The first was one of avarice. It would hold one woman at a
time, she would be compelled to hide the flower and only take it out
to look at when she was alone. The second was a desire to go into

the wild and commune with nature. This helped separate the intended prey from the protection of any technology. The third was a simple tracking spell so that Eishao was always able to find his prey. This became especially helpful if they were to escape or be rescued.

They would continue to hide the flower, which had sealed the fate of more than one female. The only thing he had to do now was find a way to place this where she would find it.

School was not an option, not only was their no way to get inside there was also no guarantee that she would be the one to find it. Her walk home was also no good, as there was an equal chance that her annoying friend would find the flower, and she was hardly a worthy bit of prey. Time had shown him that if he was patient and cautious he would find a way of ensnaring his quarry.

Smiling, he tucked the flower inside his coat pocket and lay back to think of how he would trap his prey.

22

MARTIN'S HOPE

MARTIN WAS FAIRLY certain that, as Eric would put it, he was fundamentally screwed. One of the many downsides of being trapped in a glass bottles is that they are fairly effective at blocking access to the Way. The only normal flaw would be the stopper, if it were made of cork or another soft wood. Unfortunately, from what Martin could tell when he tried to touch the Way that was not likely the case.

Following a fitful night's sleep, he had prowled around his new prison searching for any weakness. After climbing onto the roof with a lantern he found that, to his dismay, the stopper was indeed made of solid glass. As he was sitting in the kitchen considering his next move, he felt his access to the Way return. Running outside, he looked up and saw the stopper had been removed from the bottle.

One of Eishao's minions stood waving its hand back and forth over the neck of the bottle. At first Martin was confused about what the creature was doing and then it struck him. The bottle was airtight. With the glass stopper in place it would only be a matter of days until he asphyxiated. Therefore it was necessary to cycle the air into the bottle. A plan began forming in Martin's brain.

He had begun to resign himself to his fate however now he saw a path of escape opening up to him. If nothing else, it would give him something to keep him busy rather than counting the minutes that remained of his life. Opening himself to the Way, he pulled energy in and just as quickly passed it to his ring. He had created the ring, a simple construct of the purest silver, as a young wanderer and found it a useful reservoir of power. More than once it had gotten him out of a tight spot when his opponents had seriously underestimated his reserves.

Above him, the minion stopped its waving motion and replaced the stopper. As it only had one hand, it took time for it to reach down and retrieve the stopper from the table top to replace it. As soon as the stopper was in place Martin felt his connection to the Way dwindle to a small trickle. Settling himself back inside at the table, he let his body relax into the chair while he channeled the tiny bit of precious energy into the ring.

At the miniscule rate the power was flowing with the stopper in place he was not sure if the power would do any good. Unless Eishao was a fool, he would contact someone and sell Martin for renewed glory in the Court. Depending on the posturing, Martin figured he had a day or two at best. Once he was in the Court's hands, no power he possessed would save him. They would make an example of him, dragging out his abhorrent punishment for decades as a warning to any who would dare defy the Court. Pushing the thought from his mind, he focused on siphoning every ounce of the Way he could manage.

23

COOKING

ERIC HAD BEEN a little overwhelmed when he spoke to Mrs. Blair, so he had not been paying as much attention as he probably should have. When she had talked about showing more flexibility by taking different elective classes, he remembered mentioning how he would love to learn how to cook. So it should have come as no surprise when she found him after lunch and directed him to the Home Economics room.

He felt more than a little self-conscious when he entered the classroom. From what he could tell, he was one of only two guys in the entire class. Calvin Montgomery, whom he was not very familiar with, was the other boy. Calvin was tall, lanky, and reserved. He stared at Eric in surprise when he entered.

The room was laid out with a lunch counter off to one side with twelve swivel stools attached to the floor. The counter had an old Formica top with stainless steel trim like you would find in one of the converted railcar diners on the East Coast. The class seemed to use this as their desk area. Behind them was an array of sewing machines ranging from old treadle models to more modern electronic machines. On the opposite side of the room there were several full kitchens with a stove, sink and refrigerator. The kitchens were arranged in a semi-circle to allow the instructor easy access to the students. Eric took the last seat at the counter and handed Mrs. Laurel his admission form. Scanning the form, she stopped and looked at him quizzically.

"So, Mr. Green, you're interested in learning how to cook?" Eric nodded. "Very well, it's good to have an even number of students as it helps to evenly break up the class. I'll tell you the same thing I told everyone at the beginning of the semester. This is a classroom and you are here to learn. You will respect me, the room, the tools within it, and the lessons or you will find yourself in study hall. Are we clear?"

The no-nonsense way she said it reminded him of Martin and he found himself nodding without hesitation.

"Hmm," she said. "A fellow of few words. Well, let's see if we can't teach you something then." Eric listened over the next ten minutes as Mrs. Laurel described the best way to prepare vegetables. She then divided the group and Eric found himself paired with Calvin. *Thank goodness.*

As the pairs moved over to the kitchen area, Mrs. Laurel passed out vegetables and waited for the class to settle into their places. "Now, everyone listen up. You have bell peppers, celery, and onions. These are staples in many types of cooking. What you are going to do is clean and dice these in a uniform manner. They must be uniform because . . ." Eric flinched a bit as Calvin's hand shot up with most of the class at this expectant pause. "Yes, Calvin?"

Calvin cleared his throat. "Because they need to all cook the same amount and if they're different sizes some will be overdone and some will be underdone."

Mrs. Laurel smiled and nodded. "Exactly! This is a vital part of basic cooking. Some will tell you that speed is more important than precision and those people are wrong. Being finished fast and wrong just means you've got more time to try it again. Now, everyone take your vegetables and get to work."

Eric picked up half the produce and joined Calvin at the sink. At first he just tried rinsing them off, but he noticed Calvin staring at him strangely. "What? Am I doing it wrong?" Eric asked hesitantly. Calvin studied him silently for a moment before seeming to come to a decision about something.

"Okay, Green. I'm going to go out on a limb and assume that you're not just here to mooch food and make fun of what we do in here."

Eric looked at him in alarm. "Why would I do that?" Calvin regarded him a bit suspiciously.

"Why not? That's what most of the guys that started the semester were doing. Once they figured out Mrs. Laurel wasn't about to put up with it they dropped the class. Well, once they got in their digs at me that is." Eric regarded him with open confusion.

"Okay," Eric said. "Can we back the truck up for a second? I'm here because Mrs. Blair said I needed to show variety in my elective courses. She mentioned a cooking class and I jumped at it. Lately I had an eye opening experience that gave me quite a bit of motivation to learn to cook. So if you can help me catch up that would be great. I've got more interest in what I'm doing wrong than in teasing anyone."

Calvin considered this for a moment before nodding. "Well, I guess coming in to be a clown doesn't really fit your reputation. So I'm going to act like you want to be here until you give me a reason to doubt that. First thing, you need to play some catch up. A lot of what we are doing plays off things we already learned this semester. That's probably one of the reasons you are teamed with me—I'm top of the class in here."

Eric stayed silent, listening patiently and waiting for Calvin to continue. "The first thing you need to know is almost everything we get from the produce counter is covered in something. Wax if you're lucky, pesticides and fecal matter if you're not. So the first thing we learned to do is rinse them off with either a store bought or home-made cleanser. Non-toxic and safe to eat, mind you."

Turning, Calvin grabbed an opaque spray bottle from near the sink handle and began spraying down the veggies. Eric followed suit and listened carefully as Calvin showed him the steps to properly clean each item.

Once they were done they were a bit behind the rest of the class, but Calvin was careful to show Eric the proper way to cut, dice and maintain proper knife safety. Once they started cutting, Eric really started to shine. The knife felt like it had been custom made for his hand. Once he started, he found that he could easily mirror Calvin in making the uniform cuts necessary for the assignment. In fact, he was so quick, too quick, that they drew the attention of Mrs. Laurel.

"Eric, stop there for a moment! You seem to be going awfully fast. Let's check to see how uniform your cuts are."

Eric stopped, carefully wiped the knife on a towel and placed it back in the butcher block in the center of the counter, then stepped back. Mrs. Laurel pulled on a disposable clear plastic food handling glove and raked her fingers through Eric's pile. Sweeping back and forth, she nodded in approval.

"I must say Eric, I came over here because I was afraid you were not listening to instructions and were chopping too fast, but you've done a wonderful job. Have you had a lot of kitchen experience?"

Eric felt his ears go a little red at being the center of attention and shook his head. "No, until today the most I had ever done was made a sandwich."

Mrs. Laurel looked at him in astonishment. "Well, if your knife skills are any indication, you may be a natural at this." She turned to address the rest of the class, who were gaping at the new kid's prowess, "Continue on with your work, everyone."

The classroom filed with the sounds of knives on cutting boards again. Eric tried to slow down, focused on keeping the cuts he made uniform, but he and Calvin were still done far ahead of the rest of the class.

Calvin looked over his pile of vegetables with approval. "Good job, Green. I gotta say, I thought you might be playing me, but it looks like you're serious. And you seem to have some mad skills.

It'll be nice to have another guy in the class but you need to know you are going to take a lot of crap for being in here. Mostly I get gay jokes but you never know."

Smiling back at Calvin he shook his head in amusement. "Hey, I've been called just about everything for doing less, believe me. And if someone gives you any crap about being in this class, send them my way to repeat it. I can't stand bullies. A united front is usually enough to stop their verbal diarrhea, but if not, I'm sure I can help them change their ways."

Calvin grinned back at Eric. "You're all right, Green. I think I'll take you up on that if it comes down to it. I hope to be a great chef one day and would prefer not to break my hands fighting with idiots."

Mrs. Laurel came by and looked over their cut vegetables with approval before moving back to the center of the kitchens. "That is enough for today. I want you to get some storage containers and seal these up. Tomorrow we'll use them as the base for our roasts. Eric, as you weren't part of the assignment you'll have to continue to work with Calvin and will be the only one not taking home a roast. Well, unless you want to bring in a three pound roast, in which case, do so before school tomorrow and I will put it with the others. Either way, it will not impact your grade, just your ability to enjoy the fruits of your labors." She smiled and waved the class into motion.

Calvin showed Eric where the containers were stored and they again set a speed record for finishing their work. Calvin washed up the last of the dishes while Eric wiped down the counter top. Looking up mid-wipe, he saw Emily look away from across the room. He had been so focused on what he was doing that he had not even realized that she was in the class.

He rinsed his dishrag and put it over the back of the faucet automatically before going to the other side of the room to sit on one of the empty stools at the lunch counter. Calvin sat down one seat away from him and started up a conversation with a small brunette about the merits of grape seed oil in cooking. Emily crossed the room and sat down next to Eric.

"So, what do you think of the class so far?" she asked perkily.

Eric looked into her eyes and felt a moment of absolute terror before he clamped down hard on it. Looking over at Mrs. Laurel, he took a moment, as if considering his answer.

"She seems like a very good teacher. It'll be nice to actually know how to cook my own meals rather than having to depend on others to feed me." He saw a look flash over her face that he had a hard time identifying. Not pity. Not sadness. Something more complicated. It was gone before he was able to identify it.

"So I hear your team destroyed the other teams in volleyball during gym. Sounds like it was a real upset," Emily said.

He felt like she was trying to change the subject but he let it go. He was kind of happy to share his accomplishments with her. "Yeah, I can't take a lot of credit for it, though; the teams were already in place when I got to class. It was a classic case of opponents underestimating their foes. In the end, the people on my team just wanted it more than the other teams did."

Eric grinned as he thought back to the final game. They had faced off against the senior volleyball team, who had managed to destroy every opponent they'd played. Their first mistake was taunting Jan by calling her Jbird. He had asked Matt about it and found out that Jan had gone to juvenile hall after getting into a fight, and she had been branded jailbird or Jbird ever since. All they had done was piss her off, and by the time the game was over, two of the girls on the other team were nursing impressive black eyes and Jan had been warned against any more power spiking.

It was surprising how well he was able to keep everyone on the team working together. For all his talk of teamwork, he had expected everyone to start doing their own thing once they started playing. The funny thing was, every time they did, it had only taken a few words from him to get everyone back on track.

Even Mr. Fellow, the gym teacher, had commended him on his leadership skills after class. "I don't know how you did it, Green. I would never have expected that team to be able to work together like that. It looks like you have the gift for leading others, son. Good job."

Mrs. Laurel interrupted his daydreaming as she came over and gave the class a few last minute instructions and suggested helping out with food prep at home to hone their skills. The bell rang and everyone rushed out to the hallway. Eric walked with Emily down to their lockers and could not help but notice Dave nearby, seething with anger. Emily seemed not to notice as she put her notebook back in her locker and grabbed a new book.

"So we've got at least one class together now. At the rate we're going, people will start to talk." She said it in a teasing way, but something about her tone grabbed Eric's attention and he practically heard a feral growl in the back of his head. With considerable effort, he kept his tone light.

"Well, I guess if the guidance office keeps making changes anything is possible."

She looked at him for a moment before playfully slapping his arm. "Well, see you later, Eric."

"Yeah, see you after next period, Emily."

Turning, they both slipped down the hallway in opposite directions. Eric met up with an openly gaping Matt while Emily met her friend, Becky Davis, and the two of them hurried to their next class.

As Matt and Eric disappeared down the hallway, Dave Mackenzie glared after them.

"Oh, you're going to get yours, Green," he said softly to himself. "Bad things happen to poachers around here, little man. Really bad things."

24

LURKING DANGERS

THE CLANGING OF a bell pulled Eishao from his reverie in the empty apartments overlooking the school. Glancing out the window, he saw the building begin to disgorge its occupants at the close of their day. Racing down the stairs, he waited for the lovely lass to exit the doors. As before, she was walking with her friend, the one Delamar had told him was called Becky. They were forced to slow their exit due to the sheer mass of humanity in front of them and Eishao was able to take in the girl in all her glory.

Emily. The name was far too simple for such a gorgeous creature. Her beauty was almost ethereal, almost . . . wait. What if she was the power he had felt earlier? Was it possible this was a fledgling Abomination? The thought turned his stomach. If that were the case, his fun might be spoiled before it started. He had learned long ago that one did not play around with an Abomination, they were far too unpredictable. Better to put them down immediately upon their discovery. His visage soured as he walked parallel to the girls on their path from school. He had carefully explored this section of town and knew the pitfalls quite well.

Annoyed by the delays, he detoured around a large buried cable that ran over two blocks and came up over the road. Here, he was able to slide by it on the far side with only minor nausea. Swinging back, he managed to catch up just as the two girls were splitting up. Glancing after Becky, he grinned evilly. *It might be worth following her after all. If Emily is the Abomination, perhaps Becky or her family can provide some amusement. Perhaps later.*

Emily turned the other way and headed towards some older houses. Slipping from shadow to shadow he kept himself unseen using more of the Way than would normally have been necessary.

Damn technology. We should never have let these apes progress so far, it is intolerable! Intolerable! He was forced to backtrack over and over and barely caught sight of her entering an older Victorian style house near the center of the block.

The next few minutes were full of irritation and growing rage for Eishao. Every entrance seemed to be interwoven with over lashings of water pipes, fiber optic lines, electrical cables, other strange cables he could not identify and various hybrid metals. Finally, when he was about to give up, he found an alley hidden behind high bushes along the side street. Originally designed for vehicle traffic, this alley had been closed off sometime in the past and forgotten.

Now the alley was a buffer zone between the wooded area behind the houses and the large wooden fences at the end of each yard. In short, it provided Eishao a marvelous location not only to observe, but also offered a path of escape from the ever-encroaching technology. The first backyard he passed made him nearly wretch and once he moved beyond it he saw a strange, blue-glowing lantern buzzing near the back fence. He had seen one of the wretched things before and he despised them. An electrified lure for bugs that fried them when they got too close; a foul interpretation of the famous bog light lures of his people.

Carefully keeping away from the fence, he was able to come up behind the house Emily had entered. The fence here was in poor repair, unlike its neighbors. Either the owner was too busy or too lazy to keep up with maintenance. Eishao grinned gleefully. Two boards were loose and he was able to move them apart and peer into the backyard. The yard was mostly bare save for a small table and chair set positioned beneath a shade tree. At the far end of the yard was a crumbling brick patio with a peeling set of wooden stairs leading up to the rear door.

He examined the back of the house with an experienced eye. The caretaker of this place was obviously not very good at their job. The rear of the house was showing signs of neglect. They apparently thought there was no reason to go to the trouble, since no one would see it. This provided him with a wonderful opportunity. Had the fence been strong, it might have provided a barrier even against him. However, loose boards made it easy to push an opening in the fence and quietly move into the yard. Once through the gap in the fence, he moved towards the house, making sure his masking enchantment was in place. The rear windows had the curtains pulled back and he had an unobstructed view of the ground floor.

Emily sat at a dark stained oak table in the kitchen speaking with what Eishao assumed was her mother. A fading beauty in her own right, she was sadly showing too many of the passing years. *Still, if she were terrified beyond belief, she likely would provide some amusement,* Eishao thought, turning his attention back to Emily. He studied her intently. The mother had likely been attractive enough once to have attracted the attention of a Sahae. So it was possible that the girl could be an Abomination.

Her beauty did not seem natural; she was far prettier than most human females that Eishao had seen. She had captivated both he and Delamar, which might speak to more than just extraordinary beauty. Moving as close to the house as he comfortably could, he listened to their conversation.

"So, Emily, how are things going at school?"

Emily smiled at her mom and set her pencil down slowly. "Classes are fine. I had a little trouble with some of the science questions but Becky helped me out on them so I should be good."

"Well, if you need any help, your father should be able to work on it with you later tonight."

"Oh, and Eric Green got moved into the locker next to mine."

Her mother looked back at her daughter and gave a little grin. "The elusive Mr. Green, huh? Well now, I'm sure that's an interesting story. How did he happen to be moved next to you?" Emily told her mother about Dave's prank and how it had backfired.

"I think it'll be good for you to be away from that boy. He's far too pushy for my tastes; how apropos that Dave causing trouble leads to you getting more time with Eric." Emily tossed her head in irritation and Eishao felt his breath catch as her eyes flashed for a moment in anger.

Surely if she is an Abomination she has incredible control. Anger is normally the easiest way to cause them to show their true selves. Perhaps I am wrong and she is just a girl. Better to be safe than sorry, I suppose.

Turning back to her homework, Emily picked up the pencil and stiffly replied to her mother. "He's an interesting guy and I like talking to him, but I don't know what to think of him half the time. Just when I think that he likes me, he gets all weird."

Eishao felt a stab of resentment as she spoke of this boy. Not that he would ever consider having a relationship with a human. Granted, one could call the intimate interactions he had with human girls and women over the years "relationships," if one stretched the meaning. After all, there was nothing more intimate than hunting someone down, feeling their terror and hopelessness as they realized they were about to die. Nor was there anything more delicious than that final moment when the light faded from their eyes.

Yes, if she is not an Abomination, I shall quite enjoy her terror. She will be a hunt to remember. Eishao gazed adoringly at Emily though the glass. *Still, either way it might not hurt to take the boy out, not normally my brand of fun, however it might be nice to change things up. If he gets in the way, I will have no choice anyway.*

He reverently removed the jeol blossom from his pocket and placed it on a faded deck chair. Sure his presence was masked; he cast a simple spell and backed away. As the mother moved away into the kitchen, he caused the girl to hear the sound of a small animal crying in pain.

Leaping up from the table, she raced outside and froze, listening. She remained motionless for a moment and then shrugged. As she turned to go back inside, she saw the blossom and gasped in delight. Picking it up with great care she examined it for a moment before looking around and hiding it inside her shirt. She raced up the stairs and into the house. A moment later, Eishao caught sight of her in one of the upper floor windows.

Smiling in glee, Eishao started to cast a spell that would raise him in the air for a better view when he heard a strange buzzing noise and a wave of nausea fell over him. Whipping around, he saw a strange craft floating in the air above the yard. A brand of four circles were bound together in what he could only assume was a meaningful way and the craft was slowing sinking towards the ground.

As it came closer, his nausea increased. *Damn technology! Will I never be free of its fetid touch?*

Turning for a last glance through the window, he fixed his gaze on Emily and then leapt to the fence and retraced his steps away from the house. As he got to the side street, he glanced back and saw whatever the accursed craft was sinking below the level of the fence into Emily's yard. Moving back through town, he was astonished at the increased technology present.

It was as if every single person in town turned on every blasted device they owned. He headed towards the empty apartments near the school, only to find that someone had left a music machine blasting on the stairway. He nearly lost his masking spell as he headed down his main escape route and found the way barred by two new automobiles parked on either side of the road. In the end, he was forced to take to the air using the Way.

By the time he got outside the city he was shaking and utterly spent. With the last of his energy he managed to make his way back to his tree and set his minions to guarding the area. Slipping into his bed, he felt like he was forgetting something important, but before he could grasp what it was, the last of his energy slipped away and he slid into the darkness.

25

SEARCHING

"AT LEAST IT ISN'T a Class 1, sir."

Thomas Crawford snorted, glaring across the table at Tim Jomas, the area Field Agent Supervisor. "Yeah, it's an amazing break," he said sarcastically. "We go from having a Code 1, Class Level A contact that we can't find, to having a Class B contact showing up in the residential district. Super. At this rate, the town will be overrun by the end of the week."

Thomas slapped his hand down on the table and winced as pain shot up his arm. Leaning back in his chair, he rubbed his hand and ignored the expression of amusement that Jomas was trying unsuccessfully to hide. "Talk to me people, what do we know?"

At the far end of the table, Mabel Grace, head librarian of the town library and one of the oldest members of the group, cleared her throat. She was just shy of seventy with steel blue eyes and hair the color of driven snow. Her paper-thin, parchment-like skin was dotted with liver spots and her veiny, claw-like hands firmly grasped a large stack of papers.

"Well, Tommy, it is pretty bad." Thomas winced at the nickname that only Mrs. Grace could get away with using on him. "The sensors seemed to have some trouble picking up this one at all, which means he is probably pretty good at being sneaky. There was

a low-grade signal tracked from the area near the school to the residential area, however it was hard to get a fix on it. The signal disappeared shortly thereafter. We suspect that whatever it was got driven
out by the contingency plan."

Thomas nodded and glanced around the room to see if anyone
had anything to add. From the way no one was making eye contact,
he did not think any of them did. *And no one wants to have to tell the
old man that we screwed up, even if it was equipment issues and not
an actual mistake,* he thought glumly.

He rose from his chair and walked over to the bank of computers that indicated the sensor grid in town. At the moment, all of the
sensors showed green. *Green is good, but how long would it stay
green?* He rubbed the back of his neck and turned back to the group
with a sigh.

"Alright, you know the drill. We've confirmed that there's a
threat, so we'll be monitoring the sensors around the clock. I'll take
the first watch and we can cycle through. Head on home, everyone.
I'll call it in."

The group rose to their feet and hurried out, headed for home.
The only one that lingered was Mrs. Grace, who peered at him with
concern. "I could call the report in, Tommy, if you would like."

He shook his head and offered a smile. "No thanks, Mrs. Grace.
My operation, my call, though you know I appreciate the offer." She
nodded and filed out after the others. Sitting back down, he reached
for the phone and hit the button for Mr. Harris.

"Harris here," his superior barked.

"Sir? It's Crawford."

"So, what do we have?"

"It isn't good, Mr. Harris. The Class A was confirmed to be an
accurate reading. No sensor glitch is indicated. The Class B is like-
wise confirmed. We have no additional information. It's possible
that the two are connected but right now, sir, we have nothing."

"So why didn't the damn sensor net go off?"

Thomas winced at the harsh, biting tone Harris used. "We still don't know, sir. The best theory is that the creatures may be using some sort of masking spell to avoid detection."

"Great. So we can't see them and they can come and go as they please? Is the thing still around?"

"The grid doesn't indicate any fluctuations at all. We suspect that instigating the "Alpha Protocol" did the trick. Once our agents started turning on everything in the area, our last readings indicate that the being left the area. The board has remained green since then."

"Or it just cast a good enough spell to avoid detection. I don't like it, Crawford. I want the grid turned up to maximum sensitivity. I don't care if we end up chasing sensor ghosts; I want some warning before this damn thing starts eating people. Or whatever it is planning."

"Understood, sir." Thomas hesitated for a moment and then asked the question he feared he already knew the answer to. "Sir? Do you think it might just be passing through?"

The man on the other side of the line hesitated and then gave a great sigh. "Pray it is, son. We should be so lucky. If either one of these things decide to cause trouble, we need to make sure to avoid casualties as much as possible. Keep an eye on that grid and call me if anything hits. Understood?"

"Yes, sir. I'm taking first watch and we'll be monitoring the grid around the clock until further notice."

Crawford hung up the phone, made the necessary adjustments, and immediately saw sensor ghosts flicker on his screen at the edge of town near the old park and down near Elm Street, where the Class A had reported. There were more flickers at a few other spots in town. Pulling out his phone, he texted his team to double check the areas and settled down to watch the screen into the wee hours of the morning.

26

HOME COOKING

HOME ECONOMICS WAS one of the most interesting classes Eric had ever taken. After school, he stopped at the library and grabbed a few books that discussed the mechanics of cooking. As he explored the basics, he was fascinated to see how much of cooking was actually math and chemistry. The complex mixtures of compounds used to create reactions that resulted in things like rising bread dough and flaky pastry crust were amazing. By the time Mrs. Green got home, he was using minute amounts of cooking supplies to experiment on the kitchen table.

"Eric! What are you doing with all my baking supplies out? Did I forget about a bake sale?" Mrs. Green wore an expression that was teetering ominously between amusement and anger at Eric's invasion of her cook space so he hastily explained.

"I joined Home Ec. today! Sorry for the mess, I'll clean everything up. I'm just behind the other kids and I wanted to explore some of the basics that they already went over."

Mrs. Green looked at Eric in astonishment. "You want to learn how to cook?"

Eric gave her a wry grin, not quite meeting her eyes. "Well, there've been times in the past where it would have been really helpful if I had the skill." They sat in silence for a moment and when Eric looked up, he caught a shimmer of tears in Mrs. Green's eyes. Confused, he thought about asking her what was wrong, then chickened out and stayed at the table.

After a few moments, Mrs. Green finished putting away the groceries she had brought in and sat down at the counter next to him. "Well, I think it's wonderful that you're always trying to learn new things. If more people took after you, this world would be such a wondrous place. Let's talk about a few rules of the kitchen. First, please make sure to ask before using supplies, this lets me plan our meals and make sure I have everything to make them.

"Second, if you want to cook, you have to clean. I expect that you were taught in Home Economics how to clean properly, but I may require you to go a bit further here, depending on how good a job you do. Third and most important, if you're not sure about something come and ask me. While I support your desire to learn, I'll not have you hurting yourself or the kitchen while you do. Understood?"

Eric nodded excitedly. "Sure thing, Mom!" The words came out of his mouth so quickly that they stunned them both.

Mrs. Green teared up and patted him on the back before hurrying to the stove to start cooking dinner. Sitting there at the counter, Eric tried to focus on his work before coming to the conclusion that he needed to stop for now. He cleaned up his area, got a thumbs-up from Mrs. Green for his efforts, and took the stairs two at a time up to the window seat, where he flopped down.

Mom. Wow. I can't believe I called her Mom. I mean . . . God, I've been so happy here and they've been so good to me. But Mom? Seriously? He closed his eyes, relaxing back into the pillow to soak it in. He sat up with a start. *What if she isn't okay with it? What if she's all weirded out by me calling her mom? Oh crap. And Martin. How will he feel if he knows I'm calling my foster mother Mom now?*

He suddenly realized that Martin had not stopped by as he said he would. At the very least, he should have been bothering Eric about practicing his lessons and yet here it has been days without even a visit.

Nice, I'm so caught up in my own drama that I've neglected to notice that the one person who has known me since birth is MIA. Should I try to go out after dinner to look for him? No. No, stumbling around in the dark and breaking my neck wouldn't be a good idea. I can go out tomorrow and see him. It should be easy enough to follow the directions he gave me. Or will he be pissed if I leave town? Crap. He told me not to go looking for trouble. Then again he wouldn't leave me if I suddenly disappeared. Screw it, I'm going out there to find him. The directions he gave are pretty straight forward; I should be able to find his place. I can take some time after school tomorrow if I don't see him before then. Yeah, that's a good plan.

Running his fingers through his hair, he stared out the window, thinking about Martin until he saw Mr. Green walking up to the house. Jumping up, he rushed downstairs to meet him at the door. Together they walked into the kitchen.

Mr. Green stepped over and gave Mrs. Green a peck on the cheek. She squeezed his arm and smiled. "Eric, can you set the table? Dinner will be ready in just a minute. Edward, could you help me with the roast?"

Mr. Green looked at her in surprise before nodding and walking into the kitchen ahead of her. Eric moved off to the sideboard, grabbed the plates and utensils and started setting the table. A few moments after he was done, the Greens came out and placed the roast and vegetables down on a wicker trivet in the center of the table, like some delicious centerpiece.

The three of them sat at the table and Mrs. Green quickly served the meal. Dinner was outstanding and Eric ate almost five full helpings. The roast beef was succulent and full of flavor. The potatoes were soft yet firm with beef juice infused in each bite. The carrots and celery were cooked down so far that you could mash them up and eat the smooth remains. There was sliced, fresh-baked bread and sweet, creamy butter that he used to soak up the juice that ended up left behind on his plate. *This meal is more than cooking, it's art.* He realized that of all the things he had put his mind to learn, this was something he might never attain. Some things you could learn, other things required an affinity.

Finally, Eric pushed back from his plate and looked up into the astonished and amused faces of his foster parents. Grinning self-consciously, he eased back in his chair.

"Did you like dinner, Eric?" Mrs. Green asked.

"It was great, thanks, Mom." He sat back and waited to see if she would correct him. When she did not he turned to Mr. Green. "So, Dad, I was thinking of going over near the bluff tomorrow to see if I can spot any birds out of the book we were looking at the other day. Do you have any suggestions about where to go? Preferably someplace less traveled?"

Mr. Green gave him a small grin then turned serious. "Well, Eric, if you want to try near the bluff, you'll want to stay well back from the base. Rocks still fall pretty regularly and even a small one can cause serious damage. As long as you stay back, say fifty yards, you should be fine and that will keep you in the tree line. Also, stay back from the river on the other edge and you should find a large area there to bird watch. Is anyone going up there with you?"

Eric paused to think about it. Going up there alone would likely not be kosher, but the last thing he wanted to do was introduce Martin to Matt. Talk about blowing his cover. "No, I hadn't planned on taking anyone else. After all, Matt is really the only person that would go and he talks so much I'd never see any wildlife."

Mr. Green nodded thoughtfully. "Well, just make sure that you take your cell phone with you and that it has a full charge. If you get into trouble you can call me. Be back here by six. That should give you a little over an hour to bird watch and still have plenty of daylight to make your way home."

"Yeah, the birds are going to be hard to see under the trees by that time anyway. I should be able to be back here by six so you don't have to send out any search parties." The last part he said as a joke, but he could see by the set of their faces that they did not find it funny.

Mrs. Green went into the kitchen to get dessert and once she was out of the room Mr. Green spoke. "Eric, I want you to know that we're happy that you are calling us Mom and Dad. I said it when we met you and I mean it as much now as I did then. You're our son and permanently part of this family. That said, I don't want you to feel pressured to say or do anything that you're not ready to out of obligation"

"I know that, Dad. I do. I . . . I've never called any of my foster parents by those names. Truth is, I've never really stayed long enough for it to be an issue. My night terrors freaked a lot of them out. There was always some reason that they found for sending me packing. I never got too used to being anywhere. Don't get me wrong, there was some weird stuff that went on.

The first house I was placed, the water heater blew up on my second day. The next place, an electrical fire started in the attic. Stuff like that started to taint me in the eyes of prospective parents and once something odd would happen they would think I was behind it. I came back to the orphanage so many times you'd think it had a revolving door." Eric laughed at this, Mr. Green looked sad.

"It's okay, really. I learned to live with it and besides, if it hadn't been for being sent back so many times, I wouldn't have ended up here with you and Mom. I've spent a lot of time on my own, learning to take care of myself, and I guess I was just expecting the same scenario to play out here."

"Being sent back you mean," Mr. Green said.

"Well, yeah. The days went by, then weeks, then months and I'm still here. I've got to say it was confusing. Eventually I started to hope that I'd found a home, which made me even more afraid because now I've got something to lose."

Mr. Green leaned across the table and squeezed Eric's hand. "Son, you are welcome here. This is your home. We're your family. And we're not going anywhere."

Eric smiled at Mr. Green and choked back the tears that were threatening to overwhelm him. "I know that now. It took a while to get through my thick skull, but that point finally got through. It was the jacket that really clinched it for me."

"The jacket that was ruined in the locker fiasco?"

"Yeah. I mean, you guys had already supported me when I got into the fight with Moose.

Then along comes Dave pulling the locker thing and not only did you have my back, but I think Mom was ready to go over to his house and give him an old-fashioned beat down, plus replace that ancient jacket. It really showed how much you guys love me and I realized that I love you guys too."

"I am glad to hear it, Eric." Mr. Green blinked rapidly, eyes glistening with tears.

Mrs. Green bustled into the room with steaming plates of pecan pie and maple ice cream. All three were too busy chewing to continue speaking for some time after that. Finally, after his third piece of pie, Eric pushed himself back from the table.

"Okay, I've got some more reading to do before class tomorrow and then I'm off to bed. Goodnight, Mom. Goodnight, Dad." Stepping around the table, he gave his foster mom a hug and then turned and headed up the stairs. Behind him, the two stood and silently watched him walk up the stairs. Mrs. Green's hand snaked over and took Mr. Green's and the two rose from the table. Walking hand in hand down the hallway towards the living room, they smiled at each other.

27

MARTIN'S FLIGHT

IT HAD BEEN two days since his capture and Martin was finally ready. Whatever minion Eishao had set to watch him was fearful of Martin suffocating because it had been taking the stopper out of the bottle every few hours. This had allowed him to amass a huge supply of power in his ring. Things had been going well, perhaps too well. The possibility that this was all a trap had begun to worry Martin.

Well, there is the chance that Eishao called upon the Court right away and they are amusing themselves watching my pathetic escape attempts. It would be all the sweeter for them to wait until I have exhausted myself trying to escape while they waited outside to stop me in my tracks. Still, I lose nothing from trying. Perhaps Eishao is playing some game, what, I have no idea, and thinks to have some fun with me before he turns me over. If that is the case, then he will soon regret not turning me in immediately.

Martin moved around his dwelling inside the bottle, unraveling each item's weave of spells and transferring their energy into his ring. He had been at this for some time and the only items left were in the bedroom. After systematically dismantling all his furnishings and putting the power from them into his ring, he laid a spell of delayed decay on the house. It would make sure nothing was left to be used against him. Once he was finished, he lay down on the bed, the last fixture in the house, and fell asleep. It was a calculated move, balancing the need for speed and the absolutely necessity of being well-rested. In the end, not being sure when he would be able to safely sleep again, he decided to risk it.

He awoke many hours later, refreshed. Standing, he grasped the Way and dismantled the spell that had used to create the bed and sent the power into his ring. Speaking the last word necessary, he released the decay spell on the structure. He felt it slowly start to take hold of the building; within a few hours, nothing would remain of the abode. Stepping outside, he leaned against the glass wall of the bottle and waited.

It wasn't long before the glass stopper was removed. Once it was clear of the neck Martin counted silently to five, giving the creature enough time to put the stopper down, before releasing his spell. In an instant, he transformed to vapor and sped towards the opening. As he cleared the opening, he saw what looked like half a man with one foot and one hand fumbling to replace the glass stopper.

Aha! Too late, foul Pi Nereske. Your master will not be pleased with you, Martin thought as he slid fully out of the bottle. He heard the stopper clink into place and shifted his spell to make himself invisible as well.

The inside of Eishao's lair was swarming with Pi Nereske, which Martin avoided simply by skimming the ceiling. He felt the drain of maintaining the spell began to take its toll, even with the added reservoir of power in his ring. The wards were too strong on the door for him to open it in this form, so he took the risk and reappeared in corporeal form right in front of the exit.

His appearance took the Pi Nereske by surprise and before they could form up in pairs he kicked open the door and raced outside. He covered himself in a shielding spell before he hit the outer wards. The wards had, not surprisingly, been designed to keep intruders out and not secure prisoners inside. With the reserve of the ring he easily broke free, although during the escape he had nearly exhausted all his power.

Now comes the most dangerous part. In this state, even those blasted hopping dog men could bring me back. He ran down the path and headed straight for the town. His only chance was to find an area to take shelter in where the creatures could not follow. Behind him, he heard the chilling sound of the Pi Nereske taking up his trail. With renewed energy, he dashed down a walking path and headed for the nearby park.

He knew that it had a decorative iron link fence set a foot above the ground which would more than stop his pursuers. He was nearly to the park when the pack burst out onto the trail behind him.

Putting his head down, he pumped his legs furiously and was just able to leap over the fence as they caught up to him. Snarling, the pack raced back and forth along the chain, looking for a way to get to him.

He was so exhausted he could only lay there on the ground, chest heaving, while the creatures snapped at him from a few feet away. Slowly gathering his strength he edged back from the barrier until he was well out of reach and stood. He waved jovially at the pack. "Better luck next time, you mangy curs!"

As he began to turn, the dogs suddenly shot off into the woods. Without the energy left to maintain an invisibility spell Martin was forced to rely on his instincts. Leaping to the side he heard something large whip past him and crash into the ground where he had been. Leaping through a series of acrobatic dodges he tried to make it to the cover of the first set of buildings nearby.

He was nearing the first doorway when a figure stepped out of the entryway and pointed at him. Dual glints of metal glistened in the sun as Martin tried to dodge aside. He was only partially successful as one dart flew past and the other hit him in the side. Martin barely had time to feel the impact before there was a sizzling hiss and his world exploded into light before hurling him into the darkness.

28

FOREST BOUND

IT HAD NOT taken long for it to get around school that Eric was taking Home Economics. Nor did it take long for the expected ribbing to start. Even Matt had gotten a dig in early.

"Hello, Betty Crocker!"

Eric emerged from the trees and saw his friend grinning down at him from his perch atop the big blue mailbox. Laughing, he knocked Matt off the box, catching him well before he hit the ground.

"Keep it up, laughing boy, and I'll keep all the food I make to myself."

Matt stared at him in horror. "You mean you'd deprive your sickly best friend of sustenance simply because of a bit of jocularity? Unheard of! Tell me mine ears have deceived me!" Laughing, Matt dodged the half-hearted swipe Eric aimed at him before settling next to him on the path. "Seriously though, man, you've got to be ready to take some major shit for this. As progressive as this town is in some ways, it still seems deeply rooted in the nineteen fifties. Putting on an apron is going to cost you."

Eric shrugged. "So what? I can name ten famous male chefs off the top of my head. Plus, while they're waiting on someone, I'll be making my own food. If, to do that, I've got to put up with some idiots giving me shit, I think I can deal." Matt shook his head bemusedly at Eric and, for once, kept quiet.

He had to pull down a picture of a housewife in an apron with his face taped over it in order to open his locker. Chuckling, he crumpled it up and tossed it in the hallway trashcan. Emily came up beside him and opened her locker.

"Hi, Eric."

"Hey, Emily."

She pulled out her books for her first class and closed the locker before turning to him and leaning on it. "So, do you think you're going to like Home Ec.?" As she said it, she unconsciously twirled a long lock of hair, which Eric found more than a bit distracting.

"Yeah, I think it's great. I never realized how complex food preparation could be."

Emily smiled and pushed off the locker. "Well, just don't let the guys around here give you too much grief over it. Calvin had a pretty rough time when he was the last guy standing in class. You know how people can be."

Eric nodded. "Yeah, I hear that. Well, see you after next period." Emily waved as she headed down the hallway.

"Well, isn't that cute. Little Suzie Homemaker is making nice with his neighbors."

Eric sighed and turned to face Dave Mackenzie. "Yeah, you should try it sometime, Dave. Still trying to get kicked out of school before graduation?" Eric knew he said that a little louder than necessary and was amused to see Dave go pale underneath his tan.

"You got a smart mouth on you, Green. One of these days it's going to catch up with you. You know that, don't you?"

Eric felt all his good humor drain away. Glaring at Dave, his expression became so cold that the other boy actually took a step back. His voice came out so quiet and level that it even scared him a bit. "Anytime, anyplace, Dave. Eventually I'm going to stop being nice and you're going to end up in the Emergency Room."

Dave tried but failed to keep his tough facade up as he turned and walked away. At the corner of the hall he looked back, but was unable to look Eric in the eyes. Instead, he practically stomped away and disappeared from sight. Eric grabbed his stuff and hurried to class.

He managed to slip in just before the bell rang and took his seat getting a surprised look from Mrs. Garibaldi, his homeroom teacher. She also was the history teacher and was used to Eric being on time, if not early, for her class. Once the class started, things went back to normal and he put Dave out of his mind. He went back to his locker after class and met Emily just opening her locker.

"Hey, Eric."

"Hey, Emily."

They smiled at each other and headed off in opposite directions.

I could definitely see school being a lot nicer if I get to see her between every class, Eric thought happily as he headed to English. By the time Home Economics rolled around, he was feeling a lot more relaxed around Emily. He sat between her and Calvin while they waited for class to start and discussed some of the things he had read about cooking the night before.

His new classmates were amazed at the amount of knowledge he had amassed in so short a time, which made him feel a bit self-conscious. Mrs. Laurel swept in, ending all further discussion and efficiently giving the instructions for cooking their roasts. Eric had opted to work with Calvin again as he had not wanted to ask his foster mother for a roast after they had just eaten one. Mrs. Laurel took this in stride and soon had everyone separated into their respective kitchens.

As the roasts only had to be seasoned and then placed into the preheated oven, they spent the remainder of class learning about meat and meat safety. The roasts were set to slow cook and would be collected after school. Eric planned to meet Calvin to see the finished product, which also meant that Eric would be able to leave study hall early.

For the first part of his seventh period study hall he checked out maps in the library and looked at the bluff area where Martin had set up house. He left five minutes early, made a pit stop to admire the roast, then rushed to grab his bike from the rack outside.

He waved to a confused Matt, who was waiting for him at the bottom of the stairs, and peddled off towards the bluff. Eric was in such a hurry to get to the bluff that he never noticed Dave creeping along behind him in his car. Turning down a bike trail, he cut across the park and towards the bluff. Near the edge of the park, he stopped and chained his bike to a hitching post that had been placed near the woods, he assumed for people who rode horses through this area, though he had never seen any. Checking that his phone was on and set to vibrate, he jumped onto the path and headed into the woods.

He had decided to start near the water and work his way towards the bluff. There was a trail that he could follow part of the way and he figured that Martin would not have gone too far off the path for convenience sake. As he got close to the water, he felt a strange sense of unease. He was not sure why, but he pulled out his cell phone, clicked through a few screens and the feeling dissipated. Scanning the riverbank, he saw nothing of interest, though he still had the oddest feeling that he was being watched.

Two water Sahae slipped from behind the cattail plants and peered after him as he moved away from the water. Once he was out of sight, they slipped down into the water and disappeared.

Eric began to recognize the area that Martin had shown him as he moved away from the river. Halfway to the bluff, he stopped dead in the center of the trail. Off to the side of the trail, there was a perfectly circular area of foliage that had somehow been cut out all the way down to fresh earth. It did not appear to have been excavated by a machine, the edges of the cuts both in the vegetation and the earth were too perfect to have been done by conventional means. The area around it was exactly as Martin had shown him with the spell before leaving the Greens.

Magic. But Martin wouldn't be this careless. This is like a giant neon sign calling attention to him. Something must have happened. Checking the ground nearby, he noticed a strange footprint that was too large to be Martin's, but was the same style of soft-soled shoe that Eric now knew was favored among certain shadowborn. Oh crap, he thought, looking around. *If something was able to take Martin out or capture him, I'm screwed.*

He continued down the path until he was near the bluff; he saw nothing unusual. On his way back, he noticed a great section of turf that was torn up, as if from the passage of many large animals. Pretending that he was stretching from his long walk, he casually looked around and nearly choked in fear. Standing just inside the trees not too far away were two creatures that he could not believe he was seeing.

At first glance, he almost thought they were just two guys hanging out in the woods. That was until he noticed two—no, three, horrifying things. One, he could see light in between their two sides; two, in place of normal noses they had the extended snouts of dogs. Three, there were four creatures rather than two, each one possessed of one side of the head, one arm and one foot. *Sahae! Here? Did they get Martin? Are they after me?!*

Coming up from his stretch he turned to head back to the park and the creatures suddenly disappeared from his peripheral vision. He walked casually and scanned for them, hoping they had just vanished back into the underbrush. For a moment, he felt like a haze crossed his vision and he narrowed his eyes, squinting. A squirming feeling flitted through his eyes and his vision clicked into clarity.

As he blinked back tears, he saw something that he had somehow missed before. In the distance, he could see an enormous growth of trees twisted together in an abhorrent mockery of nature. Five times bigger than any tree he had seen in the forest, it had massive stress fractures throughout, where it seemed to have been forced into shape. It was impossible that he had missed seeing this monstrosity. Someone, or something, had to have used powerful magic to mask the tree. Even now he felt it trying to twist in his vision into seeing a normal looking tree, albeit a large one.

Fighting against the compulsion to see it as normal, he felt the spell's grasp on him dissipate. Looking closer at the tree, he saw that the enormous tree was in fact multiple trees that were twisted together like a small child built it from clay. The misshapen trunk had bark that seemed stretched and twisted in such a way that it set his pulse racing. Its enormous base was divided into multiple roots, twisting out in every direction.

The violence of the shape left Eric feeling like the tree was screaming in agony. Every fiber of his being wanted to run and it took every ounce of self-control, as well as all of the calming exercises Martin had taught him, to keep from hightailing it back down the path. Instead, he tried to appear outwardly unconcerned, sauntering away towards the park. With each step, he expected to hear the heavy footfalls of the dog-man creatures chasing after him, but the forest remained quiet.

Once he was out of the trees he made a beeline for his bike. As he reached down to undo the lock, he gasped in shock. The bike had been completely ruined. Both of the tires were slashed in multiple places. The tire stems were missing and the spokes were smashed as if someone had jumped up and down on them. Even the frame looked like someone had stomped on it, and the handlebars were twisted and bent in a testament to the high level of fury directed at the bike.

Glancing around, he saw no one, but he remembered how the creatures in the woods had hopped away. *Could they have done this? You would think they'd want to avoid the metal, being Sahae.* Warily, he watched the woods for any sign of an ambush as he unlocked the bike and pulled it up on his shoulder. Glancing around nervously, he walked quickly back towards his house. He opened his cell phone and texted his foster parents to let them know he was having trouble with his bike but was on his way. As he cleared the edge of the park and started down the street towards his house, two eyes stared balefully from the shadows.

Dave laughed at the look on Green's face. He had not even planned on wrecking the bike but after he saw Eric head off into the trees and disappear, he could not resist. For the first time since Emily started lusting after that jerk, he actually felt good. It was long past time that Eric Green learned his lesson. No one crosses Dave McKenzie and gets away with it.

29

TAKING AN EVENING STROLL

THE LAST GLOW of sunlight faded from the horizon as the town of Seaverville wound down from another day. The shops by the river were closed tight, with only the display lights illuminating the interior. Most of the foot traffic had dispersed, with only a few stragglers wandering home after a late outing. The sound of the town changed as the traffic disappeared and the people went inside their homes for the night. It was as if the town itself was preparing to sleep until a new day dawned.

At 320 Oak Street, the television was on in the living room. Becky Davis had her feet kicked up and was working her way through a still-warm bowl of microwave popcorn. She could hear her parents upstairs putting her brother to bed. From the top of the stairs, her father called down.

"Becky? Can you come up here real quick? Your brother wants you to kiss him goodnight."

Rolling her eyes, she pushed herself up off the couch and dropped the bowl on the cushion. "Yeah," she called back up the stairs, exasperated. Grumbling to herself, she headed up the stairs and saw her father carrying her brother over his shoulder into Nick's bedroom.

"Okay, buddy. Teeth are brushed; you've had some water and

two stories. Now your sister is going to give you a kiss goodnight and then you need to go to sleep, okay?" From the bed, a lump under a blanket sat up and two blue eyes peeked out at them.

"No! I don't want to go to sleep until Becky reads me a story!" With a long-suffering sigh, Becky caught the look on her dad's face and sat down next to the bed.

You guys totally spoil him, you know. I don't remember getting more than one story when I was his age, and then I was always right off to bed.

Of course, she would never have dared to say that out loud. The few times she had said anything like it had resulted in long lectures about being disrespectful, plus a few extra chores.

Nick waited for her to sit down and then jumped out from under the covers. "Boo!" Becky pretended to be frightened and jumped, sending Nick into fits of giggles. She tickled him and they wrestled back and forth for a few seconds until she finally got him settled under the blanket.

As she read him his story, the same story she had read a thousand times, The Three Little Pigs, she smiled in spite of herself. Nick had been an unexpected surprise for her family. Her parents had not really been trying to have another child, but they were overjoyed when they discovered her mother was pregnant. Becky had not been sure about the new arrival, but Little Nick had quickly won her over.

The four year old had the most beautiful blue eyes that sparkled when he laughed and dark, chestnut brown hair with a slight curl to it, giving him a slightly rakish look. Becky grouched a lot about all the time her little brother demanded, but in truth she loved spending time with him, even if tonight she had to miss part of her show to do it.

When the story was over, Nick tried to get a few more out of her as was his usual ploy to prolong bedtime. Becky gave him a kiss on the head and pulled the blanket up on him a few times while he kicked it down.

"No, Becky! I don't want to go to sleep here. I want to sleep in your room. Can I come downstairs and sleep on the couch with you?"

Becky laughed as each question was punctuated by a kick that dislodged his blankets. Giving him another kiss, she tucked the blanket back around him and gave him a hug.

"You know that you've got to go to sleep, silly. Here's your hug-a-snug and one more kiss. But now it's time for you to go to bed." She headed back towards the door, her hand going for the light switch.

"Becky!"

Cringing, she turned back to Nick. "Still want the light left on, Little Guy?"

Nick's eyes were wide as saucers as he looked at her and his chin trembled a little. "Uh huh," he said softly.

"Okay Nicky, you can have the lamp on, okay?" When he nodded, she went to the side table and turned on his lamp before shutting off the overhead light. With a final kiss on the forehead, she left his room and went back downstairs. Her father was coming up the stairs as she went down.

"Where are you going, hun? It's bedtime."

Becky managed not to roll her eyes although it was a close thing. The quickest way to lose an argument with her dad was to do something he considered disrespectful.

"I know, I just need to finish watching the last few minutes of my show and then I'm off to bed."

He hesitated for a minute. "Didn't you DVR it? You could just watch it tomorrow right?"

She sighed at his tone of voice. "Yes, I suppose I could. I just don't want anyone telling me how it ends tomorrow before I get a chance to see it."

To her surprise, he nodded in agreement. "Yeah, I hate when people do that. Okay, finish watching it and then get to bed, alright?"

Becky grinned. "Okay, Daddy! Thanks!" Kissing him on the cheek, she continued down the stairs and flopped back on the couch.

Reclaiming her now stone-cold popcorn, she turned the sound down and rewound the DVR to the spot she'd left off. When the show was over, she put the empty popcorn container in the sink and headed off to bed. She glanced into Nick's room and saw him curled up on the lion pillow that he loved fast asleep.

LORD EISHAO FLOATED in the night sky high above the town, watching as the lights below winked out. As the darkness spread, the irritating thrum of technology abated, easing the discomfort he had been enduring. Like a cool balm spread over a burn, the darkness enveloped him, putting him at ease. Above him, the nearly full moon shone like an angry, unblinking eye, bathing the world below in twisting shadows, reminding Eishao of home.

Melancholy threatened to damper his good mood and he pushed the thoughts of his past away. *The time has come to have a bit of fun and perhaps draw some worthy prey to me.* Grinning in anticipation, he spoke a few words and his form shrank and twisted until he changed completely into the form of a small boy. Only his eyes remained the same, a window to his dark soul. Sinking towards the home below him, he called upon his minion and set his plan into action.

AFTER BECKY WENT to bed, the house was quiet. The light from the full moon flooded the room, making the lamp on the side table in Nick's room unnecessary. Nick was curled up in a little ball in bed, his butt sticking up in the air. The window of his room, which was an older wooden model with metal latches that had not been secured, slid open a few inches before the child safety stop caught and held it into place. A silvery mist danced around the opening of the window before entering the room, settling to the floor and disappearing. The safety latch on the window snapped apart and the window slid all the way open. On the bed, Nick shivered as the draft from the window swept over him.

In his sleep, Nick began to shiver, gently at first and then more vigorously as the temperature inside the room plummeted. Pulling the covers up, he burrowed his head beneath the blanket, just as his breath became visible in the quickly cooling air. The window began to frost over as the moisture in the room condensed and froze into wild patterns on the glass.

Nick startled awake and pulled the blanket tighter around his body. For a moment, he was so afraid he did not know what to do. He was certain, absolutely positive, that there was a monster in his room. The only protection he had was his covers. He shut them tight around him to keep the cold out and willed the monster to go away.

The sound of his breathing kept him from being able to hear anything and he tried to breathe quietly. His heart was beating so loud it almost felt like it was going to burst out of his chest and he felt himself pee the bed a little. He heard a low growling sound come from outside the covers and he hid his face in his pillow. The light from the window was obscured as something large passed in front of it. What sounded like claws scraped across the floor, plodding towards his bed. Opening his mouth, he tried to scream for his Daddy but his mouth was so dry he could not make a sound. His breath started coming faster and faster and his heart beat even harder than before. The rest of his bladder emptied onto his bed and he gave a low moan of terror.

He heard the claws on the floor stop suddenly and a deep sniffing sound, like a big dog would make when looking for something. There was a rush of motion and he waited for the feeling of the teeth he knew were there to sink into him through the blanket. Instead, he felt the heavy breath on the outside of the blankets, sucking the fabric away from him with its force before pushing it back in. A low, menacing growl rolled over him, causing him to spasm in fear. The light from the window cast a huge, menacing shadow onto the blanket.

I have to yell for Daddy. He will come save me. He will. Oh

Daddy, please hear me and come get the monster, he thought. He took one more deep breath to scream for his Daddy, but another sound interrupted him.

A thump sounded from the far side of the room, like someone jumped off a chair. It came from near his window. *Oh no! I thought the window was closed. I must've left it open and now there's another one in my room. They'll eat me and Daddy and Mommy and Becky.*

The terror he felt caused him to quake so hard his bed actually started to move back and forth. From near the window he heard a voice that sounded like another child.

"Bad Doggy! You leave him alone and get out of here or I will hurt you so badly you will never be the same!" The creature near Nick moved away from his bed and he risked a peek from under the covers.

The creature was gigantic, bigger than any dog he had ever seen. It was bigger than the big bear on a nature show he had watched with Daddy. It glided across the floor towards a skinny little boy standing near the window. The boy had emerald green eyes and his skin was pale as a ghost. In his hand, he held a strange walking stick that he waved menacingly at the animal. Growling, the monster started to pounce and, quicker than Nick could follow, the boy moved, beating the animal around the body and head.

Within seconds, he had hit it so many times that it jumped out the window with a whine and disappeared. The strange child looked after it in irritation. "Stupid mutt. You better not come back here. Ever!" Stamping his foot, the boy turned towards the bed and caught sight of Nick.

"It is safe now. You can come out, he is gone," he said warmly. Nick flipped back the covers and stared at the boy in shock.

"How did you do that? He was so big, he could have eaten you!" The boy laughed and walked towards him and Nick suddenly felt a strange affinity for him. The feeling conflicted with his concern over how the boy had gotten into his room and something about not talking to strangers that flitted through his mind. Then all of that was pushed aside and he felt only embarrassment that the other boy saw that he wet the bed.

The other boy stepped forward and put his hand out. "Hi! My name is Drol. Oahsie Drol. Nice to meet you."

Nick automatically put his hand out to shake and the other boy pulled him up out of bed. Immediately, he felt his face flood with shame as the other boy saw his wet pajamas. Catching his eye, the boy laughed warmly.

"Hey, do not be embarrassed. There are grown men that would have wet themselves with a giant wolf getting ready to eat them."

Nick felt a little better and pulled the blanket around his body to hide the mess. Moving over to his dresser, he quickly started changing into the clothes his mother had left out for the next day.

"Yeah, but you weren't scared. How did you do that? I thought you were a goner for sure." The boy laughed and Nick found that he really liked his laugh. It made him feel good inside, like when Mommy would hug him or when Daddy carried him around on his shoulders. Nick smiled back at him.

"My name is Nick. Thanks for saving me. I was so scared. I still can't believe how you chased that thing away."

Drol gave a half bow and grinned. "Well, I cannot take all the credit. I have a secret that makes it easy for me to face any monster, no matter how tough."

As he buttoned his jeans, Nick turned to Drol with a hungry look on his face. "You do? Can you tell me what it is?" Drol gave him a pointed look and Nick immediately felt stupid. *Of course he can't tell me. Then it wouldn't be a secret.*

Drol looked back at him for a moment and then smiled again. The way he smiled made Nick so happy he could hardly stand it.

"You know what? I think that I could probably tell you. You and I are friends, are we not? And you can keep a secret, right?" Nick nodded so hard he hurt his neck. Drol seemed to consider for a moment before nodding. "Very well, I will tell you."

Leaning forward, he put his mouth close to Nick's ear and lowered his voice to a whisper.

"The secret that keeps me from ever having to be afraid of any monster? The thing that makes me strong enough that I no longer have to be afraid of anything? It is this . . . my magic stick!" With a flourish, he raised his stick up to Nick's face so he could see it closer.

From a distance, it had just looked a like a really big stick, the kind that Nick had played with when he went into the forest on walks with his parents. Up close was a different story. It was intricately carved with figures and strange designs and had little bits of light that seemed to seep out from time to time. Hesitantly, Nick glanced up at Drol. "Can I hold it?"

Drol snatched it back to his side and shook his head. "Nope, sorry. Only the person who collected the stick from the magic tree can hold it. That way no monster can take it away from you and no adult can take it."

Nick was crestfallen for a moment before he realized what Drol had said. "A magic tree? You mean like a real magic tree?"

Drol nodded. "Yes, it is really big and powerful. It grows out in the deepest woods and can only be found by those that are pure of heart and worthy of its power."

Nick sat down on the edge of the bed, his gaze going between his new friend and the stick he held. *If I had one of those, I would never need to be afraid again. I could sleep with the light off and everything,* he thought excitedly. "Drol, do . . . do you think that I might be able to find the tree and get a stick of my own?" His new friend looked surprised then seemed to consider it for a long moment. Nick felt his heart beating fast in his chest. A burning need to get a stick of his own began to fill him.

"I suppose it is possible," Drol finally said. "If you like, I could go with you, for protection, and that way if you cannot find it, I can make sure you get home safely." Nick clapped his hands in glee and danced over to where his shoes were. As he pulled them on he spoke to Drol back over his shoulder.

"You're the best friend ever! So, where do we need to go to look for the tree? Is it far away? Do you know how long it will take to get there?"

Drol waited for him to finish putting on his shoes before answering, twirling his magic stick in his hand. "Well, it is different for everyone. I had to go deep into the darkest part of the woods, by myself. It will be better for you because you will be with me. The first thing we will need to do is get outside of town to the woods. Then we can start from there."

For the first time since his friend had banished the big, bad wolf, Nick began to feel afraid again. The thought of going out into the dark, even with his new friend for protection, was really scary.

Drol seemed to realize that he was having second thoughts. He came up next to him and put a hand on his shoulder. "If you do not want to go, you do not have to. There are scary things in the dark. Of course, the wolf was in your room even with the light on. If it had not been for me happening to spot him coming in and following him, he might have eaten you up. A stick of your own will be all the protection you and your family will every need. If you are brave enough to go get it . . ."

Nick felt the last bit of fear he had vanish as his friend spoke. Grabbing his jacket, he pulled it on, paused to grab his flashlight from next to the bed, and turned to Drol. "I can be brave, you'll see!"

Smiling at him, Drol nodded. "Very well, you sneak downstairs and I will meet you outside?"

Nick nodded and headed for his bedroom door. "Okay. See you out front." Moving into the hall, he pulled his door shut quietly and headed down the stairs. Staying close to the wall, he avoided stepping on the parts of the stairs that squeaked and was soon at the front door.

Daddy will be so mad if he catches me. He told me never to go outside without him or Mommy or Becky, especially not at night, he thought as he clicked open the locks. He had to go into the living room to grab his plastic chair to stand on and remove the chain from the door. After returning the chair, he quietly stepped outside and closed the door, feeling a bit unsettled when the automatic lock clicked into place.

For a terror-filled moment, he turned and peered into the darkness for Drol and did not see him. *The door is locked, but if I pound on it Daddy will come downstairs and let me in. He will be mad but at least I'll be safe.* Just as he was getting ready to beat on the door, he heard a whisper from the shrub next to the stairs.

"Psst. Nick. Over here." Turning on his flashlight, a little wooden light Grandpa had given him, he spotted Drol standing in the grass motioning to him. "This way, hurry before someone wakes up."

Bounding down the stairs to his side, Nick felt immediate relief from his fear. *As long as Drol is here, I'll be fine. When I have my own magic stick, I will be brave like him.* Drol grabbed his hand and the two of them ran off into the darkness.

30

DAZED IN THE DARK

THE LIGHT WAS soft and gentle, yet it did nothing to alleviate the throbbing in his head. Trying to open his eyes was like attempting to lift huge boulders from his eyelids. Groaning softly, he tried to roll to his side and was wracked with pain. The world, for an instant, became a white-hot hell of burning torment. He felt consciousness slipping away and froze, trying to will the pain away.

As soon as he stopped moving, the pain lessened considerably and he sobbed in relief. Taking a few deep breaths, he focused on slowing his heart rate to a more normal pace. Time seemed to lose all meaning as he lost himself in the simple task of breathing in and out. It seemed like an eternity had passed when the pain finally faded to a bearable level and his breathing slowed. He was sopping wet and felt the beginning of a chill coming on from the pooling sweat beneath him.

Sliding his hand gently down, he felt the wooden surface beneath him; it was some sort of table, wide and flat. He slowly opened his eyes, squinting in pain at the light and his mercilessly pounding skull. He blinked and focused on his breathing as his eyes adjusted and he was able to examine his surroundings. He was in a simple stone room, lying on the only piece of furniture, an old wooden table. The ceiling was adorned with two metallic lamps hanging almost twenty feet above him, each with a single large bulb.

They appeared to be set to low power at the moment, something he was grateful for, the filament and wires barely showed a glow. On the far side of the room was a steel door with a small sliding window set in the top; both the door and window were closed. Setting his head back, he spread out his awareness. The first thing that struck him was the severity of his injuries. He was not sure what had hit him however he recognized the acrid taste of technology in his wounds.

That they have gained the ability to channel lightning in a small portable device is beyond horrifying. Still, I suppose I should be glad the Sahae did not catch me. I would likely be dead already.

He took stock of his injury as well as he could, given his limited mobility. The impact site was small, though the damage to his body was extensive; he was fairly certain that this could be a mortal wound. He was having trouble focusing against the pain and there was an alarming lack of motor control when he tried to move his arms and legs.

It was not difficult to feel the technology that lay beyond the stone walls. Just beyond the stone he sense steel, even encased it caused him discomfort. The steel door at the far end of the room did more than make him uncomfortable, it was making the bottoms of his feet ache. Whoever had left him here had taken care to place him as far away from the door as they could, so there was some knowledge of his kind there. From above, he felt the sharp stab of technology imbedded there. This was a feeling he had become familiar with over the last few decades.

Cameras, he thought. *They do love their little eye spies.* He chuckled at his pun but the pain turned it into a wheezing sigh. Settling back against the table, he relaxed. It was pointless to try and escape in this condition. Even in top form, the steel door would have been a challenge without his gloves, and he saw now that he wore nothing more than the simplest homespun shift, so big that it looked like a sleeping gown.

Drifting in and out of consciousness, he managed to sleep a bit and was eventually startled awake by the sound of the door opening. He could do little more than open his eyes, the pain in his body had returned with a vengeance while he slept. A single human male entered the room carrying a simple wooden chair that he set down near the table.

The door closed with a solid slam and the human sat down in the chair. Staring was considered rude in most polite circles, yet the human's eyes were locked upon him almost as if he was about to devour him and absorb all his secrets. Anger blossomed in his chest and glaring back at the human, Martin managed to speak.

"Just who the hell are you and why did you attack me?" He tried to growl this out in a menacing tone but the voice that came out sounded like it belonged to a doddering old man.

The human's eyes widened a bit, startled by the question. "Who I am is unimportant. We are familiar enough with your ways to know better than to give you a name, and by extension, power over the person who gives it. I believe your custom is to create a name to use while interacting? For those purposes, you may call me John Smith." Pulling his chair a bit closer, the human smiled down at him.

"We've been tracking your disturbances throughout the town and I'm amazed at your resiliency. You managed to penetrate defenses that we had thought more than up to the task of deflecting your kind. We nearly had you near the school however we were unaware that the two areas under construction would allow you passage. I suppose we should thank you. Because of you, our defenses will be even stronger the next time one of you tries to infiltrate us." Leaning over, Mr. Smith looked at him quizzically. "I must admit being completely puzzled by something. What exactly were you doing in town?"

Martin remained silent, more from confusion than anything else. *I never went near the school...*

"I mean, our sensors show you traveling all over town and the forest. Then you leave town and return with what? An invading force? They never even made it past the first perimeter. I must admit, you have us quite perplexed. On top of that, your condition shows no sign of improving. Consequently, I felt it necessary to expose myself to the danger of talking to you to get some answers. Let me tell you, by way of full disclosure, that we are being watched and if any harm comes to me, you'll likely not make it out of this room. That said, I've decided that the rewards could far outweigh the risks, if you and I could simply have a little chat."

Martin raised one hand and groaned in pain as he lowered all but his middle finger in Mr. Smith's direction.

"Go bugger a sheep, you wanker! One does not start friendly conversations by trying to kill the other person. I have never been near the school nor have I spent any period of time in your town. Then again, I am sure all of my kind looks alike to you. If you do not want to tell me who you are and what you want, piss off. Honestly, I hurt too much right now to care. At least I have the comfort of knowing I will not have to listen to your blathering much longer." Smith's eyebrows rose questioningly and Martin sneered.

"Between your little ambush and where you are keeping me, I am done for. The technology around here alone would kill me, and a long, slow, lingering death at that! Luckily, my wound seems bad enough that I will not have to wait around for that to happen. So quit wasting what little time I have flapping your monkey gums. If you have a shred of decency, you would let me go or put me out of my misery. Either way, you can go pound rocks into gravel, gravel into sand, and then go pound sand, you prissy little man." The last was said with horrible strain and Martin felt the room begin to fade as his head fell back onto the table.

SMILING DESPITE HIMSELF, Mr. Smith shook his head at the small blue man on the table. "Well, we can't let you go, little man. Assuming you're truly hurt and not playing possum, it would be a shame to let you die. Perhaps we can put you someplace secure that would better suit your recovery." He turned to the door and knocked briskly. His time with the little blue man was over. For now.

Once outside, Mr. Smith, a.k.a. Paul Bowers, was submitted to a barrage of tests. Hours later, he was irritated and seated with Mr. Harris, a heavyset, gray-haired man with sparkling green eyes and an impeccable pin-striped suit. This man was the final authority and Paul found himself nervously cracking his knuckles as he waited for his superior to finish reading his report. After what seemed like an eternity, he set the documents aside and looked up at Paul.

"That, young man was a damn foolish thing to do."

Paul had been expecting this, however the rebuke still stung and he felt his cheeks flush in embarrassment. "I realize that it had an element of danger to it sir, but . . ."

Mr. Harris bristled at Paul's light tone and interrupted him. "Only someone who has never faced a greater creature would say something so inane. You really have no idea how close you came today, do you? Not to being killed, no! That would be too easy. These things will kill you, have no doubt about that. If that was all that happened, you would be lucky." Leaning back in his chair he fixed the younger man with a stern gaze.

"Have you ever read Shakespeare? How would you like to live out the rest of your days with the head of an ass? Or bleeding out of your eyes but never dying from it? How about feeling compelled to eat human flesh? I have heard things about these creatures that would freeze the blood in your veins. And the things that I have seen . . . well, Paul, let's just say there is a reason I hardly sleep anymore."

Harris rose from his side of the desk and strode over to a low table that held multiple liquor bottles. He poured two glasses of whiskey and pushed one across the desk to Paul. Taking a long drink, he set the whiskey down and continued in a quieter tone.

"The protocols are in place for a reason. If you violate them again without written permission or my personal authorization, I'll see to it that you are removed from any position of authority, are we understood?"

Paul looked at him in shock. "You don't have that kind of authority . . ."

"When it comes to matters such as this, Paul, I have absolute authority. Iron-clad and set in concrete. Don't test my patience on this. I appreciate your zeal in wanting to learn more from our visitor, but remember that we have been at this for centuries. The protocols protect us all. Remember that. Now, what are your impressions of our guest?"

Paul took a moment to collect his thoughts before giving his report. *Deep breath.* He straightened his tie and rattled off the salient details as Harris nodded in approval.

"I agree with you. It wouldn't make any sense for us to let him go, but there are a few places we can put him that may help him recover on his own. Otherwise, it makes little sense for us to have taken him prisoner. Hopefully we can get him well enough to answer some questions." Harris pulled a folder from the edge of his desk and handed it to Paul.

"Here you go, Mr. Bowers. You wanted an active role and I'm going to give it to you. Hopefully you live to regret your rash actions. Since you felt obligated to break protocol, you've given us an excellent opportunity to interact with the subject. As of now, you're on assignment. Make any calls you need to and we'll make sure that we take care of any work conflicts. You'll remain in isolation with the subject until it is time for your next report. Hopefully you'll be able to find out exactly what our visitor was up to."

Paul could not keep the grin off of his face as he read through the folder. *Full authorization to interact with the subject.* There were a number of tests to run on the creature and questions upon questions to ask, but he would have the opportunity to question the little blue man on a great many things of his own choosing. The latitude he had was amazing, due largely, he believed, to the distinct possibility that this assignment could end quickly, with his murder.

None of this in any way dampened his spirits. Rising to his feet, he clasped the file and shook Mr. Harris' hand. "Thank you, Mr. Harris, sir. I apologize for my rashness earlier. I'll follow every protocol and get the information we need. I won't let you down, sir."

Harris nodded to him, a very sad look in his eyes. "Good luck to you, Paul. Remember what I said. These creatures can be deadly. I would prefer that this was not our last conversation."

Something about the way he said it managed to steal some of the joy from Paul. He had the look of a man who had given this speech far too many times, and the expression on his face was sobering. Nodding to Mr. Harris, he turned and left the room.

Anthony Harris sat down heavily in his chair and downed the rest of his drink. Reaching across the desk, he grabbed the other glass that sat untouched in front of the vacant chair. Raising it in silent salute, he drank it down, wondering if he had just sent another good man to his death.

31

LOST

ERIC WAS SURPRISED when his mom woke him early the next morning. Telling him to dress quickly, she stepped back out and he heard her go back down the stairs. Mr. Green bounded up the stairs a moment later and stuck his head in the door.

"Eric, make sure to wear boots, jeans and a heavy shirt." As he was ducking back out the door, Eric stopped him.

"Dad, what's going on?!"

He halted mid-step and looked back in surprise. "I thought your mom told you. A little boy has gone missing and the town is organizing search parties. You and I need to get down to the police station to join up before they leave."

Reaching down, Eric grabbed his other boot off the floor and bounced on one foot, pulled the boot on and quickly tying it. Taking the stairs two at a time, he ran out the front door and jumped in the car with his parents.

"So who's the little boy and when did he go missing?"

"Little Nick Davis." Mr. Green said. "I believe his sister, Becky, is your age. He's about four years old, almost five maybe, and his parents reported him missing this morning. They tucked him in last night and when they went to get him up this morning, he was gone. It doesn't look like anyone broke in, they think he might have gotten up sometime in the night and just wandered outside."

At this, Mrs. Green gave a small sob and Mr. Green reached over and squeezed her shoulder. "Now sweetheart, try not to cry. The boy could just have gone for a walk. Let's not cry unless there is a need."

Eric saw his mom work to suppress the tears and felt a lump in his throat. He was saved from coming up with something to fill the awkward silence as they arrived at the lot near the police station.

The parking lot was nearly full and what seemed like a hundred people were milling about. Almost every boy from school stood next to an adult that he assumed was their parent near the police station steps.

Mr. Green gave Mrs. Green a quick peck on the cheek and nodded to Eric. "Let's go. Your mom will head over to the community center to help there."

As they approached the crowd near the steps, Sheriff Barnes stepped out the door of the police station and raised his hands up to quiet the crowd.

"Alright everyone, listen up! We've checked a few surveillance tapes from last night and we do see that Nick left his house on his own. We're not sure why. What we do know is that he walked through town and at times hid from passing cars. He was last seen heading out of town into the woods. For that reason, we're going to start a search line. Stay a few feet from each other at the edge of the trees and slowly advance. There'll be searchers on horseback riding to the farthest distance we feel he could travel on his own. Try to make contact with him by yelling. We've got officers who will be interspersed among you. If you find something, please notify the nearest officer and he'll call it in. Time is a factor here people. Let's go!"

Moving with the crowd, Eric headed across the street and towards the woods. As they walked, he overheard various bits of conversation around him.

"Must have been sleepwalking . . ."

"How could you not notice your kid leaving the house?"

"This is why we have the chain on when we go to bed . . ."

"Oh lord, please let us find him unharmed . . ."

As they walked, officers split groups off to head north or south along the path, helping to speed the flow of foot traffic and spread out the line as they approached the woods. It took an hour to get everyone in place and another hour to coordinate the start. Soon Eric was stomping through the underbrush with his dad on one side and Officer Dan Jackson on the other.

The underbrush was maddeningly thick. Eric was glad for the gloves his dad had brought for them, as more than once they had to pry a bramble patch apart to peer inside. From time to time, they startled deer and other animals from hiding, and after several hours they had moved almost a mile from the starting point but still found no sign of the boy.

Calling a halt, the Sheriff had everyone mark their spot with a tied ribbon before stepping back to grab coffee and donuts that volunteers had brought from the community center. Mrs. Green looked wan and pale as she handed a cup to both Eric and her husband. Eric munched on a few donuts, having worked up a terrific appetite; Mr. Green declined to eat, citing an upset stomach. The break was over all too soon and Eric found himself ripping back into the underbrush.

By the end of the day, everyone was foot sore, exhausted and thoroughly dispirited. After searching the entire area, the only thing they announced finding was one of the boy's shoes and a wooden flashlight in a clearing close to a huge, gnarled tree. It was as if the earth had simply opened up and swallowed him. Eric walked back with his father and waited, leaning heavily on the car while Mr. Green collected Mrs. Green from the community center.

The ride home was silent, the quietest ride they had since Eric came to live with them. Once they were home, they had a quiet dinner of sandwiches and turned in early. Eric barely remembered his head hitting the pillow before sunlight was streaming through the window.

THE NEXT MORNING he awoke to a silent house. Stumbling downstairs, he found a note telling him that he should come to the police station when he was up to help with the search. Grabbing some cereal, milk and a few sweet rolls, he relished the taste of even the day old pastry. As he headed outside, he was surprised to see Matt sitting on the porch. He bounced up as Eric exited the house.

"Geez, man what is the friggin' dealio? Since when do you sleep late? You would be like an hour late for school right now! Well, if school hadn't been canceled for the search."

Eric realized Matt was right. The search yesterday had taken more out of him than he thought and he slept hours later than normal. As they headed through town towards the police station, Matt brought him up to speed on the search.

"Yeah, so the state police got here last night and started flying over the forest with their helicopter. It has an infrared camera so they are looking for him that way. They brought in some dogs, both the cops' and some out-of-towners', to help. So far, nothing. The weird thing is, the dogs keep shying away from the spot where they found his shoe. You'd think there was something there that scared them but there's no sign of animals near there, just a lot of footprints. They also found this huge hole that someone dug out in the forest. It is weird. There're is no heavy machinery tracks or anything, but it looks like someone dug like a perfect circle right down into the dirt." Matt continued talking but Eric had already tuned out.

The hole was where Martin's house had been. It was going to raise questions, but right now that was the least of his worries. He had not gone to the area where they found the shoe yesterday as it was outside of his search area. It had never occurred to him that the tree they had been talking about might be the gargantuan one he had fled from when he was looking for Martin. It made sense and he cursed himself for not thinking about it before. *Yep, I'm an idiot. Martin disappears, I see some weird dog guys, then a kid disappears and I don't even think to connect the dots!*

Matt smacked him on the arm, catching his attention as they

neared the station. "So she said to him, 'I don't have the time but it looks like you have the quarters!' Get it? No? Damn it, man, were you even listening to that joke? Ugh, what a freaking waste."

At the foot of the stairs, an exhausted Sheriff Barnes was handing walkie talkies to group leaders. He held one out to Eric. "Green, organize some of your classmates and take a look around. We've already gone over most of the area, but a few fresh eyes may help spot something we missed."

Eric nodded and stepped aside, motioning for a few people to join him. Matt glanced around and then hopped up on a bench and started to bellow. True to form, Matt was able to project to the cheap seats.

"Okay, Seaverville High! Get over here and form up with Eric. Let's go, people! Right frickin' now! Put the donut down and get over here!"

Eric flushed a bit at his friend's behavior, but pushed it away when he saw quite a few people he knew, including Calvin from Home Ec. and Emily walking toward him. He waited for everyone to gather before speaking.

"Everyone? We're supposed to spread out and take a look around. We're going over ground that has been searched already, but that doesn't mean we shouldn't take this seriously. We need to cover every inch and keep an eye out for anything unusual. If you don't feel like doing a search, head over to the community center and lend a hand. They gave me a radio, so if you find anything let me know and I can call it in. Anyone have any questions? No? Good deal, let's go!"

Turning on his heel, he led the way back towards the edge of town. Once they entered the woods, he followed the trail until he was back near the unnaturally gnarled tree. He paused at the edge of the clearing and waited for everyone to catch up, dread coursing through him. There in front of him was the same tree he had seen at a distance while looking for Martin.

This close, the violence of its construction was even more blatant. As his classmates gathered near him, he noticed that none of them gave it a second look, telling him the masking spell on it was showing them what he had seen before.

Just another big tree in the woods. Nothing to see here...move along. This is bad. Whatever is here is way too powerful for me to be screwing with. I should be running like Martin told me to. Martin...what happened to him? And poor little Nick Davis...

Shaking his head in resignation, he turned to the group and started pairing everyone up. At the last minute, he realized that Matt had run off with Calvin, leaving him to partner Emily. He could tell, seeing her red eyes that she had been crying. Awkwardly, he stood for a moment, not sure what to do.

"So, should we just go this way?" she suggested.

Relieved, he fell in step beside her. As they walked, he scanned the ground, the trees and even the sky, hoping to find some sign of Nick. The entire time, he felt his eyes draw back to the huge tree, his unease growing the longer they were there. As they walked, Emily started talking quietly.

"It's so awful. Becky, well, she's blaming herself. She thinks because her door is across from her brother's that she should have heard him leave. And Nicky asked to sleep in her room and she told him no. But he always asks to sleep in her room. Her parents are going out of their minds. Her dad was out here searching last night and this morning. He hasn't slept since Nick disappeared. Her mom has been searching the house and the neighborhood over and over. She has been going house to house with the neighbors, searching everywhere. She read somewhere about a little boy that hid in a washing machine and died waiting to be found so she's obsessed with looking close to home." Eric glanced at her and saw tears swimming in her eyes. Her voice shook a little as she spoke.

"Nicky is just a sweet little guy. He's the most wonderful kid. I can't understand why he'd leave the house. Did you know he's afraid of the dark? His nightlight blew out once when I was staying over and he freaked out. He ended up sleeping on the couch with me and Becky and we had to leave the overhead light on. The thought of him going outside at night, by himself, it just doesn't make any sense."

Eric found himself nodding in agreement even as his own mind turned to darker places. *What were you doing out here, Nick? Why would you come out here in the dark if you were afraid?* Moving through the brush, they re-entered the clearing with the strange tree. Eric felt every hair on the back of his head stand up. A menacing feeling swept over him like a wave. The feeling of danger was palpable. Heart racing, he tried to calm himself as he focused on Emily's conversation. She continued to describe happier times with Nicky.

The tension inside him rose and he turned to grab Emily's hand, wanting nothing more than to get them both away from the tree. Before he could act, two hands, impossibly thin and pale, came out of the tree and pulled Emily back into the bark. It happened so fast she barely had time to scream.

Calling out for her he reached for the trunk, and felt some force repel his hand. Turning frantically in a circle he yelled for help, even though part of him realized no one was better equipped to handle this than him. As he turned he saw Calvin and Matt were staring in disbelief at the tree.

"What the frak was that?!" Matt screamed. "Did that tree just eat your girlfriend?! What the hairy hell is going on!" Matt suddenly started wheezing as the stress became too much and doubled over, clawing for his inhaler.

Calvin helped him steady it and Matt took two deep hits before his breathing started to slow. "Eric," Calvin said, looking completely freaked out. "What do we do? What do we do?!"

Eric glanced back and forth between them, realizing they were waiting for him to say something.

"The two of you take this radio and go find my dad. Tell him that he needs to get back here as soon as possible. I don't know what's going on but I'm going to try and get Emily back."

Matt stared at him for a moment, stunned. "What are you going to do, Paul Bunyan? Chop the tree down?"

Eric shot back as Matt started to wheeze again, "I don't know, Matt! I missed the class where we went over what to do when a tree swallows someone! Okay? Now go do what I told you to!"

Both Calvin and Matt froze for a moment, and then sprang into action, running down the path towards the rest of the search party. Eric turned to the tree and reached out for the Way. His anger and fear lent him strength as he pulled power into himself. He not only burst the glamour that was hiding the door, but shredded the protection spells contained beneath it. The power soared through him and he felt a rush as the door itself burst into flames, ashes falling at his feet. Taking a deep breath, he slipped into the tree and out of the light.

The tree smelled of burnt wood and fungus, its irregular walls causing a claustrophobic closeness that nearly overwhelmed Eric. He was like a giant invading a twisting, wooden rabbit hole. His shoulders were soon rubbed raw by the rough edges scraping against him. At one turn, he got wedged tight and had to pull free at the expense of not only his shirt but the skin beneath. Leaving a bloody smear on the passage behind him, he moved further into the tree.

In the distance, he heard the sound of Emily screaming in fear and hurried forward. The passage opened up and he found himself at a four way intersection. He paused a moment and felt around him in the Way, casting a short spell to help locate Emily. Martin had taught him the basics of this spell, but it drained him more than he liked, even as it showed him the way forward. Taking the left passage, he dodged under spiky stalactites and found himself in a small, square room.

On the far side, he saw a partially open door and a familiar-looking sneaker, still attached to a foot being dragged through the doorway. *Hold on, Emily! I'm coming!*

Leaping forward, he snarled angrily and pulled upon the Way. He ripped the door open and saw a spiral hallway leading down.

Bounding down the ramp, he came to another intersection; this time the spell led him straight ahead. The ramp opened into a large, well-lit grotto with diffused daylight streaming down from the vaulted ceiling a hundred feet above the floor.

He stopped, dumbfounded. The cavernous room was enormous, with huge crystals protruding from the walls and ceiling catching random sunbeams of light from above, sending shimmering rain-bows of color over the walls and floor. On the left side of the room was a deep, clear pool of water that emitted a soft emerald light. The far end of the room had a raised dais with some sort of throne. Yet it was the cages on the right of the room that caught his eye. In a small, wicker cage was a small boy, asleep on a pile of hay. Next to him, in a larger wicker cage, was Emily, disheveled and bloody. She looked up as he entered and screamed.

"Behind you!"

Eric reacted without thinking, throwing himself to the side. A thin line burned down the left side of his body as he rolled aside. His assailant cursed loudly as his rapier scored a mere scratch.

"Well, hello there!"

The creature smiling at him was like something out of a fairy tale, or a nightmare. For an instant, Eric thought he was face to face with Elder, and then the differences between the two became apparent.

This creature appeared to be much younger and had different coloring than Eric's grandfather. Impossibly thin and pale, it moved with an ethereal grace that was almost mesmerizing. Luminous green eyes glared at him, belying the smile beneath. Before him stood what Martin had warned again and again to avoid at all cost. A Sahae of one of the great houses stood before him and Eric felt his blood run cold.

"What or who do we have here? Are you perhaps the hero, come to save the fair maiden? Or the affianced come to save his bride to be?" Eric slid his hand across his side and came back with blood.

"Well, my little monkey, I have bad news for you." The creature affected a mournful expression before slipping into a glee-filled smile. That little scratch of yours? I am afraid it is quite fatal. A long time ago, my people got tired of you pests so we devised a wonderful magic toxin. The effects should start any moment now.

You may say it is not very sporting of me, however I make the rules and I think it is quite entertaining to watch a monkey writhing in agony, begging for death. So feel free to get on with it."

Eric felt nothing but a slight discomfort at the scratch. He spoke a spell of cleansing as quietly as possible and felt what little poison there was slip away. Eishao bristled and shook his finger.

"What is this?! I will not have an Abomination using the Way in my presence!"

Eric tensed, waiting for the attack and was astonished when the man instead threw a spell at Emily. *He thinks Emily is a hybrid. No wonder he grabbed her.*

The creature turned with a smile and continued in a gloating voice. "Well now, that will be the last time your little Abomination girlfriend can save you. Now, where were we before we were so rudely interrupted? Ah, yes. Know that the next touch of my blade will mean your death. At least this time you are forewarned, so that gives you a small sporting chance. You have merely to defeat me without feeling my blade."

Though the tip of the blade never wavered from Eric's direction, the creature was overcome by the apparent absurdity of his possible defeat and he broke down into giggling laughter, bending over and howling with mirth. When his glee diminished, he turned hard eyes back to Eric.

"It is more honor than a primate like you deserves, however I must admire your courage, if not your intelligence, in pursuing the fetching creature here. So child of man, know that you face Lord Eishao. I have walked the world of man since before the first schism. I am feared in your land and my own. I have bathed in oceans of your fellows' blood and visited such terrors as would snap your little psyche in twain. Falling to me will be a moment of honor unworthy of your pitiful self, however if you wish to shower me with your thanks, I will give you a moment to do so before your death."

Eric had been gently feeling his opponent out in the Way and was astonished. He made Martin look like a flickering candle in comparison. Speaking the words of two spells, he stopped just before releasing them and saw Eishao turn an irritated eye on Emily.

"Foolish girl! You cannot possibly break the wards on you. Test them as you like, it will save me the time of killing you."

Emily looked at Eishao in confusion and spoke, but Eric could not hear what she said. Her mouth moved and she was straining like she was yelling, but no sound came out. Smiling evilly, Eishao turned back to Eric and made a flourish with his rapier.

"So, brave to the end, lad? Well, do not think that I will spare you. I have no mercy for your kind and it is the law that this Abomination and all she has known should be snuffed out of existence. Be glad that you are able to die at the hands of one as great as I. You shall not be remembered, however you at least die with the knowledge that your death was at the hands of your betters." Eishao raised the sword and Eric raised a hand to interrupt him.

"Three things, if I may," Eric commented.

Looking pleased with this, Eishao put his sword back in guard position. "You may proceed with your groveling though, as I said, it will benefit you naught." Eric looked at Eishao in disgust and rolled his eyes.

"First off, let me just say that you're out of your mind to think you could take the girl and get away with it. You're like a walking cliché." Eishao glowered at this, his mouth tightening into a thin line.

"Second, you're suffering from a terminal case of overconfidence. I mean, seriously? Have you never had anyone take you down a notch?" Laughing humorlessly, Eishao stretched his sword arm, preparing to finish the duel. Eric raised his hand and halted him in place.

"Third, and last, is your greatest mistake of all. Something that makes every mistake you've ever made in your life look like a minor error in comparison."

"Really, boy? And what is that?"

Eric glared back at the creature, his eyes hard and unwavering, and said with a smile, "Well, Tinkerbelle, the girl isn't an Abomination."

Eishao looked irritated at being robbed of some first-rate groveling and waved a hand dismissively. "Please, do you think your pathetic attempts at subterfuge will trick me into releasing the girl as an innocent? I know full well that she is an Abomination. Anything that you try to do to dissuade that is purely a waste of time."

Eric smiled, spread his feet apart, and with a deep breath pulled as much of the Way into himself as he could, watching Eishao's eyes suddenly widen in understanding and fear. "I happen to know for a fact that she isn't the Abomination. Because I am!"

With that, he released both spells. The first sent Emily and Nick outside the tree, free of their cages. The second smashed a fiery hammer into Eishao and sent him flying across the room, where he crashed hard into the wall. Moving forward, Eric grabbed the rapier from where it lay and held it at the throat of a thoroughly stunned, slightly smoldering Eishao.

Score one for roleplaying games, Eric thought as he watched Eishao's eyes widen. I told Uncle Martin that he was underestimating the value of some of my spells.

"You! You filthy bastard! You dare use the Way on me? I will flay the skin from your bones before I seek out everyone and everything you ever loved..." He froze as Eric poked the rapier up underneath his chin.

"Call me crazy, but I don't think the poison is going to be a factor if I drive this sword up into what passes for your brain. Now, I want to know what you have done with Martin, right now." Eric's voice was low and steady, menacing in a way that unsettled him. Eishao's eyes grew wide and then he smiled in glee.

"Oh, this is just too perfect. The great traitor is also responsible for an Abomination. I will not only wipe my own slate clean when I turn him in, I will be rich beyond measure." Eric pressed the blade hard enough to draw blood and Eishao hissed in pain. "All right, all right. He was the first one that I captured; in a great glass bottle of human creation, actually. It makes a perfect barrier to the Way. In a day or two I had planned to contact the authorities and turn him in."

Eric growled at Eishao while pressing the blade forward.

"Where is he, you simpering fop?" Eishao looked like he was about to explode in anger.

"Simpering? Fop? Oh, little boy, you had best hope your hand does not slip on that sword." Slowly rising from the ground, Eishao pointed to a small door behind the throne. Eric slowly walked him over to the door and watched carefully as he opened it and withdrew a glass bottle from within. "Here is his prison." Eric leaned forward involuntarily as Eishao motioned with the bottle. He peered into the bottle but saw nothing but some debris in the bottom.

He sensed movement behind him and turned in time to meet the rush of the several of the dog-men creatures he had seen in the forest. Their sheer numbers overwhelmed him and for a moment they held him in place. Then with a roar he threw them off and skewered one with the rapier. Unfortunately, the creature pulled the sword from his hand and he was weaponless. Switching tactics, he smashed the knee of one of the creatures, dropping it screeching to the ground.

He locked his arm around one of the creature's throats and another leapt impossibly high and came down on his back. Though he nearly fell, he used the creature he was choking for balance and accidentally snapped its neck. Flinging the creature away, he grabbed the one on his back by the hair and, whipping his body forward, smashed it headfirst into the floor.

The rest of the creatures were circling him in pairs, searching for an opening. Two leapt high, two rushed forward, and two came at him from behind. He almost leapt free but one pair of them managed to catch hold, momentarily giving the others time to grab on as well. Try as he might, he was not able to break free once they used leverage to hold him in place. A low cackle came from the other side of the room and Eishao strode forward, once again holding his rapier.

"Well, the shoe is on the other foot now, isn't it you tricky little bastard? Do you like my minions? Pi Nereske. They are an ugly, stupid lot but they do have their uses."

"Let Martin go, damn you!"

"You little fool! Martin escaped yesterday. That bottle was his prison, and it will be again when I catch him. Oh, you have been entertaining. I cannot believe that I thought that girl was an Abomination. It was you all along. I have to say, this makes me so happy." He smashed the rapier into Eric's face causing blood to ooze from his lips and nose.

"Obviously I will still have to eliminate her, as she has been sullied by association with an Abomination, though what fun I can have with her first. I will show her deviances that she has never dreamed of. Then I will make sure she dies horribly slowly. I think an hour, no a day! One day for every indignity that you have visited upon me today."

Grinning, Eishao danced around the room. "As for your wretched Martin, he has eluded me momentarily. I shall have him back again soon. Oh, what a wonderful day this has been. I have not had this much fun since…well, I cannot remember the last time I had this much excitement." Eishao gestured to the Pi Nereske and they pulled twice as hard on Eric's appendages, nearly pulling them from their sockets. Laughing in delight, he darted forward and slapped Eric hard across the face with his bare hand.

"The utter audacity! To think you could saunter in here and attack me in my own home. You Abominations! The last one I dealt with had the same self-important world view; imagined himself to be a great and powerful wizard. That worked out well for him. If I remember correctly, I think we encased him alive in crystal. Stupid little prick." He growled in irritation at the sight of the empty cages.

"And to take my prisoners! That, I will admit, was a surprise and showed an incredible amount of strength for a fledgling Abomination. Two spells at once? Well, well, well. It is a good thing I came along to snuff you out. Better for all if you had never been born."

Eric strained against the creatures holding him as Eishao ranted. Looking at the two creatures to his left, he yanked the Way through them and spoke the simple words for fire. The two creatures exploded into flames, singeing his arm and leg. The remaining four jumped back in terror when the fire appeared, leaving Eric free. Dodging a thrust from Eishao's blade, he threw himself into a roll and came up facing Eishao. With a roar of rage, Eishao threw a binding spell at Eric that glanced off his wards and struck at him again with his sword.

Eric cried out and grabbed his arm where Eishao had scored a heavy cut. As his concentration wavered the fire disappeared from near the Pi Nereske and they leapt forward to their master's aid. Taking advantage of Eric's injury they sprang forward from different directions tackling him to the ground.

His skull bounced onto the hard floor dazing him. Eishao quickly spoke words of power, barring Eric from accessing the Way. Struggling to regain his focus, Eric started tearing through the spell, fearing he would not be able to break it in time. Gesturing with his rapier, Eishao gazed furiously down at Eric.

"Foolish boy! You have an overdeveloped sense of heroism. Learn too late that you are beaten. You no longer amuse me. It is long past time that I rid this world of your vile presence. Though it pains me to defile this blade, I can always make another. Give my regards to the Gatekeeper of Oblivion!"

Raising the rapier above his head he lunged forward, and impaled not Eric, as he had planned, but Matt, who stepped in front of Eric. It was a close contest as to who was more shocked, Eishao, Eric or Matt. Jumping back, Eishao released the rapier, leaving Matt impaled. Groaning, Matt sank to his knees while Eric remained pinned by the Pi Nereske, helpless to go to his side.

"Matt! No! Where did you come from?! Eishao! I will kill you! Do you hear me?!" Eric raged and succeeded in throwing two of the dog-men across the floor. The others he flung around so quickly, they practically danced around the room.

"I think not, little half-monkey," Eishao commented, his amusement palpable. Gesturing, he caused the earth to rise up around Eric all the way to his shoulders, leaving only his chest and head free. The earth hardened into rock and Eric found himself stuck fast in the middle of a newly-formed boulder. Eishao ignored his escalating raving and turned his attention to Matt.

"Well, well, what do we have here? Another would-be hero? Hmm, they do grow them puny and utterly pathetic these days. To have come so far, simply to delay the inevitable... Well, my young gallant, in case you are joining our little drama late, you should know that my blade was poisoned. You have very little time to dwell upon your mistakes here on this mortal coil." Grinning, Eishao stared at Matt expectantly.

Eric pushed as hard as he could against both the physical and magical bonds holding him. In vain, he reached for the Way, desperate to counter the poison Eishao had used on Matt. Being fully human, he suspected that it would spread in Matt much more quickly and with deadlier results. Matt looked up at Eishao for a moment and against all reason, started laughing. Eishao frowned in confusion and the more Eishao frowned, the harder Matt laughed.

"What, pray tell, little dying boy, is so bloody funny?" Matt wiped his eyes and said something too quietly for Eric to hear. Eishao apparently could not hear him either, because he reached down and dragged Matt up to stand face to face with him. "What was that, you arrogant little prick?"

Matt laughed again, even though Eric could see he was terribly pale and appeared to be in horrible pain. "You think you're the first fairy to come running through our woods, bra? You think after all these years that we're still the defenseless dweebs that we used to be? That you could prey on us, using us as you will? This isn't the seventh century, you arrogant son of a bitch. These days we've got something on our side that lives, breathes and grows with us. A weapon that will help us squash you like the bug that you are."

Eishao looked at Matt in mocking fright while he held the boy effortlessly on the end of one hand. "And what is that, lad? Your unflappable wit?" he said derisively.Matt laughed at Eishao as he slipped his hand covertly into the pocket of his hoodie.

"Nah, you fairy douchebag. As impressive as my rapier wit is, that alone isn't enough to defeat you. Instead, I need the one thing that makes humans able to stand against your kind after so long in the dark. Our ally that will let us take your kind out if you ever screw with us again. The sword that will strike you down without mercy! Technology! Now eat it, buttmunch!" Matt's arm swept forward, smashing his plastic inhaler onto Eishao's face. As it burst, the chemical mix inside coated the right side of the creature's visage.

The effect was instantaneous and horrifying. As the contents of the inhaler spread over the skin, it dissolved it like acid. The flesh began to bubble and parts slipped free, one rather large portion started to slide right off the bone. With an agonized scream, Eishao threw Matt to the far side of the room where he hit the wall with a sickening crunch. One moment Eishao was screaming in front of Eric and the next he was gone, having swept out of the room faster than eyes could track.

The Pi Nereske that remained glanced at each other for a moment before giving forth a horrible cry of fear and fleeing the room after their master. At Eishao's disappearance the earth that encased Eric burst open and the wards barring him from the Way failed. Rushing unsteadily across the room, he picked up Matt, cradling him in his arms, careful of the rapier still sticking out of him. From what Eric could feel through the Way, there were dozens of interconnected spells unraveling with alarming speed all around them. If he was right, this was a temporary dwelling that was quickly beginning to collapse on itself as Eishao moved further away.

If they were not clear before that happened, they could be trapped inside forever or worse, crushed inside the collapsed tree. Using two simple spells he increased his speed and predicted the quickest way out. Luckily, there was a closer exit the way Eishao had gone and he quickly found himself back outside in the clearing. Moving away from the tree, he barely managed to duck behind another tree before Eishao's enormous, twisted tree dwelling blew to bits, wooden shrapnel flying everywhere.

Stumbling a bit from the blast, he managed to lay Matt down without dropping him. Pulling the sword from Matt's body, he flung it away and cast a spell to remove the venom. He felt the venom dissipate but he noticed that Matt was still barely breathing.

Blood leaked from the rapier wound however Eishao throwing Matt into the wall of the room appeared to have caused much more severe injuries. What Eric saw on the outside spoke of internal damage that was probably worse. That, coupled with their rough exit from the tree, had left his friend fading fast. Looking down at Matt, he saw his eyes flicker.

"Eric . . . did I get him?"

Eric choked back a sob as he looked at his best friend lying broken. "Yeah man, you tore him up good. Made what I did to Moose look like a love tap. You always were the badass."

Matt laughed and it turned into a bout of strange, wet coughing, as if he were drowning. "I take after my dad, man. It'd have made him proud to see his boy stand his height today." Blood bubbled out of Matt's mouth and he convulsed into a coughing fit. He spit out some blood and grabbed Eric with his good arm, the other one appeared to be broken in more than one place. "Man. I'm pretty messed up. It's gettin harder to breathe and things are starting to fade. Tell my mom...tell her I'm sorry. I should've been more careful . . ." Matt tried to say more but he did not seem to be able to catch his breath. His eyes rolled back into his head and his body started to convulse.

"No! Matt you are not going to die on me! You hear me?" Brutally reaching out, he fought against the overwhelming exhaustion and grabbed hold of the Way. Warnings from Martin were swept out of his mind as he pulled magic into his body. More power than he had ever tried to wield flowed and still he took more in. He felt like he was going to burst with the power running through him. It burned and swept through him, taking some part of him away with it and still he pulled on it, beyond caring. Channeling the power, he reached out and pulled all of Matt's pain to him. The last thing he felt was fluid filling his lungs and the sensation of drowning; then everything went black.

32

AFTERMATH

ANTHONY HARRIS TOOK a deep breath and eased himself back into his oversized leather chair. The chair creaked more than it used to, a sign that his increasing weight was taking its toll on the wheels. He did not look like his usual well-to-do businessman/politician self. His thinning gray hair, normally coiffed in a classy, fashionable style, stuck out in all directions. Bloodshot gray-blue eyes that had once held a gentle amusement now reflected the horror of one who had seen into the abyss and lived to tell the tale. He was sixty-five years old and dead tired.

His well-tailored suit jacket hung on the back of his chair, his shirt rumpled and sweat-stained, clung about his torso like a funerary frock. One of his pant legs was torn and showed a thin layer of blood from the skin underneath, which had been lacerated on some rather nasty brambles during his recent traipse through the woods. His liver-spotted hands shook slightly as he flipped through the photos. The faces of four children, found alive thank goodness, if not entirely undamaged, stared back at him.

The first was Emily Randall. Great kid, her parents were heavily involved in the community and he had spent a lot of time with them over the years. According to reports, she had been part of one of the high school level search teams. They had been sending them over previously covered areas just to be sure. Something more had happened though. She had been found with little Nick Davis at the edge of a large clearing that was filled with the broken remains of several trees. Examinations by multiple doctors had found nothing physically wrong with her. The theory they were floating now was that she had been so traumatized she had lost the ability to speak. They expected her to make a full recovery, although they could not say when she would actually be able to talk.

Then there was little Nick Davis. His parents were beside themselves with joy when he was found. Now they paced their son's hospital room wondering if he would ever wake up. Again the doctors had been nearly useless. The prognosis was positive. No physical damage had been found and he should wake up at any time. They were just a little fuzzy on the when part.

Next, and most seriously injured, was Eric Green. The foster son of Edward and Claire Green had somehow managed to get himself beaten nearly to death. Two of his oldest and dearest friends now sat vigil at the bedside of their son, wondering if he would open his eyes or if he would slip away. When he had seen them at the hospital, it had nearly broken his heart. Edward had been raging, wanting to know who had done this and what was going to be done about it. Anthony had no answers then and had even less now.

In the end, his only living, breathing, speaking witness was Matt Claughin. Normally having a witness was a good thing, however in Matt's case he came part and parcel with his overprotective mother, Mary. *God knows we would have more luck with a rabid dog than with that woman.* Matt's mother had insisted on him staying in the hospital under observation for a few days. All attempts to speak to him had been stymied by the woman. Eventually, he hoped she would calm down so that they could get the answers they needed. Leaning back in his chair, he closed his eyes and reviewed what facts they had.

One, Nick Davis had walked out into the night and into the woods. A small child, reportedly afraid of the dark, had gone into a forest that some grown men would have hesitated to enter alone. He had done so after sneaking through town and evading detection. According to the video footage, he appeared to be talking or singing to himself; to keep up his courage, maybe? It made no sense. Then there was the fact that the boy had eluded all the searchers that the town could throw at him—human, canine and technological.

Two, the three teenagers had been part of a later search party that had somehow stumbled across Nick Davis. The teens had recovered the little boy and sustained various degrees of damage or injuries.

Three, the detection equipment reported high level "Other" activity in the area where the children had been found, coupled with a massive unidentified energy surge. The sensor path showed at least one entity detected. From there they became unreliable. The different sensors ranged from a very strong Class B to a Class A. The guys from surveillance were tossing around the idea that it might have been a Class B and a Class A. Harris figured if there were two creatures they probably would not all still be here to debate the subject. Whatever the classification, the creature had been very strong and moved away from the area at an incredible rate. They were currently unable to find a trace of anything within the sensor net.

Four, although they suspected foul play on the part of the entity in the luring and abduction of Nick Davis, they were no closer now to any answers than when they started. They had no idea of the identity of the creature that fled or where it had gone.

Glancing at his watch, he saw it was almost three in the morning. *God, I'm too old for this. Though tonight might be too much for even the young to take in stride*...The desk before him was filled with pictures and DVDs which he knew held all the video he would ever want to see from tonight's fiasco. Taking one, labeled "footage-long shot," he put it in the player on his desk and switched on a small TV. The scene began with a shot of a distant crowd. The person holding the camera climbed up on something to improve the vantage point, temporarily shooting the ground until the picture stabilized on a view of the crowd.

The video showed a scene of absolute chaos in the woods outside town, where the kids had been found. Over two hundred volunteers, state police, FBI, local police and National Guard were clustered around a clearing filled with the decimated remains of over ten trees. In the center of the mess he saw himself, a harried old man in a faded tan trench coat, bellowing orders over the rising clamor from the surrounding horde. *God, is that old bastard really me? I can't possibly be that old,* he thought before turning up the sound.

"Dennis, get the Davis boy into the ambulance as soon as he's stabilized on that stretcher. Make sure that he has at least one doctor with him at all times! Bob! Bob Stewart! Make sure that Emily Randall gets to the hospital. I know she seems fine, but I don't want to take any chances. Her parents can go with her in the ambulance if they want, but I want her to be seen by a doctor immediately. Understood?" The two men raced off to their tasks and he watched himself grimace and sit down hard on a log, holding his chest.

On the screen, a flurry of activity ensued while EMTs swooped down on him as he struggled to pull out his nitro tablets. One helped him get a pill out and take it. Watching the pain consume his recorded self, he remembered the throbbing in his chest. It was a warning that he was pushing himself too hard, but at the time he had really had no choice.

As mayor, he held a profound responsibility for the townspeople, however that was only part of what drove him. Unbeknownst to most of his constituents, he was the regional director of an organization that had been helping to protect humanity for thousands of years. And today they failed miserably. Sighing, he looked at the damage on the tape; the surrounding area was a reflection of the damage done to the children.

God knows what they went through because we were caught asleep at the switch. He saw Eric Green being loaded into an ambulance that had managed to break its way through on the walking trail. *That is one tough kid to be able to survive a beating like that. What a mess. It's going to be months fixing the damage to that area,"* And *that is the least of our concerns.* He caught a glimpse of Claire Green's face, eyes streaming tears, as the doors of the ambulance slammed shut.

The camera angle swung around and he saw Matt Claughin being led behind the departing ambulance with his mother, crying and clinging to him. She glanced up and stared coldly at the camera. *Damn, if she had a gun I think we might need a new cameraman. I suppose this is just the chickens coming home to roost. Mary never did forgive us for Steve's death.* On screen, Mary turned away and returned her attention to Matt.

The camera swung around and focused on the center of the clearing, which was filled with pieces of multiple trees that had been shattered sometime during the event. The camera shot the ground again as the cameraman climbed down off the high vantage point. After a moment, the ground disappeared and a much closer shot of two men appeared. They stopped their study of the wood and surrounding area and stepped toward the camera. Tom Murphy spoke first. He ran Riverboat Collectibles, a tourist shop down near the water, during the day. His second job was as a forensic mythologist for S.P.A.R.K., and he was a damn good one. Brushing his shaggy red hair back from his face, he blew out a sigh, looking all of his forty years.

"So, I've got a lot to say, do we want to talk here or should we do this later?" The cameraman swung in a circle and Anthony saw most everyone had headed towards town, leaving just S.P.A.R.K. personnel in the general area.

"No, we should be good, go ahead and let's get it recorded," said the cameraman. "Looks like we're among friends here; tell me what you know so far."

Tom looked around and nodded. "Alright. We've done a thorough search of the area. Besides this area here, we found an odd excavation down near the walking trail. It is too large and perfect to have been done by hand and there are no signs of any equipment moving in or out of the area. For whatever reason, we suspect the entity dug the hole. Why, we have no idea."

The second man, Richard Carroll, a twenty-something college student who worked part time at the theater and was Tom's assistant, stepped up and handed Tom a sword.

"Well, this little baby is cool," he said. "This weapon is not of any known metal that we've been able to identify. We'll know more once the lab gets a chance to look at it. Whatever it belonged to is obviously not here now, but we can't say for sure where it went."

Turning back to Tom, he waited for his superior to speak. Sighing heavily again, Tom gestured to the shattered bits of trees on the ground. "From what I can tell, we had a powerful Class B entity, regardless of the sensor data. I can't explain the Class A readings except to say that it's possible that there was something else here. Regardless, these trees were apparently the Class B's center of operations and also where it likely took the children. The debris reflects what you would expect from an explosion, but we have no signs of accelerant or explosive residue."

At this, the camera panned around and showed clean wood that looked like it had simply burst apart. "Being this far out, we have no eyes on this location and it is well outside of our main sensor grid. Had we upgraded the path with the new posts I recommended, the ones with lights and hidden cameras and sensors, we would know more."

Anthony growled at the recording. "Yes, now is the right time for an 'I told you so' from a budget meeting two years ago. Good man, but damn annoying sometimes."

On the tape, Richard stepped back into center frame. "The good news is, we found something." Richard stepped out of frame and returned with a backpack. Unzipping it he pulled it open to reveal a specimen jar.

"Whatever those kids did to it, the thing looks like it was pretty badly wounded. It lost part of itself while it was fleeing. We should be able to analyze this and set defenses to immediately destroy the thing if it comes within miles of town now." Anthony peered at the lump of flesh in the jar. It almost looked part of a melted Halloween mask until you saw the edges.

"We'll get it back to the lab as quickly as possible for the detailed report," Tom added. "We should be able to learn quite a bit about the creature from that. The clean-up teams are going to scrub the area in a mile radius. They will record, tag and bag anything of interest and then sanitize the area. By the morning, there will be no traces as per protocol . . ."

Switching off the set, he grimaced. It was no better the second time around than it had been live. "We had a Class B creature, apparently a pretty powerful one, camping out in our back yard and we couldn't even find it when we were looking. And we may have had a feuding Class A that either disrupted its plan or just wandered by at the same time selling cookies. What a cluster." He knew he wasn't being fair, either to himself or his people.

The fact remained that they had Class A readings and then they totally missed a mid-range Class B. The system had at least tracked the second creature until it passed out of range. To be fair, according to the reports in the archives, entire cities had been wiped out by Class B creatures, leaving only a few survivors to tell the tale. It galled him that here, in a relative stronghold of human technology, the thing had not only gotten in but had likely lured a child right out of his bed. *At least we still have our prisoner. If he recovers we may finally be able to get some answers on what is really going on. If we can get him to talk.*

Rising, he crossed the room and grabbed his suit jacket, not bothering to put it on. Moving to the door, he gave one last look at the mess on his desk and with a sigh, clicked off the light, stepped out, and locked the door.

As he walked away from the main door and headed across the entryway, he clicked a remote in his pocket. The door to his private elevator opened up, spilling light out that shone on the wall behind him. Over the entryway was a single word spelled out over the doors.

S.P.A.R.K. - Scientists Practitioners Artisans and Recorders of Knowledge

EPILOGUE

EISHAO

THE PAIN WAS beyond imagination. Every pore, every speck of his being was aflame in a way he had never thought possible. Each rushing step he took towards the gateway inflamed his agony. It felt as if every being he had ever tormented was now revisiting that agony on him tenfold. He was blind in one eye and his vision was fading from the remaining orb. His flight seemed to reach on for an eternity yet finally his goal was at hand.

Once he stood in front of the gate, he barely had the power to activate the keystone. Sliding past the threshold, he felt immediate relief as the shadows of Sahae surrounded him. The weariness he felt was worse than anything he had ever known. Time lost all meaning as he moved towards the last place he thought he would ever return.

Set upon the crest of a flowery meadow overlooking a lake of inky darkness sat the holiday cottage of his family. A place filled with grand memories of millennia of happy times before the Great Blight. He could not even appreciate the beauty as he blindly made his way to the front door. Instinctively, like a wounded animal, he had fled to the last place he felt safe. As he crossed the threshold, his heart twisted in his chest. Everything was the same, even the familiar scents of his lost family lingered in the air. Then the smell faded under the stench of his burned flesh.

Clawing his way up the stairs, he made his way to his old room and slid between the sheets. Letting his mind slip into darkness, he relaxed and let the healing sleep overtake him. As he dropped into slumber, his last thoughts were of the human and Abomination who had bested him. Soon, they would pay. Dearly.

ACKNOWLEDGMENTS

A HUGE THANK you to my cover artist from Indie Book Covers – Michelle Warren.

I would also like to thank the following people for Beta feedback, editing and content feedback and support: Michelle Mankin, Maggie Evans, Keelyn Taylor, Mindy Badgett, Michelle Warren, and of course Michelle Pace.

To anyone I might have forgotten to mention I hope you know I appreciate any help that you gave me on this

ABOUT

THE AUTHOR

L.G.PACE III HAS SPENT several decades pouring creative energy into other things besides writing. He began his current journey by telling his two daughters bedtime stories about a magical realm and a hero named Terel. Though that story is still sitting unfinished in the electronic universe he has managed to bring two other stories out of the dark maelstrom of his mind for others to enjoy.

He dwells in the great state of Texas with his wife, novelist Michelle Pace and their children.

For more information about L.G. Pace III and his books, visit:

GOODREADS
https://www.goodreads.com/author/show/6982344.L_G_Pace_III

TWITTER
https://twitter.com/LGP3Author

FACEBOOK
https://www.facebook.com/LGPaceIII

www.ingramcontent.com/pod-product-compliance
Lightning Source LLC
Chambersburg PA
CBHW050016180626
46810CB00002B/436